THE SOUND OF HOME

LANGLEY PARK SERIES

KRISTA SANDOR

CANDY CASTLE BOOKS

COPYRIGHT

A NOTE TO THE READER

This book is intended for mature readers. It contains descriptions of adult relationships, sexually graphic situations, and adult language. If such things offend you, this book is not for you.

1

"Come on, Em. You're eighteen now. You've got to learn to live a little."

Mary Michelle MacCaslin, known to her friends and family as Em, exited the car and met the gaze of Zoe Stein, one of her oldest friends and her only real link to normal teenage life.

"I mean, seriously, Em. Have you ever even been to a field party at Sadie's Hollow?"

Zoe knew she hadn't. "It's not really a field," Em shot back.

"You have to walk *through* a field to get there," Zoe countered, removing a small flask from her backpack and taking a long pull. She held it out, but Em waved her off. "Come on, one little taste. I promise you'll find Mr. Daniels to be quite the social lubricant."

"Mr. Who?"

Zoe pulled two sleeping bags from the car. "Christ on a cracker, Em! Jack Daniels. It's whiskey. Come on, Virgin Mary. Take a swig."

"You know I hate it when people call me that."

"Can I call you *Wunderkind*? That's what the paper calls you, and I don't see you getting all pissed off with them."

Em rolled her eyes. Zoe could really be a pain in the butt sometimes.

A beat passed, and Zoe let out an audible breath. "Okay, okay. I take it back. But that outfit, Em..."

"What about my outfit?" she asked, fingering her pearl necklace while throwing a quick glance at her plaid skirt.

"It's way more Great Aunt Ethel than it is naughty schoolgirl, Britney Spears, circa 'Hit Me Baby One More Time.'"

"Zoe, you know I had a performance tonight. I'm lucky my dad let me go out at all."

"I know. I know," Zoe replied and placed the flask in Em's hand. "That's why you need to drink this. We've only got a few more weeks before everyone starts leaving for college. Tonight is about being stupid, having fun, and being stupid."

"You said *being stupid* twice."

"Yes, because we need to be double-double stupid tonight. And no writing in your little datebook. I don't want to see *drank alcohol in excess* written in your quasi-obsessive-compulsive log."

Em gave her a sideways glance. Zoe had always teased her about her many journals and datebooks.

She wasn't going to acknowledge her friend's little dig, so she changed the subject. "I know I've only done online high school, but I'm pretty sure the word you're looking for is *doubly*."

Em MacCaslin didn't live the life of a typical teenager. Scratch that. Em MacCaslin's entire existence had been quite different from most people's. When she was four years old, her parents enrolled her in piano lessons. She was playing complicated pieces by Chopin, Rachmaninoff, and Beethoven before she turned five. At six, she had taken up the violin, and the results were the same. Newspaper articles from her hometown of Langley Park, Kansas, proclaimed her a "Wunderkind" and a "Child Musical Prodigy." By twelve, she'd focused solely on playing the violin and was living out of a suitcase, traveling to study with master teachers all over the world and taking part in elite competitions.

Zoe put on her puppy dog eyes. "Please, Em. We get the whole night. Your dad thinks you're spending the night at my place, right?"

Em never lied to her father, but Zoe had been begging her to go to

Sadie's Hollow all summer. She grabbed her backpack and met Zoe's gaze. Her friend had added an exaggerated pouty lip to her puppy dog eyes.

Em glanced at the ground. "Do you think Michael's going to be there?"

Zoe's lips curved into a wry smile. She knew she had won. "I'll answer that question after you take three pulls off my pretty little flask of Jackie D."

Em glanced at the flask. "I mean, it doesn't matter if he's here. I just thought it would be nice to see him."

"That's it? You just thought it would be *nice* to see him? He is your next door neighbor, isn't he? Are you telling me you haven't seen him since you've been back?"

Zoe was right. Michael MacCarron was her next door neighbor. Just about every childhood memory she had included him. Born on the same day at the same hospital, Midwest Medical in Langley Park, Kansas, Michael Edward MacCarron and Mary Michelle MacCaslin came into this world looking like twins with their small tufts of auburn hair and fair complexions.

Em twisted her pearls. "I haven't been around that much. You know that, Z."

She had been traveling nonstop for the last three years. Two stints in Vienna and then zigzagging back and forth between London, New York, and Tokyo. It had been thrilling, but it didn't leave any time to visit Langley Park.

She had been back a few weeks to perform at several fundraisers for the Kansas City Symphony and had only caught glimpses of Michael. But from her brief glances, it was safe to say, he was no longer the lanky boy, all knobby knees and sharp elbows, shooting hoops while listening to Nine Inch Nails. Earlier that morning, she had peeked out her window and watched him mow the grass. She couldn't take her eyes off the boy she used to share a plastic kiddie pool with when she was a toddler.

During her time away, he had transformed into an Adonis of a man with sculpted shoulders, long, strong legs, and a back that rippled with muscles.

Not that it mattered.

She had no time to worry about boys. Soon, life on the road was going to end. She had received a full-ride scholarship to attend The Juilliard School in New York City. In less than two weeks, she was going to be something she hadn't been since grade school: an ordinary student.

Maybe ordinary wasn't the right word to describe her.

She was as ordinary as someone who had played a private audience for the Queen of England. Em knew her reputation might intimidate some of the students; but she hoped as they studied and played together, they'd come to see her as a real person. A person who needed music to survive just as one needs air to breathe. A person who couldn't imagine a day without Beethoven, Mendelssohn, or Tchaikovsky. Her life was always going to revolve around music, and now she was going to be surrounded by people her age with the same passion and drive.

Zoe gestured to the flask, her cocky smile still in place. "You give me something. I'll give you something."

Em brought the flask to her lips and swallowed the burning, bitter liquid. "This stuff tastes even worse than it smells."

"Come on, *Wunderkind*. You've got two more sips to go."

The alcohol from the last two pulls settled in her belly. "This stuff is terrible."

"Aw, quit your complaining and take a sleeping bag. We need to get a move on."

Em took the sleeping bag and looked around. "Where the heck are we?"

They had driven at least an hour south of Langley Park and were now squarely in what looked like the middle of nowhere.

"The tiny little town of Lyleville," Zoe replied, leading Em into the darkness. "We just have to pass through this field and hang a left at the cemetery."

"Cemetery?"

"I didn't tell you?" Zoe asked, taking another long pull from the flask before handing it to Em. "That's what's so great about this place. Sadie's Hollow is this little crater near the Lyleville Cemetery. Cops can't see us if they drive past, and the townspeople—what's left of them—don't come here because of the legend."

"Zoe, stop messing with me."

"I'm not messing with you, Wunderkind. The legend goes, a long ass time ago, a girl named Sadie Wilson was supposed to meet her true love here. Her father, some wealthy merchant back when this place was a real city, had forbidden them to marry. So they decided to elope. Except, he never came. Sadie's so-called true love ended up running off with another woman. The next morning, Sadie was found hanging dead in a tree. They never knew if she was murdered or if it was suicide."

Em glanced over at the old headstones. A chill crept up her spine. Sadie Wilson's headstone glowed eerily in the moonlight like a warning beacon. She swallowed hard and started down a set of limestone steps leading down into the hollow when she heard Zoe let out a shriek.

"Hey," Zoe said, grabbing onto her backpack and pulling her off the steps. Her friend's wry grin was replaced with a stern glare. "Don't go on those steps. I'm serious."

"Why not?"

"People say those are The Steps to Hell. They also say that when it's a full moon, you can see Sadie sitting on them, calling out for the man who betrayed her."

Em shook her head. This was crazy talk, but that didn't stop another shiver from running down her spine.

"The whole 'Sadie's ghost thing' is probably just some stupid campfire tale, but why tempt fate?" Zoe added, softening her tone.

Em nodded and followed her friend down the steep incline. The Jack Daniels was making her limbs feel lighter and her head a blissful kind of fuzzy as the overlapping sounds of various conversations permeated the humid night air.

They emerged from the trees and passed into a clearing. Em saw at least forty, maybe fifty kids standing in clusters. Small tents dotted the hollow while flashlights bobbed back and forth like fireflies, and teenagers moved from group to group, laughing and horsing around.

"I can see why you guys come here," Em said, surveying the large oak and willow trees that enclosed the area. But Zoe wasn't paying attention to her.

Zoe increased her pace. "I see Gabe. Let's go say hi."

"Do you have a thing for Gabe Sinclair?"

"No way, nothing like that," Zoe said and took a long pull from the flask.

But before Em could ask another question, Zoe was hauling it down into the hollow.

"Hey! Look who's back in town."

He handed Em and Zoe cups containing a blue liquid.

Em sniffed the cup. "What is this?"

Gabe took a sip from his own cup. "It's called Blue Dinosaur. It's Everclear and Blue Raspberry Kool-Aid."

"Just drink it, Em," Zoe said, scanning the crowd, then focused on Gabe. "Is your brother going to stop by?"

"Yeah, Sam will be by. He said he would drop off some beer."

"How is Sam?" Em asked, surprised at how easily the blue dinosaur punch went down compared to the burn of Zoe's whiskey.

Gabe smiled. "He's good. He still thinks he can tell me what to do, classic older brother complex, but he's been a lot more chill since he met Kara."

"Who?" Zoe asked, the dyed pink tips of her bob flying across her face as she turned her attention to Gabe.

"Kara's his new girlfriend," Gabe answered, looking over Zoe's shoulder. "I think that's them now."

Em and Zoe turned to see the outline of two people walking hand in hand, the larger of the two carrying a case of beer.

Zoe stiffened and turned her attention to a tall guy walking by wearing a Portishead T-shirt.

"Ladies and gentlemen, the psychedelic pharmacy is open. If you want it, I've got everything you need to forget about your troubles.

Anybody want to take a trip to Mary Jane Land?" he asked, shaking a baggie. "Flights are departing."

"Me!" Zoe said. She dropped her sleeping bag and backpack on the ground then turned to Em. "Can you just drop our stuff in front of an empty tent? Michael always sets one up for me. I'll find you in a little bit, okay?"

Before Em could even respond, Zoe was halfway inside a tent surrounded by clouds of hazy smoke.

Gabe gestured toward Zoe's pack and sleeping bag. "Do you want any help with that?"

"No thanks, Gabe. I'm good," Em answered.

She drank the last few sips of the dinosaur punch and blinked her eyes. The light from the electric lanterns hanging from the tent posts blurred into the night. She blinked again, trying to focus her gaze.

"Zoe's tent is the blue one at the end of the row." Gabe put a steadying hand on her elbow. "And, Em, go easy on the punch. When that Everclear kicks in, it hits like a motherfucker."

That made her laugh. She giggled as she set off for their tent and threw the packs and sleeping bags inside. Someone handed her another cup of punch, and she downed the tasty liquid in seconds.

She surveyed the hollow and smiled. These were ordinary kids partying at Sadie's Hollow before they went off to college—and tonight, she was too.

She walked the perimeter of the hollow and searched the teenagers' faces as they passed by in fuzzy blurs of shrieks and laughter. Even though she had left Langley Park when she was twelve to study abroad, she recognized many of the kids from grade school. Their once rounded, rosy cheeks were leaner now, but she could see reminders of the children she remembered.

It was as if she had hopped into a time machine and fast-forwarded into the future.

"I'm Dr. Who, time traveler extraordinaire," she giggled.

She stretched her arms toward the sky, tried to focus on the full moon, and twirled with her head thrown back, watching the moonlight dance on her fingertips.

Magic fingers.

That's what her first violin teacher, Tom Lancaster, had called them. She smiled and made a mental note to stop by and see him before she left for New York. But just as she was about to tuck the thought of Mr. Lancaster away, her foot hit a rock, and she pitched forward. Just as she was about to fall flat on her face, two strong hands gripped her around her waist.

"I didn't think you would be able to stay upright for much longer, Miss Time Traveler Extraordinaire."

A solid body pressed into her back. She turned, wanting to learn the identity of her rescuer, but drew a blank when she gazed into the eyes of a young man with sandy blond hair.

"You don't remember me, do you?"

Em shook her head and tried to clear the alcohol buzz. "Wait. I do. You're Kyle, Kyle Benson. I'm Em MacCaslin."

"I know who you are, Em. Everybody knows who you are."

"You took violin lessons with me when we were little, right? See I do remember!" Em added. Her tongue tingled and felt heavier than usual when she spoke.

Kyle let out a laugh, his hands still wrapped around her slim waist. "That's right, but you were always the best."

"You were pretty good," Em replied. "Do you still play?"

"Nah, I quit a few years ago. I was good enough to compete in some state and local competitions, but nothing close to your level."

"Now it's photography, right, Benson?" came a voice from the darkness.

Em's heart skipped a beat. She would have recognized that voice anywhere.

2

"Michael!" Em exclaimed and clasped his hand.

Michael tightened his grip. "I can take it from here, Benson."

Kyle deflated a notch and stepped back.

"Here," Michael said, pressing a camera into Kyle's chest. "You must have set this on the ground. I'm sure you don't want anything to happen to it."

"Thanks, MacCarron," Kyle replied, his tone void of even a shred of gratitude. "I was just making sure Em was okay."

"She'll be fine. I'm here."

Michael met Kyle's gaze, and a testosterone charge rippled between them. An age-old game of chicken. The only question was who would duck out first?

Kyle broke the standoff. "It was good to see you, Em." Conceding defeat, he turned and walked toward a clump of teens standing around a keg.

"What are you doing, Em?" Michael asked. His first impulse was to continue holding her hand, but he let go when an uneasiness settled in the pit of his stomach.

Em smiled up at him. "I was spinning. Zoe's gone to Mary Jane Land, and I've mostly been walking around with blue dinosaurs."

His lips quirked into an amused smirk.

"What I mean is, I've been walking around *drinking* Blue Dinosaurs."

Michael chuckled. "I see you've tried the punch. How much have you had?"

Em held out her hand. She raised her index finger, then slowly added her middle finger. Her eyes narrowed as if muscle control required a supernatural level of concentration.

Michael shook his head. "Em, you can't even weigh a hundred pounds. I think you've had enough."

"I've missed you, Michael," she said, her gaze abandoning her fingers and meeting his.

He felt the urge to touch her. He wanted to brush his fingers over each tiny freckle that dusted her cheeks.

Knock that shit off, MacCarron. This isn't one of your groupie cheerleaders vying for attention. This is Em.

"Let's sit down on the rocks," he said.

He stuffed his hands into his pockets and led her over to a cluster of large boulders. They settled on one, and Em leaned into him. The alcohol was loosening her inhibitions, and he liked it—he liked it more than he wanted to admit.

He couldn't stop throwing glances her way. Had she always been this pretty? The last time he saw her was three years ago when she had returned to Langley Park to spend Christmas with her father. Em's parents divorced when she was young, and she used to split her time between Langley Park with her father and Sydney, Australia, with her mother. But once she began traveling to study violin all over the world, he had seen her less and less.

Em smoothed out the pleats of her skirt, and he bit back a chuckle. While most of the girls at the party were wearing cut-off jean shorts and tank tops, leaving little to the imagination, Em had on a plaid skirt, a short-sleeved cardigan, and a string of pearls.

Fucking pearls.

"Why are you looking at me like that?" she asked, attempting to look incredulous.

"You wore pearls to a Sadie's Hollow party," he answered. He'd never thought pearls and plaid were sexy before tonight.

"I'll have you know," she raised her index finger, "that tonight I helped raise quite a bit of money for the Kansas City Symphony. Like big-time dollars."

Jesus, she was an adorable drunk. "You did, did you?"

"I most certainly did," Em replied, coming to her feet and pretending to play an air violin.

"What did you play?" he asked, unable to hold back a grin.

She closed her eyes and began to bow with her right hand. "Just Paganini. *Nel cor più non mi sento.*"

"Oh, yeah, *just* Niccolò Paganini's most difficult composition, and arguably one of the most technically challenging pieces ever written?"

She opened her eyes and met his gaze. "Just that."

Holy shit, she was stunning.

"Could you lose the air-violin for a minute and sit back down. I'd hate to see you fall on your ass again."

"I *almost* fell on my bottom. Thankfully, Kyle Benson was there to catch me," Em replied and settled herself on the rock.

"You can say *ass,* Em. Nobody will hear you."

"I know."

"Then say it. Your dad's not here."

She twisted her pearls.

"You can't do it, can you? Once a good girl, always a good girl."

"Hey," Em said, grabbing his hand. Her touch sent a rush of electricity surging from the point of contact. "Do you remember when we played "Heart and Soul" on the piano back when we were in kindergarten?"

"How could I forget? Your dad let us stay up late and watch *Big.* You lost your mind watching Tom Hanks and that old dude jump around on the giant keyboard."

"Do you remember your part?" she asked, her face hopeful and glowing creamy white in the moonlight.

Sweet Christ, she was beautiful. When the hell did that happen?

Michael tried to push any sexual thoughts from his mind. He had to remind his twitching cock that nothing could happen with Em.

He released a breath. "I could knock out my part if I had to."

"Let's do it," she said, then turned toward the long, smooth boulder.

Em positioned her hands on the rock as if it were a piano. She gestured with her chin for him to do the same. "Ready, and..." she said, and began to play. She watched him with a furrowed brow as he pretend-played alongside her. "You're doing it wrong. The notes are more staccato."

"Em, we're playing on a fucking rock. How can you even tell?"

"I just know, Michael. It's like the music talks to me, like it lives inside of me. It's always been with me."

Fuck, he could get lost in her eyes. Did she still wear those little cotton panties, the ones with tiny flowers, like she did when she was just a girl?

Enough, MacCarron!

He mentally punched himself in the mouth. Of course, she didn't. She wasn't eight. She was eighteen, a woman. The little girl he used to play piano duets and flashlight tag with had grown up.

Em nudged him with her shoulder. "Put your hand on top of mine. Then you'll be able to feel how the notes were meant to be played."

He draped his large hand over hers. For a second, he thought Em trembled, but then she began to play. As her fingers danced across the imaginary piano keys, Michael felt each note and could hear the music almost as if he was inside her, connected to her.

"See, if you played each note with a bit more—"

He silenced her with a kiss. Her body tensed. He pulled back a fraction, allowing his teeth to nip at her bottom lip. The contact made his head swim. Her lips parted, and he deepened the kiss. She sighed into his mouth, her breaths becoming shallow. If kissing Em was the last thing he would ever do, he would die a happy man. But he wanted more. He slipped his tongue into her mouth and caressed her in a hot, desperate rhythm, begging her to match his intensity.

Em was sweet. So fucking sweet. He tasted the raspberry punch on her tongue, but it had an edge to it. She must have been drinking something before the punch, something spicy like whiskey or rum. The two flavors assaulted his senses and teased his cock. He knew Em MacCaslin was innocent, everyone did. But the intensity of this kiss told him there was something deeper, something darker inside her even she didn't know existed.

Then it hit him. He was kissing Mary Michelle MacCaslin.

Jesus, what was he doing?

His second-guessing ended when she whispered his name, her voice hungry with need.

"Oh, Michael."

Em spoke not only to his cock, which was begging for release like a bull in a bucking chute, but to his soul. When she guided his hand across the pretend piano keys, an almost spiritual awakening burst inside him, like standing at the crossroads of a tornado and a tidal wave.

He lifted his hand from where it rested on top of hers and slid his fingertips up the length of her arm. He trailed them across her shoulder and found the string of pearls resting around her neck. Slowly, he wrapped the delicate necklace around his fingers and pulled her in closer. Each time he twisted another segment, Em gasped as if she was moving closer and closer toward something her body never knew it wanted and could no longer deny.

His breath grew ragged, and he nearly came in his pants when her hand moved to rest on his thigh. "Em, you taste like every color of the rainbow," he whispered. He pulled on the necklace, forcing her to turn her head and allow him to kiss and lick the delicate skin of her neck and the sensitive area behind her ear.

"Michael," she breathed again.

When she said his name, it sounded so new, an enduring melody locked in his heart.

He released the necklace and cupped her face in his hands. "What is it, Em?"

She smiled up at him. "That was my first kiss."

The admission was so honest, so real, so raw. He could only answer it by pressing his lips against hers.

"Um, Michael?"

Dammit. That wasn't Em's voice. It was Tiffany Shelton's.

Tiffany's tone was like the screech of an emergency brake on a speeding train. He released his grip on Em's pearls. "Hey, Tiff."

Tiffany kept her gaze locked on him, her snub nose, which he once considered cute, now looked childish. "Gabe says all the equipment is ready to go. This party is fucking L, A, M, E, *lame* without decent tunes."

Michael turned to Em. "I deejay most parties. I'm getting pretty good."

"Pretty good?" Tiffany barked. "You are the fucking boss."

Michael didn't even acknowledge Tiffany's praise. "Let me get the music going. Do you want me to get you another drink first?"

"Got that covered," Tiffany said, holding out a red Solo cup of the blue punch.

Em took the cup. She smiled up at him, and her swollen lips made his cock strain against his shorts. "I'll be fine. I'll go find my tent. I want to change into more comfortable clothes."

Tiffany snorted. "I guess nobody told you it's a strictly no plaid zone at Sadie's Hollow."

He threw an irritated glance at Tiffany, then took Em's hand. "Let me get the music going. I'll come find you in a little while."

Em nodded, then took a sip of the punch.

He rose to his feet and followed Tiffany. They weren't fifty feet away before she pulled him behind a tent. "Do you think Miss Grandma Pearls over there would know what to do with this." She palmed his hard cock through his cargo shorts.

Michael couldn't help his response. He was already worked up from that kiss with Em. Tiffany wasn't his girlfriend, not even close. They had hooked up at every Sadie's Hollow party, and she was hot, a cheerleader with killer legs. With Tiff, it was fucking, pure and simple.

What would it be with Em?

Nothing.

It wouldn't be anything because he wasn't going to fuck her—not at a high school Sadie's Hollow party. That's not what Em deserved. And she wasn't just *some girl*. She was literally one of the foremost violinists on the planet.

The fucking planet.

Em was going to go on to a glowing career, playing all over the world. And what would he be doing? He wanted to study music. He wanted to mix and produce tracks. He wanted to feel the thump of the bass as he layered sounds one on top of the other, creating something that was powerful, emotive, and real. But what would he be doing instead? Following his father's plan. The law school plan. The plan to carry on his father's legacy.

"You know where I'll be after you finish rocking the shit out of this party," Tiffany purred. Still facing him, she took several steps back. She was trying to come off as alluring but only succeeded at looking cheap.

"Damn noisy birds," Michael moaned, rubbing the sleep out of his eyes.

He untangled himself from the long leg draped over his thigh. He was a fucking idiot. He'd let Tiff bring him beer after beer while he was playing his set. And just like every other damn night at the hollow, he ended up fucking her doggie-style in a drunken haze.

He climbed out of the tent and surveyed Sadie's Hollow. Other teenagers were emerging from their tents, shielding their eyes from the morning sun like zombie-vampire hybrids. He saw Zoe walking around in a crumpled Portishead T-shirt.

She smiled at him, but her face fell when Tiffany crawled out of the tent.

"Michael!" Zoe called out, eyeing Tiffany Shelton. "Where's Em?"

Michael scratched his head. "I figured she found you. I haven't seen her since—"

"Since you had your tongue down her throat then dropped her ass for this twat waffle."

"Oh, screw you, Zoe," Tiffany tossed back, then tried to pull him in for a kiss.

"Give it a rest, Tiff," he said, turning away and walking over to Zoe.

He crossed his arms. "What do you mean, you don't know where she is? This isn't her scene, Zoe. Somebody could have taken advantage of her. She was pretty drunk when I left her."

"I know this isn't her scene, but I saw her with you! I figured she'd be safe with you of all people. I didn't think you'd ditch her for Tiffany "easy fuck" Shelton. Aren't you over that shit yet?"

Michael shook his head and rolled his neck from side to side. "Let's search the hollow. She couldn't have gone far. She probably just passed out somewhere."

A layer of sticky sweat coated his skin, but it wasn't from the muggy Kansas humidity. "Do you see her?" he yelled out to Zoe who was searching the opposite side of the hollow.

She didn't answer back, but her pace became frantic as she shook tents, waking the sleeping inhabitants, none of whom were Em.

"Let's check the trees," he called out. "You don't think she would wander into the cemetery, do you?"

Zoe's face drained of all its color. "How would I know? Jesus, Michael, where is she?"

"Shit!" His gaze was drawn to the ground, and he scooped up a broken string of pearls.

"Oh, shit," Zoe said, taking the pearls out of his hand.

"The steps," Michael called out and ran toward The Steps to Hell.

Long auburn hair fanned out over the limestone stairs. Em was still wearing the same plaid skirt and cardigan, but her clothes were crumpled and dirty with dustings of grayish powder like she had bumped into a blackboard covered with chalk. Her knees were scraped and bloodied.

"Em! Em! Are you okay?" He scanned her face, her torso, her legs, and then he saw her hand. Her left hand. The hand that was responsible for playing some of the most beautiful pieces of music ever composed.

Zoe fell to her knees. "Fuck! What happened to her hand, Michael?"

He ignored Zoe's words and gathered Em into his arms. "Em! Wake up!"

She was breathing, the rise and fall of her chest gave him some hope until she opened her eyes and panic spread across her face. "You never came back, Michael. You never came back! And then there were the tall men! The tall men came after the bridge! And Paganini! He was there, too!"

Zoe fell to her knees and cupped Em's cheek in her hand. "Michael, she's burning up. And, dammit, look at her eyes. Somebody gave her something, maybe Ecstasy? Shit, I don't know."

Beads of sweat glistened on Em's upper lip, and her dilated eyes flooded with fear. Michael clenched his jaw. Fuck, he was an idiot. "I think she's on LSD or some shit like that. She's not making any sense. She must be coming down from a bad trip."

MICHAEL GUNNED the engine of his old Range Rover and merged onto the highway. "What about your dad, Zoe? We can take her to your house, and your dad can fix her hand."

Zoe sat in the backseat holding Em in her lap, a towel wrapped around her left hand. "Jesus, Michael! I think she's got at least two broken fingers and that gash on her ring finger. I can see right down to the bone. What are we going to do? She's supposed to leave for Juilliard in a few days."

"Zoe, focus! Your dad is a surgeon. Can't we just take her to your house?"

"My parents are in Phoenix this weekend meeting my brother's fiancee's mother. They don't get back until late tonight. Should we just take her home?"

18

"Fuck, no, Z. We have to get her to a hospital. It's her left hand that's all mangled. Do you know what that could mean?"

Zoe stared down at Em. "Just get us to the hospital, Michael. It has to be my dad's hospital. It has to be Midwest Medical in Langley Park. It's the closest level one trauma center. They'll be able to get a hand surgeon there faster than any place else."

He pressed his foot on the gas pedal, pushing the car well over the speed limit. He glanced back at Zoe in the rearview mirror and watched her face crumple as tears streamed down her cheeks.

3

———

"I need a doctor! I need some help!"

Michael burst through Midwest Medical Center's Emergency Room doors carrying Em in his arms.

He bit back a curse when he saw the nurse rushing toward him. Anita Benson. Kyle Benson's mother.

"Mrs. Benson," he said. His cheeks burned with shame. "Em needs help. Something happened to her hand, and I think she's—"

"She's on drugs," the nurse replied, hands on her hips, eyes begging Michael to deny it.

"Yes, I think it may be acid or LSD. But it's something that's making her hallucinate."

Em reached out with her good hand and batted at something imaginary in the air.

Nurse Benson pursed her lips. "You think?"

Zoe ran through the ER doors, and the pink tips of her bob slashed side to side across her cheeks.

"And you, Zoe Stein? You're involved in all this, too? I can't imagine your father would be pleased to have you mixed up with drugs."

"We don't know what happened, Mrs. Benson," Zoe said, echoing

Michael. "We just found her like this about an hour ago. She needs help."

Two other nurses rushed over, and Nurse Benson gestured for Michael to place Em on a gurney. "We'll take it from here," she said and vanished behind a set of double doors.

EM STARED at the dish of hospital Jell-O, the color mimicking the dinosaur punch from Sadie's Hollow.

Zoe sat on the edge of her hospital bed. "What are we supposed to tell the doctors, Em? They're going to want to know what happened. Jesus, what are we going to tell your dad?"

Bile coated her throat, thick and bitter, and she pushed the Jell-O away.

What happened?

Her thoughts bounced around like a pinball machine. Memories would materialize only to disappear in the blink of an eye just as a new image burst into the tangled mess of her consciousness. But three things kept popping up in a loop of disjointed color, sensation, and sound: *Paganini. A bridge. Tall men.*

Paganini made sense. She had played the Paganini piece at the donor event before going to Sadie's Hollow. But a bridge? She couldn't picture it. She could only feel it—a jostling bumpy sensation in her bones as if she had ridden in a vehicle crossing over something rickety. Was she in a car when she went over the bridge? She and Zoe didn't cross any bridges on the way to the hollow. Did she cross a bridge on the way to the donor event? No, she didn't. And tall men? The words tall men were cemented in her mind. But she couldn't picture anything about any actual men: tall, short, or otherwise.

She let out a breath. "I don't know what happened. All I remember is—"

"I know, Em." Zoe cut her off. "Tall men, the bumpy bridge, and the Paganini piece, *Nel cor più*, whatever. You kept repeating it over and over in the car. I don't know what any of it means."

Em tried to focus. She had to put the pieces together. But her brain felt fluid and fuzzy. The ER doctor had given her a mild tranquilizer. It helped stop the panic and crippling fear, a remnant of whatever drug she had been given, but her mind was left unable to parse out the real from the delusional.

Michael ran his hands through his hair. "Did someone offer you something that looked like a sticker? Do you remember who you were with?"

She ignored Michael's questions and attempted to flex her fingers. The nurses had told her not to move her hand. She kept trying, but nothing happened.

No movement.

No pain.

Nothing.

There was damage to at least one of the tendons in her left hand. Her inability to bend her ring finger spoke to the probability of a flexor tendon injury. The hand surgeon was on her way, but no one at the hospital could say if she would be able to play the violin with the same level of precise dexterity she had known her entire life.

Michael stuffed his hands in his pockets. "Em, come on. You've got to be able to remember something."

She closed her eyes. "This is going to ruin everything, isn't it?"

No one answered. The silence spoke volumes until the sound of hushed voices in the hospital corridor snaked through the air.

"Now, the good Lord knows I'd be the last to judge, but look, just look at what God gave that girl. And what does she do with all that talent? She throws it away to drink and do drugs and act like a harlot. Brought it all on herself, she did. And of course, she says she can't remember anything."

Nurse Benson's words hung in the air.

Another nurse entered the room and inspected her IV. "Your father is on his way, and we're going to get you prepped for surgery." She wrote a quick note on Em's hospital chart then glanced over at Zoe and Michael. "Your friends are going to have to leave."

"Em, it'll be okay," Zoe said, fear and exhaustion lacing her words.

"We'll be in the waiting room. We'll come to see you the minute you get out of surgery," Michael said, leaving the bedside to stand next to Zoe.

Em couldn't even stand to look at them. "Just go."

Zoe wiped back a tear. "We won't be far. It's going to be okay."

Em's head jerked up, and she met Zoe's weepy gaze. "*Okay*? It's going to be *okay*?"

"I just mean that—"

"She just means that we're here for you, Em," Michael said.

The room was quiet for one beat, then two.

"GET OUT!" The words tore through Em's throat, cutting the air like a million shards of glass.

No one moved. The room stilled like they were frozen in a suspended state of disbelief. Anger flooded Em's system. A surge of pain and rage and bitterness coursed through her veins. This was their fault. Michael and Zoe's fault. They had ditched her. They had abandoned her.

Em sprang from the hospital bed, and the IV ripped loose. Medical equipment beeped in a frantic cacophony and churned the charged air.

Em lunged at her friends. "GET THE FUCK OUT OF HERE. I NEVER WANT TO SEE EITHER ONE OF YOU AGAIN!"

The nurse grabbed her around the waist. But a switch had flipped. To Em, everyone was a threat, and her only choice was to fight.

"I need some help in here," the nurse called out. "We've got a code green."

Em's gaze bounced between her friends' faces. She liked the fear and shame she saw reflected in Michael and Zoe's eyes. It was like fuel for her rage.

A nurse ran in with a syringe. A prick and burn spread through her arm as a wave of fuzzy numbness washed over her body. Her heavy eyes met Michael's gaze. "You never came back. You never came back for me, Michael."

4

PRESENT DAY — OCTOBER 30

"Holy cow! I never thought anything like this would ever happen to me!"

Dammit! He was talking again.

Em straddled the mild-mannered computer programmer, and her skirt hiked up around her hips.

She had flown directly from Sydney, Australia to Los Angeles seated next to a priest who was more interested in saving her soul than getting into her panties. But her luck changed when she'd transferred planes for the last three-hour leg of the trip from LAX to Kansas City. She sat next to Adam something or other. She hadn't even tried to remember his name when he'd introduced himself and offered her a stick of gum.

Gum, for Christ's sake.

She had declined the gum but helped herself to two Jack and Cokes during the flight.

She should have ordered a third.

"The less talking, the better," she said and shifted her body. She should have asked this guy what kind of car he drove before she decided to fuck him. Screwing in a Prius inside an airport parking garage was no easy feat. But she did like the nerds. They were harm-less and easy to control. She was probably a legend on Reddit by now.

"Mary Michelle," the programmer said. Two words. Four sylla-bles. She stopped going by her nickname, Em, and started going by her real name more than a decade ago after the accident at Sadie's Hollow. But here, in Kansas, it sounded wrong. In her hometown of Langley Park, she had always been Em because of him. The very person she would never forgive.

She tried not to look annoyed. "What is it, Aaron?"

"It's Adam."

"Of course, it is," she said. She lifted her shirt and revealed a black lace bra. If this didn't shut him up, nothing would. Nerds loved black lace.

As if on cue, Adam's hands found her breasts. He pulled the thin lace down and buried his face in her cleavage.

"Condom," Em said, pulling the Trojan packet out of her pocket.

"Right, right. Do you want me to..."

She pressed her breasts into Adam's face and lifted her body. She tore the condom wrapper open with her teeth, unzipped the programmer's fly, and reached for his cock—which felt pretty substantial. That was a pleasant surprise.

"You really know your way around a guy, don't you?" Adam asked, his voice a mixture of fear and desire.

She sank down on his sheathed cock. "I know a thing or two about a thing or two."

Em rolled her hips. If she rode this nerd hard, he'd come in thirty-seconds, and she needed him to last. For the most part, sex had become a tool to distance herself from her emotions. In her world, sex meant power, and power meant control. But her mind didn't always cooperate.

"Aaron, I'm going to ride you like a cowgirl."

The programmer's eyes widened, and his fingertips dug into her hips.

She grabbed onto the headrest and rocked her body up and down, building up speed like a freight train. She closed her eyes, and a barrage of images, sounds, and sensations flashed like a strobe light inside her mind.

Paganini. The complex twist of notes flowed through her body.

The wooden bridge. Each thrust mimicked the choppy motion her muscles remembered.

Tall men. This never made sense. But the words were cemented in her brain.

She blinked open her eyes. She needed to stop the flood of memories, not allow them to come rushing back.

"I'm getting close, Mary Michelle. So very..."

It was over, and the wave of memories receded into the hidden depths of her mind.

"Do you want me to call you?"

Poor, Aaron—or was it Adam? She'd forgotten again. Em glanced down at his tousled brown hair and his eyes, dreamy with gratification. "No, you don't have to call me."

"Thanks, I guess. Thank you for..."

"For the fuck," she said, climbing off his lap and onto the passenger seat.

"No, I mean, well, yes."

"You're sweet." She tapped on an interior light, adjusted the rearview mirror, and checked her face. Her blue eyes were lined thick with black eyeliner and smoky with gray eyeshadow. She noticed the faint freckles on her cheeks taunting her. She could hide behind the makeup, hide from herself, but beneath it all would lie her creamy white skin sprinkled with freckle after freckle: the face of Em MacCaslin.

Adam removed the condom and tied it off. He adjusted his boxer shorts. They were adorned with musical notes.

He offered Em a sheepish smile. "They were a gift from my grandmother. I played the piano when I was younger. I haven't touched one in years, but my grandma still shops for me like I'm a six-year-old."

A muscle ticked in her jaw.

"Do you play? I mean, did you ever play an instrument?"

Em opened the car door. A tingle of electricity pulsed through her fingers as if they were begging for recognition.

She clenched her fists. "No, I don't play any instrument."

"YOU GOT ANY PLANS FOR HALLOWEEN?"

Em met the cabbie's gaze in the rearview mirror and shook her head.

"I live over in Lenexa," he said, resting his arm across the front seat, "but I think my wife and I are going to bring our daughter to Langley Park to trick-or-treat tomorrow night. They do it right, you know—the botanic gardens are all lit up, the shops passing out treats, music in the town square. We went last year, and my little Becky loved it."

The cabbie turned onto Langley Park Boulevard, and the Midwest Medical and Psychiatric Center came into view. An ambulance with its sirens blaring turned into the emergency room entrance.

"You okay back there, miss?"

She had cradled her left hand like a wounded bird, holding it to her chest and massaging the scar on her ring finger. She dropped her hands. "I'm fine."

"You from around here or just visiting?"

"My dad lives in Langley Park."

"That's nice! Real nice! I bet he'll be glad to see you."

"He's sick." She took in a sharp breath. The words just flew out.

The cabbie's brow creased in the mirror. "I'm sorry to hear that, miss. Is he over at Midwest Medical?"

"No, he just moved to the Langley Park Senior Living Campus."

Why was she unloading on this guy? It wasn't like her to spill her guts.

"That place is the gold standard for senior care. At least, that's what I've heard. They've got a topnotch Alzheimer's care center. Is that why your father's there?"

"No, he's not there for Alzheimer's. He's got COPD."

The cabbie tilted his head.

"Chronic Obstructive Pulmonary Disease. It's a breathing disorder," she added, leaning her head back and closing her eyes.

It was a breathing disorder her father had because of her. Her accident had driven him back to smoking. He had quit when she was a baby, but after her injury, stress and guilt had led him back to a pack-a-day habit.

A few beats of silence passed before the cabbie spoke again. "Someone must be having a wedding or something at the Botanic Gardens Lake Pavilion."

Em sat up and glanced out the window. The glow of the pavilion's white lights reflected off the dark water of Lake Boley. How many times had she played there as a child? How many times had she performed there? Her fingers twitched.

"I gotta tell, ya. I love driving into Langley Park," the cabbie said as they passed the lake and drove into the town center, all traces of their somber conversation gone.

It had been more than a decade since she had been back. During the first few years after her accident, her father would visit her in Australia. Those visits were hard. They never talked about her injury, and the guilt loomed large over every interaction. Their visits went from once a year to every few years, and now, here she was, driving into Langley Park. It had been three years since she had seen her father. On his last visit to Australia, he'd tried to hide the smell of tobacco with mints and gum. He'd blamed a near-constant cough on allergies. Em knew the minute he left her, he was lighting up.

She swallowed back the lump in her throat. "It's changed quite a bit since I was last here."

"You must have been gone a long time. Ten, fifteen years ago, it was mostly old people and lots of empty shops. But now, it's like Beaver Cleaverville around here. Everybody's buying up the old houses and renovating them. You'd never know Kansas City was only a few miles away. It feels like Smalltown, USA."

With a population of almost four thousand, the small municipality of Langley Park was a walkable, bicycle-friendly haven for families and young professionals clamoring to live in the charming

Tudor, Federal, and bungalow style homes built in the 1930s that encased the town center to its north, south, and west. The Langley Park Botanic Gardens, which sat adjacent to Lake Boley, bordered the town center to the east.

"You want a little tour of the town center before I drop you off? They've got it all decorated for the trick-or-treaters."

Em nodded. She needed a little more time in the safety of the cab. Once she stepped out of that car, it would all become real.

The cabbie passed her street, then turned right at the next block and headed north on Baneberry Drive. Even at nine o'clock on a cool October evening, the town was alive with activity. The Langley Park town center ran four blocks east to west, and three blocks north to south. Packed with professional offices, hip boutiques, and restaurants, locals clad in trench coats and scarves strolled along the streets. The Scoop, the local ice cream parlor, still had families lined up for their homemade milkshakes and double dips. The tiered fountain in the town square was lit by strings of white lights that crisscrossed the space and swayed in the night breeze.

"Want me to keep driving, miss? The yoga studio over on Mulberry Drive has a pretty great skeleton display up in the window."

"That's okay. I've seen enough." Langley Park had changed, but echoes of her past life remained. A thousand years could pass, but she would always recognize this place. It was in her bones, a part of her. It didn't matter that she had moved halfway across the world, this was her hometown. She had been the golden girl here, once upon a time. Now she prayed nobody would recognize her.

Her father's house was located in the neighborhood a few blocks south of the town center. The cab turned down her street, Foxglove Lane, and her pulse quickened. All the streets in Langley Park were named after plant life native to Kansas, but the Foxglove flower, with its bell-like shape and vibrant petals, used to hold a special meaning to her. Digitalis purpurea, the scientific name for the plant, means "finger-like."

When she was a girl, she wondered if her ability to play the piano and violin came magically from the Foxglove flowers that grew in lovely bunches all over Langley Park. Only later, after the accident, did she learn the beautiful bud was extremely poisonous. It was ironic how her fingers, the fingers she once foolishly thought were magical, were now responsible for her father's illness.

"Here we are, miss. 718 Foxglove Lane."

She stared up at the house.

"Hey, is that one of those American Foursquare houses? You don't see many of those around here."

The majority of homes in Langley Park were Tudor style with some Colonial, Federal, and cozy bungalows sprinkled in. While the American Foursquare did share some similarities with the boxier Federal style, the Foursquare sported a large central dormer and a pyramid-like, low hipped roof that left a bit of an overhang. As a child, she used to stand against the side of her house and press her little body into the scratchy bricks to stay dry during summertime thunderstorms. But a jolt of anger crushed the sweet memory when she remembered who was pressed up against the house next door smiling back at her.

"And look! There's another American Foursquare right next door!" the cabbie exclaimed.

The American Foursquare next door to hers was dark, but a light was on inside the freestanding carriage house situated at the end of its driveway.

"Yep," she replied. Her tone dripped with venom. "Two American Foursquares, side by side."

5

"Good bless the Irish."

Em set her suitcase down and eyed the bottle of Teeling Single Grain Irish Whiskey sitting on a sideboard in the living room.

She poured herself a glass and walked through the darkened house, trailing her fingertips along the wall. Hints of tobacco smoke scented the air. Somebody else would be living here soon. Strangers would be cooking in the kitchen and sleeping in the bedrooms. Maybe a family would live here. Maybe they'd have a little girl.

Stop! Get that happy ending, dreamer bullshit out of your head.

A week ago, her father had called. But this call was different from their bland check-ins. He had moved into an assisted living cottage on the Langley Park Senior Living Campus. It happened fast. Two weeks prior, he'd suffered six breathing attacks and spent a combined ten days in the hospital. The doctors told her father that unless he wanted a life that revolved around emergency room visits, living on his own was no longer a viable option. So when a coveted unit on the assisted living campus became available, he took it.

Em sipped the whiskey and surveyed her childhood home. The American Foursquare was, as the name suggested, a big square. A large rectangular living room separated in the center by a small foyer and staircase made up the front of the house while the dining room and kitchen sat side by side in the back of the structure. Four tidy, square bedrooms made up the second floor.

Her Steinway baby grand piano still sat in the corner of the living room. The light from the street lamp glinted off the polished mahogany finish. Em flexed her fingers. The smooth spruce keys whispered like a siren's song beckoning to be played. She resisted the urge to run her fingers across the keyboard's long expanse of black and white. She hadn't turned on any lights, and the house remained shrouded in darkness. She needed it to be dark. The darkness muted the tangle of memories wrapped up in this house.

A high-pitched squeak came from the kitchen. Em furrowed her brow, took another sip of whiskey, and went to investigate. The sound stopped as she surveyed the space. The digital clock on the oven read 10:27. She stood there a beat and listened. There it was again. It was coming from the window. She ran her finger along the ledge, found the latch, and pressed it firmly in place, silencing the rickety hissing sound. The October breeze must have picked up and rattled the latch open. Her American Foursquare was solid brick and mortar, but the original windows from the 1930s, while charming, did little to combat the Kansas wind.

She opened the refrigerator, and the interior light illuminated the snug kitchen. A large bag of Halloween candy sat on the counter next to a wilted, generic-looking houseplant. The butcher block counters looked worn, and the dim light highlighted the scratches and nicks plaguing the old cabinets.

She took out a carton of milk, sniffed it, and grimaced at the sour smell. A hunk of cheddar with mold creeping across the edges sat on a plate next to a takeout box from The Park Tavern Grill. She shut the door and ripped open the bag of candy.

She was stalling.

Em popped a Kit Kat into her mouth and walked over to the stairs. She had to go up to her room. Eyeing the bottle of whiskey, she refilled her glass, then ascended the stairs. Her bedroom door was closed. She touched the doorknob cautiously as if she was trying to ascertain if there was fire on the other side.

It was ice cold.

She turned the knob. The hinges squeaked. She swung the door open, and a stale smell filled the room.

She took two tentative steps inside. The moonlight shined in through her window, and she gasped. "He never touched a thing."

Broken plaques, bent trophies, and torn up photographs littered the floor. Her room was a time capsule. A shrine to the last day she had spent in this house.

"We can't say definitively if you'll regain the same level of function and dexterity."

Dr. Neil Stein, Zoe's father and Chief of Surgery at Midwest Medical and Psychiatric Center, sat on the edge of the bed, but Em wouldn't meet his gaze.

"I didn't perform the surgery, but I've looked at all the notes and pictures from Dr. Medina's repair. It was a clean tear of the tendon, and she noted that the digital nerve and artery remained intact. That's a good thing, Em."

Em cradled her splinted finger. She hadn't spoken a word since her outburst in the hospital. A week had passed since the surgery. Even with her mother's arrival, she still hadn't uttered a word.

"You'll need to wear the splint for several weeks and do the hand exercises," Dr. Stein said, modeling the exercise by gently moving his ring finger with the other hand. "Make sure your good hand is doing all the work. We don't want you bending the repaired finger on its own. The tendon needs to heal, but moving it will help to lessen the chance of the tendon sticking to the nearby tissue."

She watched Dr. Stein's hands, but her mind was on the A string, the third string of the violin, and how her ring finger would dance and slide and pop nimbly along it.

Dr. Stein patted her leg. "Em, honey? Do you have any questions?"

She didn't answer.

Her mother had braided her hair that morning. A lovely fishtail braid that snaked around the back of her head and came to rest several inches below her right shoulder. She shook her head and stared at the braid. She wanted Dr. Stein to leave. His words only solidified what she already knew. There would be no Juilliard. There would be no life playing the music she loved.

"All right, then. Take care, Em."

As soon as Dr. Stein left, Em sprang to her feet, closed her door and locked it. She pressed her back against the hard wood and surveyed the room. Trophies lined every shelf and ribbons and certificates hung neatly, filling every inch of wall space. All these reminders of her past were taunting her.

You've lost everything, and it's all your fault.

"Shut up," she whispered. The words tasted like shards of glass.

A volcano of anger tore through her body. She ripped the blue ribbons from where they hung tacked to the wall. It felt good tearing down these symbols of her old life. She swept her hand across the top of her dresser. The satisfying clamor of metal striking metal rang out as trophies toppled to the floor. Endorphins raged through her body, and she pressed on like a marathon runner hitting mile-marker twenty-five.

There was no stopping now.

Her parents banged on the door. She ignored their pleas and focused on the violin case sitting on her desk. She opened the lid and lifted the violin from its velvety enclosure. Over the years, she'd had the privilege of playing some of the most exquisite stringed instruments ever created worth hundreds of thousands, if not millions of dollars.

Stradivarius, Vuillaume, Guarneri.

Em had held history in her hands as orchestras accompanied her all over the world. But that bit of wood and string that she held in her hand now, affectionately nicknamed Polly, brought her to her knees.

Made of Swiss chalet pine, her gaze swept over the instrument: a Paul Bailly full-sized violin crafted in 1880. It was a gift from her parents. It wasn't in the same league as the Strads she had played on loan, but this violin came at a significant cost to her father. He'd joked that, while some little girls wanted a pony, his little girl wanted a violin made by a renowned luthier trained by the legends Jules Galliard and Jean-Baptiste Vuillaume.

Em held the violin out in front of her like someone skeptically appraising an item at a yard sale. She assessed the scroll and gazed down the neck past the delicate f-holes.

Smash it.

Rip out the pegs.

Tear off the strings.

This isn't your life anymore.

The angry voices in her head beckoned her to destroy this tangible link to a life that would no longer be hers. She squeezed the neck of the violin as her breath came in short pants. It felt wrong to be holding the instrument in her right hand. Her right hand was for bowing, and her muscles tensed with the unfamiliarity of the position. She looked at her splinted left hand, hanging limp and useless at her side, and her chest tightened with emotion.

She needed to hold her Polly one last time. She balanced the neck of the violin on her splinted hand. Her chin connected with the chin rest as her body found perfect alignment, and her muscles relaxed into position. Like the final goodbye between lovers at the end of an affair, she inhaled the scent of wood and rosin. She closed her eyes and remembered the last piece she'd played, Paganini's *Nel cor più non mi sento.*

Translated from Italian: In my heart, I feel no more.

From this moment on, she would feel no more. A dark voice rattled around her mind. Anger and rage would provide a sanctuary from the torment of her lost dreams. She eyed the instrument, and her vision blurred. She knew what she had to do.

EM ENTERED her childhood bedroom and retrieved a broken picture from the floor. With only the moonlight, she could still make out the image. It was a picture from her first summer at Shelter Island, NY, where she had attended a prestigious camp for a few dozen of the world's most gifted youth musicians.

She had assumed her father had thrown everything out, or at the very least, put these reminders of her past into a box, left to sit abandoned and forgotten in the corner of the basement like old high school yearbooks.

She finished the last of the whiskey and set the glass on her desk next to a closed violin case.

The wounds of her past, once hidden under layers of anger and forced indifference, prickled as she touched the jagged scar on her left ring finger. She laid down on her bed, tucked into the corner of the room, and glanced out the window only to see the darkened bedroom window of the house next door. Michael's childhood room. But before her thoughts could drift to Michael MacCarron, to his crooked smile and the way he always smelled of spearmint and lemongrass, something small and bumpy dug into her shoulder. She reached around and pulled a long string of beads. The necklace must have been lying on her bed. As she fingered the tiny orbs, the breath caught in her throat.

Her grandmother's pearls.

A gift passed down to her from her Australian grandmother. It was the cherished heirloom she wore when she used to perform. Her fingers touched each bead reverently, methodically, as one would pray the rosary. But something was missing. The square-shaped vintage clasp. The clasp was long gone, lost to the night she couldn't remember.

That damned night.

Even after more than a decade of trying to piece the events together, it remained an enigma. Cloudy and distorted like a chalkboard erased in haste, leaving only obscure fragments of images and words.

Em swallowed hard. She needed to stop the storm of grief and heartbreak that threatened to overtake her heart. She wrapped the broken necklace around her hand and slid it inside her panties. She pinched her eyes shut and rubbed the pearls against her sensitive bundle of nerves, feeling arousal take hold.

She was going to take those pearls and show them who was in charge now. Rage and lust coursed through her body. She pressed the pearls into her sweet spot and made small, rhythmic circles, sparking her sex to throb beneath her touch.

The house was still as she reached her peak, and she cried out in a tumble of fury and relief.

6

"I'm here to see Bill MacCaslin. I'm his daughter."

Em stood at the security gate of the Langley Park Senior Living Campus and shielded her bloodshot eyes from the sun.

She had polished off the whiskey late last night and succumbed to a fitful sixteen hours of sleep. She dreamed of playing the violin. A dream she had every night; and, while anger insulated her from the pain of her loss during her waking hours, the pull of the music was no match for her subconscious mind.

"Bill MacCaslin's daughter," the security guard parroted back and narrowed his eyes.

"Yes, he moved into one of the assisted living cottages last week. I'm here to visit him."

The security guard was an older gentleman who looked to be in his early sixties. Did she know him from somewhere? He didn't look familiar.

"You know, you broke your father's heart."

Em hardened her gaze. "Do I know you, sir?"

"No, you don't know me. But a long time ago, you meant something to this town, and everybody saw what happened to poor Bill after you threw away your future to get drunk and high. Your little accident didn't make the papers, but people talk in Langley Park. I remember Bill used to come into the coffee shop on his way to teach at the university. I'd see him from time to time before I started my shift working security at the hospital. He'd be grinning ear to ear, telling the whole shop about you playing violin in this fancy place and that fancy city. He was never the same after your *accident*. It broke this town's heart to watch that poor man live with that kind of sorrow."

Her nostrils flared, and she clenched her hands into tight fists, but the twist in her gut told her he was right. His words also confirmed her worst fear: the whole town knew about what happened in Sadie's Hollow, and they blamed her.

Em lifted her chin a fraction and swallowed back her guilt. "My father is expecting me. I think we're done here."

With one last sneer, the security guard handed her a map then buzzed her through the gate.

She continued up the sidewalk that ran parallel to the main drive. The campus was only a ten-minute walk from her house on Foxglove Lane. She could have driven the 1980 candy apple red Mercedes-Benz coupe her father kept locked in the carriage house garage, but she needed the walk to clear her head.

She clutched the map and forced fresh air into her lungs. She couldn't arrive at her father's cottage all worked up.

Em scanned the lawn. This place looked like an infomercial for active seniors. There was a group doing Tai Chi on the lawn while several stately gentlemen played bocce ball nearby.

The entirety of the Senior Living Campus was nestled into the southwest corner of Langley Park across the street from the Langley Park Botanic Gardens and less than a five minute's drive to the Midwest Medical and Psychiatric Center. The gated complex consisted of townhouses for seniors who still lived independently and individual assisted living cottage homes for those requiring in-home care. A memory care center for individuals with Alzheimer's and dementia was housed inside the main building.

Em looked at the map. In addition to the main building housing the memory care unit, it also contained a dining area, a coffee bar, crafting rooms, a wellness center with an Olympic-sized pool, a movie theater, and even a ballroom.

This place couldn't come cheap.

She passed the main building and headed toward the neighborhood community consisting of a grid of four streets dotted with townhomes and cottages. It reminded her of a small village she had visited in the English countryside after she performed with the London Philharmonic.

She was just about to turn down her father's street when a man riding a bicycle with a covered bench attached came barreling through the turn.

"Sorry, dude," the rider called out unfazed as two gray-haired ladies sat giggling and clutching each other like school girls in the backseat. "Teddy-cab, coming through!"

Em jumped out of the way. "Take it easy, *dude!*"

She shook her head, but the man continued down the street unfazed. She checked the map, found her father's cottage, and knocked on the door. A sign was posted in the front window: No Smoking. Oxygen In Use.

"Hey, kiddo, I was wondering when you'd get here."

Em tried to mask her surprise. Her father was wearing a small backpack with a portable oxygen canister. The clear tubes from the cannula delivering oxygen into his nose traced back across his cheeks and curved around his ears. His blue eyes had dimmed since she'd last seen him.

"Don't look at me like that, Em. The ladies in the eighties knitting group tell me I'm still quite a catch."

Until last year, Dr. Bill MacCaslin had been a professor in the education department at the University of Missouri-Kansas City. That's where her parents had met thirty-five years ago when her mother, fifteen years Bill's junior, had come from Australia to finish her doctoral work on the learning styles of children in the deaf and hard of hearing community.

"I'm sorry, Dad. I'm a little off with the travel, and then some surfer guy nearly ran me down with a rickshaw."

"That's just Ted from the bike shop in the town center. He comes over a couple of times a week to give us old folks a ride around the campus in his pedicab."

Em nodded, and they lapsed into a pocket of silence as the gentle hum of the portable oxygen reminded her that the breathing disease her father was battling was all her fault.

"Well, come in, come in," Bill gestured.

Em entered the cottage. The smell of fresh paint lingered in the air. One lone picture sat on an end table. A black and white photograph of her holding up a trophy twice her size—her first violin competition. Her father was so proud of her that day. If she had turned the camera and taken a photograph of her father, she would have captured him grinning ear to ear, the dark auburn of his beard highlighting the rosy glow of his cheeks.

"The cottage is really nice, Dad," she said, pulling her gaze from the photo and taking a seat at a small kitchen table. "How are you feeling?"

Bill adjusted the oxygen tube. "I'd give my right arm for a cigarette. Probably not the answer you wanted to hear, but I think we're past half-truths and walking on eggshells with each other."

Em rubbed at her scar beneath the table.

Her father took two deep breaths. "You've been to the house."

It was more of a statement than a question.

"Yes, I got in late last night. My room—it's exactly how I left it."

"Your mom and I agreed a long time ago that it wasn't our place to clean it up or decide what happened to any of its contents."

"Why can't you guys just hate each other like every other normal divorced couple?"

Bill laughed, breaking the tension, but the laugh morphed into a cough.

"Your mother and I will always care for each other. Her research took her back to Australia and mine kept me here. We were always the kind of people who were married to our work. The gift we both got was you."

Over the past two decades, Em's mother had been an instrumental player in creating a formal educational curriculum for deaf children in Australia. Her work had taken her to the Royal Institute of Deaf and Blind Children, Renwick Centre in Sydney. After the accident, Em spent time with her mother at her office. She was fluent in sign language thanks to spending time with her deaf Australian grandmother, Grandma Mary. At first, Em could only use her right hand to sign, but as she healed and continued helping her mother with her research, she volunteered in the classrooms and was eventually hired on as a teacher's aide.

"How are things going at the Centre, kiddo?"

Without thinking, Em signed, "It's good."

Her work at the Renwick Center had been the only thing that had gotten her through the first few years after the accident. The children and the silence insulated her from the musical world while also giving her something other than her anger at Zoe and Michael to focus her energy. Renwick during the day, and drowning her sorrows with Jack Daniels at night, had become her routine.

But the music was always there.

Anytime she would catch a melody playing below the chatter in a crowded restaurant or pass by someone whistling on the street, her fingers twitched. Her thoughts would turn to scales and harmonies, quarter notes and rests. The language of music, living dormant in her soul, would spring to attention only to be shoved back down by sex or alcohol or work like cramming the puppet back into the Jack in the Box.

"Dad, you don't have to sell the house right now. I could give you the money to cover what you owe for the cottage. Grandma Mary left me plenty in her will. More than I need, Dad."

A flush lit Bill's cheeks. "The money your grandmother left you is yours. I won't accept a penny of it." His gaze softened. "Kiddo, I need to sell the house. I'd like to get it on the market after the new year. That gives you about two months to go through everything."

Her father's chest rose and fell in short, punctuated breaths. She didn't want to upset him, but she knew he loved that house. The thought of strangers living in the home they had shared together broke her heart.

"But, Dad, if I hadn't. If I didn't..." Em trailed off. She couldn't say it. She couldn't admit she was the reason her father had started smoking again. She was the reason he had Chronic Obstructive Pulmonary Disease. She was the reason he was forced to sell his home.

Bill raised a hand. "Em, let's just get something out in the open. I blame myself for what happened to you. Maybe I should have insisted you had a more conventional childhood. You were always traveling and playing all over the world. I was so proud of you, kiddo, but I never considered the fact that you didn't get to be a kid. You had all the responsibilities of an adult before you could even drive a car. Hell, maybe you wouldn't have felt like you had to lie to me if you'd grown up going to parties, dating. Doing the things ordinary kids do."

She had never mentioned the tall men or the bridge to anyone but Zoe and Michael. As far as her father knew, she had lied about spending the night at Zoe's to party at Sadie's Hollow where she'd made the poor choice to drink, do drugs, and then injured herself.

The heavy weight of her shame settled in her chest. But before it was able to crush her spirit, an idea took hold.

There had to be more to the night of her accident. Someone had to know something. Someone else must have played a part in her injury. And now, she had two months to figure out the truth. Two months to piece together what had happened that August night. Two months to show her father she hadn't thrown her life away.

Em rubbed her scar and met her father's gaze. The gray in his beard had overtaken the auburn. He looked tired.

"I'll get the house ready to go on the market, Dad. You don't have to worry about a thing. Just rest. I'll be back to visit soon."

Her father reached a hand toward her, and she placed her left hand into his. He looked down at the scar on her ring finger then gave her hand a gentle squeeze. "Thank you, Em. Thank you for coming home."

She nodded. "You look tired, Dad. You should take a nap."

Her father nodded. "That's not a bad idea. Will you do me a favor?"

"Sure. Anything, Dad."

"Will you pass out Halloween candy to the trick-or-treaters tonight? There should be a bag of chocolates on the counter in the kitchen."

Her father had always loved celebrating Halloween in Langley Park. Em forced a smiled. "Yeah, Dad, I can hand out the candy to the trick-or-treaters."

She settled her father into bed, took one last look at the photograph on the end table, and turned to open the front door. Before her hand even reached the handle, the door swung open, and she was face-to-face with Anita Benson.

"Mrs. Benson, I didn't expect..."

Anita narrowed her eyes and met Em's gaze. Twelve years may have passed, but the woman's smug, self-righteous expression was as fresh as ever. "Look who finally made it back to Langley Park."

Em opened her mouth to speak but shut it when nothing came out.

Anita was dressed in blue nursing scrubs. She was holding a dolly with an oxygen canister. "I've come to swap out your father's oxygen tank. I hope you haven't upset him. He's had a rough couple of weeks."

Em bit the inside of her cheek.

"I assume you're here to help sell your father's house?"

Em lifted her chin. "That's between me and my dad."

Anita's eyebrows shot up. "I see. Well, as far as your father's care goes, you should know a nurse will be in every day to check his oxygen and make sure he's taking his medications."

"Are you his nurse? I thought you worked at the hospital."

"My, my! You have been gone a long time. I left the hospital years ago. I only work part-time now. I'm here at the Senior Living Campus three days a week. It looks like we'll be seeing a lot of each other while you're back."

Anita Benson was the last person Em wanted to run into at the Senior Living Center. The woman's pointed gaze oozed with judgment. Em wanted to yank that oxygen tank off its dolly and hit her over the head with it, but she clasped her hands in front of her. "Thank you for helping my father, Mrs. Benson."

"Why, it's the least I could do. He's been through so much. And all on his own."

Anita's words twisted like a knife in her heart, but they also added fuel to the fire of urgency burning inside her chest. She had to figure out what happened that night. She had to show her father that her injury wasn't his fault. And now that she was back, she was going to learn the truth and show everyone she hadn't squandered her talent and thrown her life away.

EM FOUND a second bottle of Teeling Irish Whiskey in the pantry, poured herself a glass, then popped a miniature Snickers bar into her mouth. She thought about the run-ins with the security guard and Anita Benson. She had to learn the truth, but where to start?

She went up to her room and braided her hair into an elaborate inverted fishtail braid. The floor was still littered with reminders of her past, and her fingers moved like the gears of a clock as she tried to recall the last thing she could remember from the night at Sadie's Hollow. But the sound of someone knocking on the front door broke her concentration.

She went downstairs, flipped on the outdoor light, and opened the door to find a pint-sized little girl dressed as Harry Potter. "You are my first trick-or-treater."

The kid cocked her head to the side. "Your light's off. Nobody will knock on your door if your house is dark."

A smirk lit Em's face. She liked this little smart-ass. "You knocked."

That seemed to stump the mini wizard. Em bit back a chuckle

and held out the large bowl of candy. The little girl's skeptical expression was replaced with one of delight. The kid started thumbing through the chocolates when a man's voice called out, "Em, is that you?"

It was surreal to hear someone other than her father call her by her nickname. After leaving Langley Park, she had gone by Mary Michelle. It was easier. She needed to distance herself from the person she was and dropping her nickname had been the first step in letting go of her dreams.

"It is."

The little girl grabbed a few chocolates and skipped down the porch steps. Em followed behind but stopped on the bottom step.

"It's Ben Fisher," the man replied.

Though she hadn't seen him for well over a decade, Em knew damned well it was Zoe Stein's older half-brother, Ben. She had known him her whole life. He used to make pillow forts for them in the Stein's living room. Her gaze traveled past Ben and over to the sidewalk where she saw a willowy blonde, Barbie-look-alike standing next to the last two people she ever wanted to lay eyes on, Zoe Stein and Michael MacCarron.

Barbie walked up and stood next to Ben, and Em clenched her fists.

"Em, this is my wife, Jenna, and our daughter, Kate." He gestured to the smiling Barbie doll and the mini Harry Potter who was now petting a dog in the front yard.

"Em," the little girl echoed then glanced back at Zoe. "Is this one of your favorite gingers, Auntie?"

Em vibrated with anger. Who the hell was Zoe of all people to tell her niece that she, *she* was one of her "favorite gingers"?

The air hung heavy and charged as if the tiniest of sparks could ignite a massive explosion. Em looked away from the little girl and settled her simmering gaze on Zoe, who had opened her mouth to speak, only to snap it shut.

Jenna-Barbie took a few steps forward and extended her hand. "I love your hair."

Em turned her attention to the tall woman and, without thinking, shook her hand.

"Maybe sometime you could show me how to do that," she continued, gesturing to Em's braid. "Kate's obsessed with braids, and I'm sure she'll be asking me to do her hair like yours when we get home tonight."

"Yeah, sure," Em answered with a forced smile. She was here to sell her father's house and figure out what happened at Sadie's Hollow. If she had even one shred of luck, this would be the first and last time she would see Ben Fisher and his Barbie dream house family.

Barbie was talking again, saying goodbye or something along those lines. But Em couldn't concentrate on her words. Only a few yards away, Zoe and Michael stood slack-jawed as if they had seen a ghost.

The temperature seemed to drop. Em's eyes darted back and forth between her two closest childhood friends. Michael's gaze went to her left hand. She pulled her sweatshirt sleeves down so that only the tips of her fingers remained visible.

She knew what Michael was thinking, and she wasn't going to give him the satisfaction of gawking at the jagged scar that spanned the length of her ring finger.

"I didn't know," Michael began, his words laced with apprehension.

His voice. God, she'd missed his voice. It was deeper now, different but still the same. It was like hearing a treasured song you had forgotten how much you'd loved.

Enough.

This is the man who abandoned you when you needed him the most. This is the man who kissed you then left you to go screw some slutty cheerleader.

Michael shifted his weight from foot to foot. "You're—"

Em smirked. Michael MacCarron, always so at ease, always so in control, was talking like his mouth was full of marbles. A surge of triumphant heat filled her chest, prickly and hot, the anger wrapping tighter and tighter around her heart.

Michael stilled. "You're back."

His words hung in the air as the sound of children's far-off laughter floated into the space between them. The anger burned hotter inside Em's chest with each spoken syllable.

You're back? That's it? That's what he has to say after all this time?

She could yell. She could call them selfish assholes. That's what they were, right? She could tell them she had been stuck, unable to move forward because of their self-centered choices. They'd ditched her, left her, and she had paid the ultimate price for trusting them.

She met Michael's gaze and remembered the boy with the auburn hair. She remembered her body pressed up against her house, staring at Micheal's pressed against his house, laughing as they dared one another to run into the downpour and come over to the other side.

Michael always ran to her. He was always the one to brave the storm. Sopping wet, he'd sprint across their driveways and flatten his body against the side of the house next to her. Em could almost feel his wet shoulder pressing into hers as they laughed and listened to the rain, a symphony of sound—the drops echoing off the roof.

Em pushed the memory of a smiling Michael, water dripping down his cheeks, from her mind and let the anger take control.

Fuck them. Forget them. It didn't matter that regret seemed to be wafting off them like the scent of roadkill decomposing in the hot sun. What they did was unforgivable.

Unforgivable.

The word rolled around her mind. It bolstered her resolve and annihilated any fond childhood memories from permeating the fortress of anger constructed around her heart.

She lifted her chin and met Michael's gaze. Then, without a word, she walked back inside her house and slammed the door shut.

7

"Did you know she was back in town?"

Michael shook his head.

"Jesus, Michael! She never even opened any of the letters I sent her after she left for Australia."

Michael crossed his arms and remembered the shoebox he had stashed in the back of his closet filled with letters stamped *RETURN TO SENDER.*

"Come on," Michael said. "Let's go talk in the carriage house."

Nearly all the homes in Langley Park came with a carriage house, a separate one or two-story structure set back in the corner of the property. The size of a two car garage, most folks parked their vehicles inside and sometimes built out the second floor to be a storage room or even a studio apartment. Michael's carriage house mirrored the carriage house on the MacCaslin's property. Standing one story tall, Michael's contained the Range Rover he drove in high school, a well-used punching bag, and his digital audio workstation for mixing and producing musical tracks.

"You don't want to go in the house?" Zoe asked.

Michael shook his head and whistled for his golden retriever, Cody.

They walked down the packed gravel driveway in silence. The crunch of the tiny rocks sounded too loud to his ears. A light flicked on inside the MacCaslin Foursquare, but he didn't dare look over at the house. He unlocked the side door of his carriage house and ushered Zoe inside as Cody padded in and curled up on an old futon against the back wall. He turned on a space heater and sat down in the chair at his workstation then swiveled around to see Zoe pacing back and forth.

She crossed her arms. "At least we know how she feels about us. I mean, Jesus, you just helped Dr. MacCaslin move into the Senior Living Campus. He didn't mention anything to you about Em coming home?"

"You know he wouldn't. After Em left for Australia, Bill barely spoke a word about her."

Zoe tugged at the ends of her shoulder length hair. "Micheal, I know she lost a lot. I know she deserves to be angry. But we lost part of ourselves that night, too. I know it wasn't the magnitude that Em lost, but, we—we paid for that night."

"I know."

"I couldn't even make it at Gwyer College. My parents had to come and get me after the spring semester ended. I just couldn't keep pretending I was okay. I thought being surrounded by total strangers would be the best thing for me, but..."

Michael met Zoe's gaze. He knew all about Zoe's breakdown, knew the guilt she carried over Em's injury had become too much to bear.

"I know, Zoe. I know."

"It's taken me a long time to get here. To get to someplace where I don't absolutely hate myself. If it wasn't for my mom." Zoe put her hands on her hips and raised her gaze to the ceiling. "I don't know where I'd be."

After Zoe's breakdown at Gwyer, she shared the events of the night at Sadie's Hollow with her mother. Zoe's mom, Kathy Stein, a retired social worker, had worked with her daughter and Michael during the summer between their freshman and sophomore years of college.

Kathy never called it therapy, but every couple of days, she would call over to the MacCarron law practice in the town center where Michael was working for his father during the summer. She would ask if he could come over and assist her and Zoe in a gardening project. There would always be something heavy to lift or a lawn ornament to move. While the three of them worked in the Stein's backyard, they would talk. At first, it was difficult for him to discuss his feelings, but after a few weeks, he'd found himself watching the phone at his father's law practice, hoping the next call would be from Kathy Stein.

He never forgot Kathy's words: *You can't force someone to forgive you, but you can learn to live with the knowledge that you did everything humanly possible to try and make it right.*

Zoe patted the hood of his old Range Rover. "I can't believe you still have this."

"She does great in the snow and ice," he answered, but that wasn't the only reason he kept the old car.

Zoe nervously ran her hand over the hood. "I thought this would be easier. You know, seeing Em for the first time. I didn't think I'd stand there like some sort of dunderfuck."

"Jesus, Zoe," Michael said and shook his head. "Where do you come up with these words?"

She brushed a tear away and released a shaky breath. "We never wanted anything terrible to happen to Em. We were young. We could have made better choices, but what's happened has happened. We spent years reaching out to her. We tried to apologize."

Zoe was right, but still—just seeing Em nearly tore his heart out. The guilt and shame seeped back into his chest as fresh as the morning they found her sprawled across The Steps to Hell.

Zoe wiped her cheeks. "I better go."

"Do you want me to give you a lift?"

"No, my car's just over at Ben's. I think the walk would do me good."

A cab pulled up in front of Em's Foursquare as Michael and Zoe made their way down the driveway. They stood in the shadow of the house and watched Em, clad in sky-high boots and a skirt that resembled a scrap of fabric step off the porch and head toward the cab. She opened the door.

"Where to, miss?"

"The Levee."

MICHAEL CURSED under his breath and flicked on the Audi's turn signal. The car gripped the road as he turned onto Westport Road and headed toward The Levee. The Levee was a Kansas City institution. A bar that had been around for years, it offered live music on the main floor and a sports bar upstairs. Tonight, it would be crawling with patrons celebrating Halloween.

After he had said goodbye to Zoe, he let Cody back in the house and grabbed his worn University of Missouri-Kansas City School of Law hoodie. Em may not have anything to say to him, but he wasn't going to let anything happen to her. He didn't care if his intentions were antiquated. He'd be damned if he was going to stand by while she went bar hopping alone on Halloween.

He parked on the street a few blocks away and entered the bar. Just as he thought, it was packed, teeming with costume-clad adults out celebrating. The bar was buzzing and boisterous as a band played, and patrons knocked back shots and sipped on local Kansas City craft brews. Em wasn't hard to find. Her braided red hair may have looked childish on someone else, but on her, it was stunning—auburn with hints of gold and fiery like the sun. He hadn't noticed her leggings were ripped, giving everyone a glimpse of her creamy thighs. Her blue eyes seemed larger outlined in dark smoky makeup.

Christ, she was sexy.

Em had an edge about her, something that said, *I might be small, but I will fuck you up.* Petite and curvy in all the right places, she moved toward the bar like she owned the place.

She hadn't noticed him. He planted himself on a stool near the far end of the bar. He hunched forward and pulled up the hoodie, trying to disguise his six-foot-four-inch frame. From his vantage point, he was able to observe Em's every move. She was a siren. His jaw twitched watching man after man vie for her attention. She'd let a few buy her a drink, but her eyes kept scanning the crowd like a wolf.

A trio of men settled in at the bar next to her, and Michael breathed a sigh of relief as he took in the group's apprehensive posture. These were not your typical bar brawling, pickup artists. These guys were the type more at home in a lab or deciphering lines of code. Nerd could not be Em's type. That he thought he knew for sure, until she turned on her stool, tapped one of the men on the shoulder, and flashed him an alluring smile.

The nerd had taped a shit-ton of gray paint samples on his t-shirt. Fifty shades of actual gray. Christ almighty, this is what Em liked? She leaned in and fingered one of the samples, pulling Fifty Shades in closer. Michael rose to his feet. He needed to get a closer look.

It was easy for him to watch her but still stay out of her line of sight. The place was packed with several layers of patrons standing around the bar, many trying to jockey their way in to order drinks. Michael settled in next to a large group. His jaw tightened as he watched Fifty Shades lean in and whisper something into Em's ear. Her legs were crossed between his, revealing more of her thigh. The position looked intimate, and Michael nearly charged the bar when the guy placed his hand on her knee, but his attention was drawn lower as Em rubbed her boot against the nerd's leg.

Like a black widow luring in a mate, Em was in control. Michael saw the assertive glint in her eyes, the confident lift of her chin and grew hard. Watching Em toy with this nerd was the hottest thing he'd ever seen. What would he do if it were his hand gripping her thigh? He'd rip those leggings and press her up against the bar. He'd fuck her right there in the middle of all these people. But just as he was about to lose himself in the fantasy, Em stood and led Fifty Shades over to the dance floor.

From his vantage point, he could still keep Em in his sights. His erection strained against his pants as she snaked her arms around the nerd's neck and pressed her body into his. She moved her hips in rhythmic circles, grinding into Fifty Shade's cock. Michael's system flooded with a torrid mixture of anger and arousal.

The guy smiled like a kid on Christmas and lowered his hands to rest above her ass. Michael's fingers twitched, and he forced them into fists. His gaze was locked on her perfect ass wrapped in that little skirt, and another barrage of filthy thoughts flooded his mind.

Jesus Christ—had he ever felt this kind of attraction?

Or was he bewitched by Em like the poor guy she was toying with on the dance floor?

He ran his hand over the auburn scruff on his face. He had to stop thinking about what it would feel like to be inside her—fucking heaven if his cock had anything to say about it. He needed to make sure this guy, or any other joker, didn't get the chance to find out either.

What the hell was he going to do? Storm in and throw her over his shoulder like a caveman? Punch Fifty Shades in the jaw for reacting to Em in the exact way he had? Luckily, Em seemed less concerned with the guy as her gaze focused on the band.

A local progressive bluegrass band was on stage tonight. Michael had seen them a few times in Langley Park when they played the neighborhood bar and grill, Park Tavern. The five-member group included a fiddle player. Em watched him intently and her brow creased in agitation. She pulled free of Fifty Shades and walked over to the side of the stage.

She gestured to the fiddle player, a young man, who probably thought she was going to try and hit on him as a cocksure smile lit his face. He crouched down to her level, but his smile disappeared when she yanked him by the collar and shouted in his ear, his eyes moving back and forth between Em and his instrument.

Michael crossed his arms. What the hell was she doing?

The song ended, and the lead singer addressed her over the mic with a curious grin. "What's going on, Red?"

Em lifted her chin. "I was trying to help your violinist stop fucking up the music."

The singer laughed, and the bar went still. "It's a fiddle. He's my fiddler."

"Fiddle or violin," Em said, stepping onto the stage, "they're the same fucking instrument. The difference is only the type of music that's played."

Michael's jaw dropped. But she was right. The violin could be considered a fiddle when playing bluegrass, folk, country, or more danceable tunes. The instrument was considered a violin when playing classical music and jazz. But neither of those were hard fast rules.

"Looks like we've got a real know-it-all with us tonight, folks," the singer said, but the smile of his face appeared more amused than irritated. "You care to show my lowly fiddle player how it's done, Red?"

Em's chin fell a fraction, but then she had it back in place. "I don't know if you'll be able to keep up."

Who was this woman? Not the sweet, innocent girl he had kissed back at Sadie's Hollow.

The crowd was loving this exchange. A patron in zombie makeup yelled out, "Charlie Daniels Band, "Devil Went Down to Georgia." Put your money where your mouth is, Sweetheart!"

"That song's not usually in our set, but I think we can accommodate the zombie-gentleman," the singer replied. "What do you say, Red? You up for the challenge?"

The bar cheered as the fiddle player handed his violin to Em, arms outstretched with an exaggerated bow that sent the audience into chanting, "Red, Red, Red!"

She stiffened but took the instrument.

The singer gestured for her to stand next to him center stage.

She stepped into the spotlight. "It's been a while since I played."

"Is that the way it is, Red? Are you all talk? You can always hand the fiddle back."

Em brought the violin to her chin and lifted the bow.

The breath caught in Michael's throat.

She met the singer's gaze. "Try to keep up."

The drummer played four quick beats, and what happened on

that stage brought the crowd to complete silence as Em pulled the bow across the strings. The singer, visibly shocked at her talent, stumbled over the first few lyrics but recovered. The crowd joined in, dancing and singing along.

Em's fingers moved at lightning speed, and a smirk graced her lips. She leaned in toward the singer. They looked as if they'd been performing this song for years.

The crowd was loving it, but Michael was paralyzed.

He'd seen her play plenty before the accident but only classical pieces. While she was always captivating to watch, her body becoming one with the music, this was something altogether different. This was sexy and powerful.

Em turned toward the other musicians, and they jammed together in perfect synchronicity. The energy from the stage was pulsing as they finished the song. The crowd cheered, and the singer picked Em up around the waist and gave her a twirl.

"And that," the singer said into the mic, breathless and grinning ear to ear, "is how you play the mother fucking fiddle, ladies and gentlemen!"

The crowd called out for an encore. Em smiled and raised her hand to block the bright stage lights. She looked out into the sea of people, and her euphoric expression changed to one of horror as she met his gaze.

8

E m pushed her way through the crowd. The cold October air
sliced her skin as she burst through the bar's exit and onto the
sidewalk.

"Em," Michael called out from behind.

She kept walking. Why the hell was Michael there?

Then, like a bullet penetrating flesh, a thought pierced her brain.
She had played the violin. She'd held the bow, let her fingers caress
each string, let the music take over and flow through her body just as
oxygen entered her lungs. Nothing had felt this real since the last
time she had held Polly—the night she played the Paganini piece
before she met up with Zoe to go to Sadie's Hollow.

The night her friends ditched her.

Anger gripped her heart and contracted like a fist.

"Mary Michelle MacCaslin! I'm talking to you."

She stiffened. The sound of Michael calling her by her real name
sent shivers up her spine.

"Oh," she said and turned to face him. "It's Mary Michelle now, is
it?" Puffs of air billowed into white bursts of sound as she bit out each
word into the freezing night air.

"Em, you can still play?" Michael's eyes were wide with disbelief.

She shook her head. "I don't play anymore. I can't. I have you and Zoe to thank for that, don't I?"

His eyes pleaded with her. "Em, I just saw you. You were incredible."

What the hell had gotten into her? Why didn't she leave the bar when she saw the band playing? She had stayed far, far away from music over the last twelve years. Spending time with her deaf Australian grandmother and helping her mother with her research with deaf children had allowed her to live a life with little exposure to music. But now that she was back in Langley Park, the rules and limitations she had relied upon to insulate herself from the world of music were disintegrating like sugar cubes in a scalding mug of tea.

She squared her jaw and met Michael's gaze. "I will never, never be able to play like I used to." She raised her hand and revealed the long scar that zigzagged down her ring finger. "This is why I will never be able to play."

Michael took a step back.

"It's what you wanted to see, right? I saw you looking at my hand after Zoe's brother and his Barbie-doll family left."

Michael winced.

She knew it! All she was to him was some carnival attraction that peaked his curiosity.

The wind whooshed down the street, and an icy rain fell from the sky. Em shivered and pulled her jacket across her body.

Michael stripped off his hoodie. "You're freezing. Put this on."

The gesture made her laugh. "You have got to be kidding me. So *now* you care about my well-being?"

"I've always cared about you, Em," he said, his words thick with emotion. "Now take the hoodie. You're not dressed for the cold."

"Excuse me? You don't get to have an opinion on how I dress!"

She wasn't about to wait for his reply and walked away. She didn't know where she was going, but it needed to be someplace where she didn't have to look at Michael MacCarron's face. Somewhere she didn't have to feel the intensity radiating off of him. They were like two live wires dancing precariously close to each other. If they were to touch, sparks would fly.

She quickened her pace, but his heavy steps followed behind her. The heels were a bad choice, and within seconds, she pitched forward on the ice-slick pavement and fell into a group of people clustered together on the sidewalk.

"Easy does it," came a man's voice.

She looked up and tried to place the person who was holding on to her elbow. "Do I know you?"

"Em's fine, Kyle," came Michael's clipped voice. "I was about to take her home."

"Kyle Benson?" Em asked, finding her balance.

A look of shock crossed Kyle's face, but he replaced it with a hesitant smile. "Looks like you remembered me. It's been a long time, Em."

She glanced at Michael. He was glaring at her and clenching the hoodie in his hands.

She ignored Michael's seething gaze. "Did you drive here, Kyle?"

"I did. I'm parked across the street. Do you need a ride?"

"She doesn't need a ride anywhere," Michael growled.

"Actually, Kyle," Em said, meeting Michael's stony gaze, "I would love a ride home. I'm staying at my dad's place."

Michael blew out an audible breath. "For Christ's sake, Em! We live right next door to each other."

"It's no trouble," Kyle said, fumbling with a set of keys. "I still live in Langley Park. It won't be out of my way at all to bring you home."

"At least take the hoodie." Michael draped the worn sweatshirt over her shoulders.

He pulled the soft cotton around her neck. She inhaled his scent, and hints of spearmint and lemongrass sent her reeling back to the night he kissed her. His warm fingers pressed into her bare neck, and a flash of those fingers twined with her grandmother's pearls flooded her mind. She shivered, but it had nothing to do with the cold.

"And Kyle," Michael said, his hands skimming her collarbone, "head straight home. This sleet may turn to ice, and I don't want you driving Em anywhere in an ice storm."

She wanted to tell Michael to fuck off. Who was he to make any demands? But her body was too preoccupied with his fingers as they brushed against her neck. She didn't even notice the sleet creating an icy layer on the pavement.

Damn this stupid crush she'd always harbored for Michael MacCarron. Damn that tiny space in her heart that would never forget the way he kissed her.

A hand pressed against her lower back. She recoiled and arched away from the touch. It was Kyle's hand. She stepped back and gave him an apologetic smile.

Michael shoved his hands into his pockets, but his eyes stayed locked on her. She met his gaze. They were like children in a staring contest, neither giving any indication of conceding defeat.

Kyle broke their standoff. "We should go, Em. Michael's right about getting ahead of the weather."

EM RUBBED at the scar on her ring finger. Coming back to Langley Park was like entering an alternate reality. A reality where she could play the violin and everything she had tried to forget about Michael MacCarron came hurtling back at her at lightning speed.

"Em, are you okay?" Kyle asked.

She blinked. "Did you say something. I'm sorry, I'm all in my head right now. What was it you asked?"

Kyle pressed a button on the car's console. "Are you warm enough?"

"I'm fine," she replied curtly, then decided to temper her response. Kyle was kind enough to take her home. She had no reason to be cruel to him. He didn't make her play the violin. He didn't ask Michael to follow her to the bar. "Thank you for driving me home. I hope I didn't ruin your plans. I saw you were with friends."

Kyle flipped on the blinker and turned his F-150 pickup truck onto the Langley Parkway. "It's no bother. I was just leaving a small fundraising event nearby."

"What were you raising money for on Halloween?" Em asked, relieved to focus on Kyle and take her mind off Michael MacCarron.

"It was for me."

"For you?"

Kyle adjusted his grip on the steering wheel. "Yes, some folks would like to see me run for state representative."

"Kyle, that's wonderful! I never knew you were interested in politics. I thought it was…"

"Photography," he supplied.

"Yes, photography! Is that still a hobby of yours?"

"It's my profession."

"Is it?" Em asked, settling into the front seat and relaxing her hands in her lap.

"I do a little of everything, but my passion is nature photography."

Em nodded and looked out the window as they passed by the Langley Park Senior Living Campus.

Kyle tapped his fingers on the steering wheel. "I don't mean to pry, but my mom mentioned your dad moved into the assisted living cottages."

Em rubbed the back of her neck. Just the thought of Anita Benson made her tense. "Yeah, he went through a real rough patch with his health. A cottage opened up, and his doctors urged him to take it. I'm in town for a couple of months to get the house into shape so he can put it on the market. Then I'll head back to Australia."

"My mom mentioned running into you." He said it almost like an apology.

She let out a nervous laugh. "I don't think I'm on the list of her favorite people."

"There are days I'm not even sure if I'd make that list. She's an intense person. She expects a lot, but her heart is always in the right place."

Em rubbed at her scar. "Your mom was the nurse who admitted me after I was hurt at Sadie's Hollow."

"I know," he said, fingers still drumming. "My mom said you didn't remember what happened that night."

She nodded. "I hardly remember anything—and everything I do remember doesn't make any sense."

He gave her a sympathetic smile. "I'm sorry. That's got to be terrible."

Em sat forward. "Do you remember seeing me that night? I mean, I remember bumping into you, but after that, everything gets fuzzy."

"I'm sorry, Em. There were a ton of people. I was just hanging out with everyone."

"I really need to know what happened that night, Kyle. Even if my injury was all my fault, I just need to know."

"What do you think could have happened?" he asked, turning onto Foxglove Lane.

"I don't know. Maybe I left the party and wandered into the town. But somehow, I got back to Sadie's Hollow. Michael and Zoe found me on those steps near the cemetery."

"The Steps to Hell?" Kyle asked.

"Yes, The Steps to Hell," she echoed as her darkened house came into view.

The lights were on at Michael's next door. He'd beat her back.

"Here we are," Kyle said, slowing the truck.

Em looked at her house. She wasn't ready to go home. She wasn't ready to be surrounded by her old life. And she certainly wasn't ready to be a stone's throw from Michael MacCarron.

"How about we go grab a drink. I'm not ready to call it an evening yet."

Kyle's expression went blank.

"Unless you have somewhere you need to be," Em amended.

"No, no! Of course, we can grab a drink," Kyle said. "Let's try Park Tavern."

He drove around the block and turned onto Mulberry Drive. The town center buzzed with Halloween activity. The trick-or-treaters had gone home hours ago, but the adults were still out enjoying Langley Park's bars and restaurants.

Kyle circled the block looking for parking. "I'll drop you off at the door. You can grab some seats at the bar. I'll meet you inside after I find a parking spot."

She left the warmth of Kyle's car. The icy rain had subsided, and the town center sparkled under the warm glow of the street lamps. Her eyes widened as she looked into Park Tavern's front window. Sam Sinclair was behind the bar chatting with a couple dressed like *Game of Thrones* characters.

Sam.

Sam had been the big brother she'd never had. He was Michael's cousin, but they looked more like brothers, sharing the same auburn hair and green eyes. Sam spent a lot of time at Michael's growing up. He would be tasked with taking them to the park or over to the botanic gardens. Always tall for his age, Sam was a gentle giant whether he was pushing her on the swings or lifting her up to pick a leaf off a tree branch.

A gust of wind ruffled the bare branches of the trees lining the street, and Em inhaled the spearmint and lemongrass scent of Michael's hoodie. She'd forgotten she still had it on. She pulled the jacket around her. But before she had a chance to lapse back into thoughts of Michael, her gaze traveled across the tavern to a high-top table near the back. Zoe sat alone, picking at the label of a beer bottle, her eyes locked on Sam.

After all these years, was Zoe still pining away for Sam Sinclair?

The anguished look on her face gave her the answer. For a moment, Em's anger toward her old friend waned. She watched Sam meet Zoe's gaze with a clueless smile as he waved to her from the bar. Sam had no idea how Zoe felt.

A mix of exhilaration and triumph washed over her. It whispered, "Zoe deserves Sam's indifference. You've lost so much. It's only right that Zoe feels her fair share of misery."

A hand tapped her shoulder, and she whirled around.

Kyle raised his hands in mock surrender. "It's only me."

She pulled the hoodie around her. "Sorry, Kyle." She glanced into Park Tavern. A moment ago, she was ready to bask in Zoe's pain, but now, all she felt was shame. "I don't think this place is my scene. I'm just going to walk home."

"I could drive you, or we could try somewhere else."

Kyle was the sweet puppy dog type she preyed on, but she couldn't go there with Kyle—especially with his mother of all people caring for her father.

"That's sweet, but a little fresh air would do me good." She started to go but turned back to face him. "Maybe we can grab a coffee while I'm in town."

Kyle reached into his pocket. "Here's my card. All my numbers are on it."

"Thanks for driving me back to Langley Park. You were a lifesaver tonight. Do you think..." she trailed off.

"What? Do I think, what?"

She slid the card into her purse and chewed her lip. "I told you. I was going to try and figure out what happened to me the night I was injured."

Kyle nodded.

"If I have any questions about Sadie's Hollow or the towns near it, do you think you'd be able to help me with that? It's been a long time since I've been home. I'm just not as familiar with the area anymore."

He brightened a shade. "Of course. I'll help you out with whatever you need."

THE CLAP of her high heels clicked on the pavement as she turned onto Foxglove Lane. The Tudors and bungalows once lit for Halloween trick-or-treaters were now dark with carved pumpkins sitting stoic and still on porch steps.

Michael's house was dark, and so was his carriage house. She let out a relieved sigh. He must have gone to bed. Something on the sidewalk in front of her porch step twinkled in the light. She bent down and picked up a Kit Kat. Ben Fisher's daughter must have dropped it.

She shook her head and smiled, thinking of the sassy little girl. She was about to pocket the candy when a man stepped out of the shadows.

9

Em shrieked and hurled the Kit Kat at the dark form looming on her porch.

"Christ, Em! It's just me."

"What the hell are you doing out here?"

Michael stepped out of the shadows, and the moonlight lit his face. His features were pinched like an exasperated parent waiting up for an unruly teenager breaking curfew. He rubbed the back of his neck then crossed his arms. "What took you so long to get home? And why the hell were you walking? Did Kyle Benson try to make a move on you?"

Em pushed past him and unlocked the front door. "I'm sorry. I didn't get the memo that you had any say about what I do or who I do it with. And for your information, I eat guys like Kyle Benson for breakfast."

Michael put a hand on the doorframe. "We need to talk."

She ducked under his arm and went inside. "I have nothing to say to you, and there's nothing you can say to me that would change anything. So, I don't see the point."

She went to the sidebar and poured a whiskey. "I'd offer you one." She held up the glass and tossed back its contents. "But you're leaving." She picked up the bottle of Teeling and poured another three fingers.

Michael switched on a lamp. The soft pool of light might as well have been a spotlight magnifying the significance of every stick of furniture and every framed photograph. Em's gaze rested on the baby grand.

"I bet you could still play that, too," he said, walking over to the piano, his voice softening. He lifted the cover and ran his fingers soundlessly across the keys.

She joined him and dropped her gaze to where his index finger rested on middle C.

"Em, you know Zoe and I tried to contact you. We wrote letters. We called. We knew there was no way to make it right, but you cut us off. It really wrecked Zoe. She had to come back home after her first year of college."

Em skimmed her index finger over the keys, leaving it to rest only millimeters from Michael's.

"Em," Michael continued, "I'm sorry. Zoe is sorry. If you'd only read our letters, you'd have seen. You would have understood. We never wanted anything to happen to you."

She set her empty glass on the piano and licked her lips. Her eyes adjusted to the dim light, and she met his gaze. His green eyes were clouded with guilt and pain. Had she not come armed with anger, she may not have been able to resist him.

She took his hand and pulled him to sit on the piano bench. He complied. She released his hand and stood between his thighs and rested her palms on his shoulders. Now they were eye to eye.

"You're sorry?" She said the words like a black widow weaving her web.

He nodded.

She ran her fingertips down his jawline. The scruff tickled the pads of her fingers, and a warmth grew inside her core. But this wasn't about sex. This was about power. This was about showing Michael MacCarron he didn't get to dictate her forgiveness. The anger that had sustained her all these years snarled and writhed with delight. She lifted a leg and hooked it around Michael's. His expression turned to confusion as she hooked her other leg around his. She straddled his lap, her tiny skirt riding dangerously high up her thighs. His hands fell to her waist, and she circled her hips.

Michael shifted. "What are you doing, Em?"

"What does it look like I'm doing?" She lifted her hips a fraction. He was responding to her advances. The evidence of his arousal pressed hard against her center.

She smirked. This power trip made her core buzz with excitement.

"You don't like this?" she asked, whispering into his ear.

His fingers flexed and tightened around her hips. She was winning. She was in control—or at least she thought she was.

She inhaled, and Michael's scent filled her nostrils, evoking the memory of their kiss at Sadie's Hollow. It took every ounce of anger she had to bury those thoughts deep in her mind. She closed her eyes and focused. She would treat him like she treated all the men she fucked—like a toy, like something she used to scratch an itch.

Em slid her hand down and palmed his cock through his pants. It twitched and begged for her touch.

She lowered her head and met his gaze. His shallow breaths came in soft puffs against her lips. She unbuttoned his fly, and his hand moved from her hip and into her hair. He laced his fingers into her braid and cradled the back of her head with his large palm.

She had Michael MacCarron right where she wanted him.

"Em," he said. The word came out in one tight syllable.

"Hmm," she replied, swiveling her hips and grinding as she worked to release the next button on his fly.

He wrapped his fingers around the tail of her braid and pulled like he'd done with her grandmother's pearls. Her resolve slipped a fraction. The anger driving this escapade was dangerously close to collapsing into full-blown desire, and she couldn't surrender to that emotion.

"Em," he whispered. He pulled harder, forcing a moan to escape her lips.

"Yes," she answered, her shallow breaths meeting his.

He maintained his grip and met her gaze. "You're not in charge here."

"I think I am," she answered, grinding into his cock until another swift, deliciously painful yank of her braid forced her to stop.

"I'm not some boy you can manipulate, Mary Michelle."

She shivered at the sound of her real name and bit her bottom lip. She narrowed her gaze in an attempt to regain the upper hand. She had to turn the tables. The only way she could overcome her feelings for Michael MacCarron was to make him a conquest and use him like she used all the other men she had dominated.

Michael MacCarron as her equal was too frightening a prospect.

"I watched you all night, Em. I know your game. I know you think you're in control right now, but I have some fucking bad news for you." He released her braid and moved his hands to grip her ass.

She inhaled sharply.

He pressed his lips against the shell of her ear. "You're not in control. Not even close."

In one clean movement, Michael stood and lifted her into the air. She tightened her legs around his waist as he turned and pressed her back against the wall. The sharp contact sent electric pulses racing to her core. Her center grew hot and wet. Anger was losing, and desire was taking over. She softened her gaze, but Michael's eyes hardened. He took a step back, and his hands moved from her ass to her waist. Her boots made a sharp click against the wood floor as he pried her body away from his and set her down.

"We're going to talk, Em, but not like this."

She parted her lips to respond. But she couldn't speak. A pang of anxiety burst through her chest. None of her tricks were going to work with him. All she could do was stare into his eyes for one brief moment before he turned and walked out the front door.

MICHAEL UNLOCKED the door to the MacCarron law office Monday morning and set three steaming cups of to-go coffees and a bouquet of sunflowers on his desk. It was still early, but he knew the occupants of the architecture office next door would already be in. He clicked his computer to life and checked his appointments.

His father, E. Noland MacCarron, Esq., had opened the law office more than three decades ago and quickly became the lawyer Kansas City families turned to for all their trust, will, and estate planning needs.

He saw his dad in every corner of the space. Pictures of his father receiving Kansas City's Most Prestigious Lawyer award and golf trophies lined the shelves. A photograph of his mother and father on their wedding day sat next to a vase of wilted sunflowers.

After his mother passed away seven years ago, his father had insisted on keeping the vase filled with his dead wife's favorite flower. Michael discarded the drooping sunflowers into the trash and replaced them with the fresh bouquet. He stared at the flowers. It had been ages since his father had stepped foot into the office. Michael didn't have to continue the sunflower tradition. But come Monday morning, his first stop was always to the florist in Langley Park's town center.

He ran his hands through his hair and shook his head. He'd barely slept a wink last night, and when he did manage to sleep, his dreams exploded with images of Em. Her eyes wild, blue, and flashing. Her body pressed against his. Her sweet scent like the tang of freshly cut oranges. It had taken every ounce of strength to resist her last night.

It wasn't like he hadn't been with other women. He dated different people through college and law school. But nothing ever stuck. Every relationship lacked something he couldn't put his finger on. When his father's health deteriorated, his dating life went from sparse to nonexistent.

He blew out a frustrated breath, picked up the coffees, and headed next door. A petite, older woman's eyes lit up as he entered the architecture office of Fisher Designs.

"Morning, Mrs. G," he said, handing the woman a coffee.

"Benjamin tells me Em is back."

Mrs. G wasn't one to mince words.

Mrs. Rosemary Giacopazzi, known to everyone in town as Mrs. G, had been the beloved third-grade teacher at Langley Park Elementary School before retiring and coming to work as the office manager for Ben Fisher's architecture firm, Fisher Designs. There was hardly a person in Langley Park who wasn't touched by her kindness. Michael himself had been her pupil along with Ben, Zoe, his cousin, Sam, and Em.

Michael took a sip of his coffee, and his shoulders relaxed a fraction. Just being near Mrs. G made him feel better.

"I had no idea she was coming home. Dr. MacCaslin didn't mention anything to me—not even when I helped him move into the assisted living cottage."

"Well, honey," Mrs. G said, giving his forearm a squeeze, "you know he wouldn't say anything about Em. That man's never gotten past what happened to his daughter. I'm sure he blames himself. I don't think he's spoken a word about her to anyone in over a decade."

Michael nodded. Mrs. G was right.

"And how's your father doing?" she asked, but before he could answer, Ben Fisher emerged from behind the closed conference room door.

"Thank God for coffee," Ben said with a smile. He picked up the steaming cup and took a sip.

"Late night?" Michael asked, grateful for the change of subject.

Ben's grin widened. Michael marveled at how the once rigid and stoic architect had changed since Jenna had come into his life six months ago. Ben's first wife had committed suicide leaving him to raise his young daughter, Kate, alone. Michael was glad to see that Ben and Jenna had found each other. He envied the contented grin that came so easily to his friend these days.

"I think there should be a law that if the day after Halloween happens to fall on a weekday, they cancel school," Ben said with a chuckle.

"Amen to that," Mrs. G echoed as she organized a stack of blueprints on her desk.

"Kate was a bear to wake up this morning and demanded Kit Kats for breakfast."

"It's your wife I feel sorry for today," Mrs. G said. "It takes the patience of a saint to deal with children coming down from Halloween sugar hangovers."

Ben's wife had previously worked as a traveling reading specialist going city to city setting up a reading program that targeted inner city elementary students. Now she worked as the reading intervention teacher at Langley Park Elementary.

"I agree. I hope you have something nice planned for Jenna tonight," Michael added.

A mischievous look crossed Ben's face.

Michael shook his head. "Christ, Ben! I meant like you cooking dinner or bringing home a bottle of her favorite wine."

Mrs. G looked up from her perch at the reception desk. "First of all, watch your language, Michael Edward MacCarron."

Ben and Michael shared an amused look, but like good little boys, they straightened up and bit back their smiles.

"Second, here's your stair design, Michael," Mrs. G said, handing Michael a piece of paper.

Michael looked at the paper and swallowed hard. The phone rang, and he was grateful Mrs. G's attention was pulled to the call.

"I better get this day started, too," Michael said. He tucked the paper under his arm and picked up his coffee.

Ben walked him out. "I hope you don't mind me bringing this up, but it seemed pretty tense with Em last night. I could tell it was a complete shock to Zoe. Do you know why Em's back?"

"I've been helping Dr. MacCaslin with all the legalities of moving to the Senior Living Campus. He's going to be selling the Foursquare." Michael didn't mention that Em's father had to sell his home to afford the assisted living cottage. "I assume Em's here to go through the home's contents and decide if there are any items she'd like to keep." Michael also kept to himself that he'd glimpsed inside Em's room. It was trashed, and the layer of dust coating each broken trophy and photograph suggested the damage had been done many years ago.

Ben shook his head. "It's a shame what happened to Em."

Even though Ben was Zoe's older brother, Michael knew Zoe never shared the details of Sadie's Hollow with him. Ben knew as much as the rest of the town—Em got hurt while partying, ending any chance of a career in music, and she had left Langley Park to go and live with her mother in Australia.

"It is," Michael answered, but his attention was pulled to an approaching red Mercedes coupe.

A woman holding a large to-go cup from The Drip Coffee Shop with a map spread out over the dash passed by oblivious to their presence on the sidewalk.

It was Em. But where was she going?

"Looks like Dr. MacCaslin's old coupe is still drivable," Ben said as both men watched the car pass.

Michael frowned. "The tires are bald, and I'd bet it's been at least five years since the oil was changed."

"She's probably going to visit her father," Ben said, patting his shoulder with a good-naturedly, big brother kindness he'd shown Michael since they were kids.

Michael nodded, but his mind was racing.

Em wouldn't need a map to find her way to the Senior Living Campus.

10

E m passed by Michael's office every morning that week, and the scene had been the same each day: Em holding a giant to-go coffee from The Drip with a map spread wide across the dashboard of the coupe. She wouldn't get home until late at night. He would hear the Mercedes pull up the packed gravel driveway and the slam of the garage door as she locked the car inside her carriage house situated three feet from his.

He would be inside his carriage house tinkering around with his digital audio workstation when she would finally return. A hobby he practiced in secret.

Who would trust their estate planning to a lawyer who spent his free time mixing techno beats?

No one.

His father never supported his love of music and especially didn't understand his affinity for thumping bass layered with electronic melodies. Em's talent was something his father could understand. Of course, it was all right for Mary Michelle MacCaslin to follow her dreams. She was a renowned classical violinist. And what was he? According to his father, just some kid making noise.

Michael had given everything to the MacCarron law practice. For the last five years, he had not only run the business, he had made it even more profitable. But it didn't come easy. He'd worked his ass off day in and day out. His father had started the firm almost forty years ago and built a rock solid reputation. People would come from all over the state to have E. Noland MacCarron Esq. comb through their finances and craft meticulous wills and trusts.

Michael drummed his fingers on the dashboard. He kept his Audi parked in the driveway and was sure Em would recognize it. So today, he opted to take the car he drove all through high school and college —his trusty old Range Rover. Em had only ridden in it once, and he winced remembering that drive from the Hollow to the Midwest Medical Center.

It was ten past seven in the morning. Em had gone by around this time every day this week. Now Friday, a cold November drizzle peppered the air and darkened the pavement. He adjusted the car's rearview mirror. Like a hunter waiting for its prey, he sat and watched for the Mercedes to pass by. He'd rescheduled all his meetings until next week. His Friday was wide open, and he needed to find out where the hell Em was going every day.

A jolt of adrenaline heightened his senses when he spotted the cherry red car. Built for summer drives, it looked silly traversing the slick late-autumn road. He would insist she drive his Audi or even his Rover while she was home. The coupe would be paralyzed in an inch of snow and was no match for the ice storms that could ravage the state in a matter of minutes. Then he remembered the fire in Em's icy blue eyes and the way she thought she could so easily seduce him. She wasn't the innocent girl next door anymore. It would be a fight to get her even to consider borrowing one of his cars.

Em passed by the Rover—coffee in hand and map wide open. Michael slid his vehicle into traffic and followed a few cars behind her. The Mercedes coupe would be easy to keep in his sights. Swimming in a sea of sedately colored sedans and SUVs, the coupe screamed, "Here I am world!" and the beautiful girl with auburn hair driving would have been a distraction even if she was in a beat-up Buick.

He followed her south, leaving the Kansas City area until they merged onto Highway 169 and the city skyscrapers were replaced with dormant fields and roaming livestock. They drove nearly a half an hour before she took the US 59 exit, and then it clicked.

Em was going to Sadie's Hollow.

Traffic was sparse. She could easily identify him if he continued to follow her into the small town of Lyleville, Kansas, population fifty-one. He pulled off the highway and drove into the nearby city of Garrett, a whopping population of three thousand four hundred—a behemoth compared to Lyleville—and pulled over to the side of the road.

He cut the ignition. He wanted to give her a head start. More importantly, he wanted to catch her doing whatever the hell it was she was doing in the hollow.

But he couldn't wait long.

After a few minutes, his knee bounced with nervous energy. He started the car and drove the familiar route to the old high school hangout.

The Mercedes was parked alongside the road in front of the cemetery. A knot, heavy and menacing, formed in the pit of his stomach. He hadn't been back to the hollow since the night of Em's accident. The night he had left her to fend for herself while he swam in the accolades of teenagers dancing to his music and the attention of Tiffany Shelton.

He zipped up his jacket and walked past the cemetery. He eyed the limestone steps that led down to the hollow.

The Steps to Hell.

The very steps where he had found Em sprawled out like a rag doll—her hand mangled, her clothes dusted with a chalky film. The memories came flooding back as easily as pressing play on a movie you had watched a thousand times.

The thick summer foliage that encased the hollow was gone, the leaves blown to the ground by the dogged Kansas wind. Naked branches were spread thin and bare across the sky allowing Michael to watch Em investigate the hollow. The space looked smaller to him.

As a teenager, the hollow, filled with tents and teenagers, seemed almost magical. Anything was possible under the stars and away from his father.

The misty drizzle changed to a biting sleet, and Michael adjusted his ball cap, pulling the bill low on his forehead. Em was wearing a black trench cinched tightly around her waist. He frowned. After he persuaded her to drive a more appropriate car, he would insist she purchase a decent winter coat. But his irritation dissipated as he watched her methodically trace her steps around the hollow. She stopped at a small cluster of rocks and ran her fingers across the rain-slicked surface. Her other hand went to her throat and lingered, and he could read her thoughts.

His lips on hers.

His fingers wrapped in the string of delicate pearls.

The press of her slight frame against his hard angles.

He let out a ragged breath. That perfect kiss would always be tangled and marred by Em's life-altering accident. But before his guilt could take hold, it was edged out by wonder.

Em raised her arms, palms up. The cold rain fell onto her outstretched hands. She turned in slow circles as her body fell into position and she began playing an invisible violin with her right arm bowing gracefully.

It was like watching someone else's dream. Em's hair, wet and loose, flowed like an auburn mane. Her slight body moved in sync with some tune locked inside her mind. She was spellbinding, and he wanted to touch her like he had that night all those years ago. He closed his eyes, and the memory of their kiss transported him back in time.

"What the hell are you doing here?"

Michael blinked. Em stared up at him, her hands no longer playing the violin, but in tight balls against her hips. An embarrassed blush crept up her exposed neck, and her cheeks bloomed scarlet.

"What am I doing here?" he asked, walking toward her through the barren trees. "What are you doing here?"

"It's none of your damned business what I do," she said. She narrowed her eyes. "Did you follow me here?"

Michael stuffed his hands into the pockets of his jeans. It was the only way to restrain them from pulling the hood of her trench up over her head. She had to be freezing.

"Somebody needs to be looking out for you. For one thing, the tires on the coupe are nearly bald. You could get into an accident. Icy roads are no fucking joke—especially out here in the middle of nowhere."

Her eyes were blazing. "So, we're back to this. The "Michael Really Cares About Em" show, huh?"

"Christ! How many times do I have to tell you, I'm sorry. I've never stopped caring for you. Never!"

Her eyes were lined with the black eyeliner he had seen her wear Halloween night, and the makeup had smudged making her look like some dystopian fairy. He gathered his resolve and softened his gaze, hoping she would dial back the anger.

"You could have fucked me on Halloween," she challenged.

Michael blew out a breath. "That's not what you wanted. Sex had nothing to do with that little stunt you pulled."

She shook her head, pushed past him, and headed toward the cemetery. He followed behind but stopped when she went to take the steps.

"Em, don't walk on the steps!"

He knew the legend of The Steps to Hell was a silly tale passed down from generation to generation to keep restless youth from defacing the ancient tombstones. But his words still came out in a hoarse gasp.

Em looked over her shoulder, lifted her chin, then ascended the first few steps. She stopped midway as he walked up the sloped grass next to her. Her expression flashed something that reminded him of the innocent girl he remembered, but then her eyes hardened into blue ice.

"Em, I—"

She cut him off. "Do you honestly think The Steps to Hell can hurt me now? There's nothing left to take away, Michael. I could tap dance up and down the length of them all day, and nothing could hurt me."

She was holding tight to her anger. He could feel it radiating off of her. Her eyes burned with it. But beyond the rage, there was sorrow buried in the depths of her gaze.

"Come on, Em. This isn't you. Talk to me."

She turned away and headed for the coupe. Her hands were shaking, and she dropped her keys as she tried to unlock the car door.

He retrieved the keys. Her back was to him. Her shoulders rose and fell with her breath in angry pulses. She turned and leaned against the car. Her gaze swept over him like a mathematician evaluating an equation.

"You really want to help me, Michael?"

She rubbed her hands together. The tips of her fingers were red from the biting cold. He pocketed her keys and folded her small hands inside his. She tensed under his touch, but she didn't pull away.

"Yes, I want to help you."

For a moment, he saw the girl he kissed on the rock. The girl who used to sit at her window, flashlight in hand, as they signaled back and forth late into the night. He saw Em, back pressed to the side of her house, smiling and calling him to run through the rain and join her.

She blinked, and the girl he remembered disappeared.

"If you want to help me, you'll leave me the hell alone. You're the last person I'd ever trust."

She tried to pull her hands from his grip, but he held tight. Her words stung. Her words cut him to the core, but he knew she was lying. She might not realize it, but he did. Rage and anger may have been her default setting these past twelve years, but it wasn't who she was.

Michael released her hands, but instead of letting her go, he cupped her face. "You forget, I've known you your whole life. I don't care if it's been twelve years or twelve thousand years, I will always know your heart."

Em's bottom lip trembled. She relaxed a fraction, and he brushed his thumb across her lips. He smiled, but his expression fell when she pushed him back.

"You don't know me, Michael, not anymore." She held out her hand. "I have to get back to Langley Park. I want my keys. Now!"

11

E m rubbed her hands together and quickened her pace toward the Senior Living Campus. The icy November sleet had subsided, but the sky remained gray and bleak.

It would have made more sense to drive, but the four shots of Teeling she downed after returning home from Sadie's Hollow still had her head swimming. This town already thought she was a selfish, reckless fool. Adding a DUI to her list of accomplishments would only prove them right—and it would kill her father.

She pulled the sleeves of her trench over her fingertips, and a surge of hot anger bloomed in her chest. Michael was right. She didn't come prepared for the cold. Her cheeks burned thinking about him following her. She must have looked like a lunatic prancing around the hollow. But it was the only place she could think to start. Unfortunately, after a week of retracing her steps, she wasn't any closer to unlocking the events of that awful night.

To add insult to injury, Michael had watched her linger over the boulders where he'd kissed her. She hated how vividly she remembered his kiss. That kiss awakened a part of her she had never known existed. She had gone to the hollow a girl. That kiss had made her feel like a woman. She bristled with embarrassment. The whiskey hadn't helped her forget his warm hands cradling her face or his earnest green eyes filled with concern. She pulled her trench tight across her chest and walked the last block to the Senior Living Campus.

A young man was working the security post. He waved her through with a smile—a much different reception from the tongue-lashing she had received from the last guard. The main parking lot was filled, and she watched families pile out of minivans and head inside the main building.

She reached her father's cottage, but before she could even knock, he opened the door.

"Kiddo, we've got to head over to the main building. The concert's about to begin," Bill said, a broad grin stretched across his face. He was carrying a portable oxygen concentrator, and the gentle, airy beat of the small machine hummed expectantly.

Concert? Her father hadn't mentioned anything about a concert. When he had asked her to join him for an event on the main campus, she figured they were going to join a canasta tournament or play checkers. She didn't have a clue as to what people did in this kind of community.

"What do you mean, a concert?" she asked, trying to keep her voice steady.

"Tom and Mindy Lancaster are having their students perform for the residents. They bring the kids to play here several times a year, I'm told."

The Lancasters had been her first music teachers. Mindy taught piano and Tom, the violin. Tom had been instrumental in connecting her with the elite classical music world. A professional violinist, playing with the Kansas City Symphony, he'd invited her to play for the symphony's conductor who had confirmed her talent was the kind that only came around once in a lifetime. It was Tom who convinced her parents that her talent went far beyond just being good. It was Tom who had encouraged her to set the classical music world on fire.

Guilt settled thick and heavy inside her chest. She had never contacted him after her accident. He had reached out. She'd listened as her mother spoke with him over the phone weeks after the accident, but she didn't have the strength to take his call. He was just another person she had disappointed.

Em matched her father's pace as they left the cottage and headed to the main building. A smiling gentleman with a little girl in his arms held the door open for them. The lobby of the main building smelled of cinnamon and spice. Tasteful displays of pumpkins and gourds adorned every table, and a red garland was draped dramatically across a grand staircase. Children of all ages dressed in their Sunday best skipped up the steps with sheets of music in hand.

Her father squeezed her shoulder. "Are you ready to head up?"

Her throat was tight. "Of course, Dad."

They entered a large ballroom on the second floor. Residents and families sat together as children stood near the front of the room tuning violins and taking turns warming up on the piano. Em flexed her fingers then pulled her sleeves down. It was too loud. The squeaks of bow meeting string cut through her like razors. Her shallow breath mimicked the rapid beat of her heart. She took an aisle seat next to her father and forced her gaze to the floor.

"I ran into Tom Lancaster a few days ago on campus," her father said, settling the portable oxygen on the floor between them. "I told him you were in town, and he asked me to invite you to the recital."

Em nodded. There was no escape. She had to get through the next hour or so. She scanned the students. Seven children ranging in age from maybe six or seven to late teens all stood quietly, violin in hand. Nine children holding sheet music formed a queue next to a grand piano. Tom and Mindy were moving from student to student. They were young newlyweds when Em was a little girl. Now in their early fifties, they had barely changed from how she had remembered them, except Mindy's wrist was in a cast.

Tom clapped his hands twice, and the room quieted as a small group of residents entered the room accompanied by several nurses.

"Those are some of the people from the Memory Care Center,"

Bill said, gesturing to the group. "The Campus has one of the best Alzheimer's and dementia care facilities in the country."

The cabbie had told her the same thing the night she had arrived.

Em's eyes grew wide when Michael entered the room, pushing his father in a wheelchair. He parked the chair and kept a hand on his father's shoulder. A nurse stopped to speak with him and his brow creased as they spoke.

E. Noland MacCarron had been a force of nature. But the slight man she saw sitting in a wheelchair looked confused. He rocked from side to side, scanning the room like he was trying to figure how he had gotten there.

Tom and Mindy welcomed everyone, and a little girl with feet dangling from the piano bench kicked off the recital with a choppy variation of "Twinkle, Twinkle Little Star."

The recital progressed with child after child nervously announcing their performance piece and then working their way through the song. There were the customary squeaks and misplayed notes, but families and residents alike applauded for each young musician.

At first, Em focused on the airy beat of her father's portable oxygen, worried the memories of her old life would overwhelm her. But soon, she caught herself smiling—the memories of her happy, musical childhood temporarily muting her anger.

The final participant was finishing his violin piece when a man's raised voice cut through the air.

Noland glared at Michael with rage in his eyes. "Who the hell are you? Get your goddamned hands off me!"

The ballroom grew still. Michael and a nurse crouched down to comfort him, but Noland persisted. "I need help! These people want to kill me!"

Noland drew his arm back. The crack of fist against cheek echoed through the room. Michael's head twisted from the blow. But within seconds, he was back trying to calm his father.

Em jumped to her feet and found a teenager holding a full-sized violin. "Can I borrow this?" she asked, gesturing to the girl's instrument.

The teen nodded absentmindedly, her attention fixed on Noland.

Em took the violin, lifted the instrument to her chin, and raised the bow. She exhaled and drew the bow across the strings.

C #, B, A, A

The first four notes of the eighteenth-century hymn, "Come Thou Fount of Every Blessing," rang out through the ballroom. One of the earliest songs Tom had assigned her to memorize, she had fallen in love with the calming melody. She repeated the hymn as she walked across the ballroom and stopped in front of Noland. He'd quieted and watched her with childish wonder.

Em lowered herself to her knees and repeated the hymn. The audience faded away, and the music, hypnotic in its elegant simplicity, seemed to transport Noland to another place and another time.

E, F#, G#, A, G#

A curious expression overtook his pained features. His glassy gaze moved from her face to her hands.

F#, E, F#, E, C#

Again and again, she repeated the hymn. The slide of her fingertips cascading up and down the strings and the rhythmic dip and glide of the bow seemed to awaken Noland. He met her gaze, and the confusion she had seen in his eyes disappeared.

Em began another repetition of the hymn when several novice violins joined in and played the first measure along with her. She glanced back. Six children playing tiny violins concentrated as they worked to stay on tempo. Like a sunrise so stunning it looks otherworldly in its beauty, the music took on a haunting, ethereal quality as the sound of the seven violins combed gently through the air, lulling the audience into a mesmerized state of awe.

Noland smiled, and Em saw the man she had known her entire life. Continuing to play, she rose to her feet, turned toward the children, and mouthed, "Once more."

They played the hymn one last time before Em brought their impromptu performance to a close. She took a breath and met

Michael's gaze. A magnitude of joy and pain hung in the air between them. Every fiber of her being wanted to go to him, to comfort him, but she didn't move. Her eyes flicked to the audience sitting slack-jawed in the ballroom. The crowd remained silent for a beat, then a round of thunderous applause echoed through the room drawing the attention away from Noland and onto the children beaming proudly.

"Em, is that you?" Noland gazed up at her. His intelligent, green eyes shined with emotion.

"It is," she answered, dropping back to her knees.

He reached out and touched her face. "You've changed," he said. His displeasure with her heavy eye makeup was written all over his face.

She chuckled. "So have you, Mr. MacCarron."

He took her hand. "I've always loved that hymn. Your father and I used to sit on your front porch and listen to you play it over and over. Didn't we, Bill?"

Em glanced over her shoulder and saw her father, his nostalgic expression mimicking Noland's.

Bill put a hand on the man's shoulder. "We sure did, Noland."

"Michael's missed you, Em," Noland said, glancing up at his son.

Michael gave her a weary smile. "Come on, Dad. We should get you back to your room."

Noland nodded but returned his attention to Em. "You'll come to visit me soon, won't you? Maybe with a little less of that?" He gestured to her eyes. "You don't need it, honey. You've got nothing to hide from."

Em swiped a tear from her cheek and nodded.

Michael released the brake on his father's wheelchair.

She glanced up and met Michael's gaze. The sharp edges of her anger didn't cut quite so deep when she looked at him. Instead of the careless teenager she had held frozen in the dark recesses of her heart where time stood still, she now saw a man carrying a heavy burden. His green eyes spoke of deep loss, anguish, and remorse. It was easy to paint Michael and Zoe as villains. Black and white. Right and wrong. Sinner and saint. After her injury, she had needed to compartmentalize every part of her life into rigid categories to survive.

He must have sensed the shift in her response, but before he was able to respond, Anita Benson emerged from the crowd.

"Michael, dear, we should be getting your father back to his room."

Em's skin prickled as she watched Michael and Noland follow Anita out of the ballroom.

Tom and Mindy Lancaster were speaking with students and parents trickling out of the ballroom. Noland's outburst forgotten, families were gushing about the group performance of the hymn.

Tom worked his way through the families and waved. "Em, Bill, it's so good to see you both! That was something, Em. How did you know that song would help Noland?"

"I didn't know," she answered. "It felt like the right thing to do."

The teenage owner of the violin walked over looking starstruck, and Em handed her the violin and bow. "A little more rosin on the bow next time. But other than that, you're taking great care of your instrument."

The girl beamed and gazed at her violin lovingly before excusing herself.

Tom glanced over at his wife who was busy helping children put their violins and sheet music inside their cases. "Are you in town for long, Em?"

"I'll be here through the holidays," she answered. Her post-performance fingers trembled, and she clasped them together.

A hopeful look crossed Tom's face. "Can I ask a favor of you?"

She shared a glance with her father. "Sure."

"Would you mind helping out with the music at the Senior Living Campus? Mindy usually handles all the musical needs at the SLC during the winter holidays, but she's injured her wrist. I'm still with the symphony, and the performance schedule is crazy over the holidays. Otherwise, I would have taken over for her."

"Tom, I'm not sure—" Em said, shifting her weight from foot to foot.

But Tom cut her off. "There are a few family members of SLC residents who usually help out. You wouldn't be stuck doing this alone. It would really help Mindy and me if you did this for us."

"You should do it, kiddo," Bill said. His eyes shined with emotion.

Tom's face brightened. "It's mostly background music for a few holiday events. Give me your email address, and I'll send you the details."

What was she supposed to say? She had sworn off ever playing again, except she just performed in front of a packed ballroom.

She mustered a weak smile. "Of course, Tom. I'm happy to help."

12

M ichael slid headphones over his ears and settled into his chair tucked in the far corner of the carriage house. He stared at the screen of his digital audio workstation. His run in with Em at Sadie's Hollow and his father's outburst during the recital left him hollowed out. He ran his hand over his jaw. It was tender, but no real damage was done.

Noland's behavior was becoming more erratic. Maybe they needed to reevaluate his meds again?

Michael closed his eyes and released a weary breath.

It was a shit idea to bring his father to the recital. The doctors had mentioned that behavior problems could occur more frequently during the late afternoon and evenings as his father's Alzheimer's progressed. Sundowning, that's what they'd called it. And it was exactly what happened this evening—until Em played the violin.

Michael rubbed his eyes. Christ, he was tired. He was close to nodding off when Cody, who had been sleeping blissfully on the futon, jumped down and wagged his tail.

"You need to go out, boy?" Michael asked, shaking off sleep.

The old retriever pranced and turned in excited circles as the door to the carriage house opened.

Em stepped into the carriage house and crouched down. "Cody, you're such a big boy now." She scratched behind his ears, and the dog leaned into her.

"Last time I saw Cody, he was a puppy," she said.

Michael set his headphones on the table. He rubbed at the tense muscles in his neck. "I don't have it in me to fight with you, Em." He had gone into lawyer mode. His tone was curt and void of emotion.

"I didn't come here to fight."

He watched her pet Cody. No ripped tights or stamp-sized skirts. She was dressed comfortably in yoga pants and his hoodie. Her red hair fell in loose waves past her shoulders. He wanted to gather the strands into his hands and twist his fingers in the auburn waves. He pushed the thought out of his mind and met her gaze. His stomach clenched.

Her eyes weren't filled with the simmering ferocity he had come to know since she arrived back in Langley Park.

Her eyes were brimming, but not with kindness or even the lust he'd seen when she tried to seduce him. There was no mistaking what he saw in her sapphire blue eyes: pity. He clenched his jaw.

She could keep her goddamn pity.

"I know what you're going to say, Mary Michelle, and I don't want to hear it," he said, coming to his feet.

He could spot pity coming from a mile away. Five years ago, when his father's health declined, he could barely step foot into the Langley Park town center without someone giving him that look.

So sorry to hear about your father, Michael.

I'm sure this is very difficult for you, Michael.

"I didn't know about your dad," Em said, giving Cody one last pat on his head before she stood to face him.

"Your dad didn't tell you?" he asked, still in lawyer mode.

Em twisted the hoodie's sleeve. "My dad and I never talked about Langley Park. After the accident, after I left for Australia, we didn't talk about anything from the past."

Michael nodded. Em had completely cut him and Zoe out of her life. It wasn't a far stretch to imagine she wanted to forget everything about this place.

Em took a step toward him. "Talk to me."

He crossed his arms. "Quid pro quo."

Em frowned. "What's that supposed to mean?"

He maintained a neutral expression. "You answer one of my questions, and I'll answer one of yours."

She crossed her arms. "Fair enough, what happened to your dad?"

"I figured your father would have filled you in on all that after my dad's outburst at the recital."

Em broke eye contact. "He told me Noland was diagnosed with Alzheimer's. He said your dad's health declined quickly."

Michael ran a hand through his auburn hair. "It started about six years ago, after my mother's death."

Em flinched, and Michael knew why. She hadn't come back to Langley Park for his mother's funeral. Her mother had traveled across the ocean to attend, but she had remained in Australia.

Her finger twisted into the cuff. "I'm so sorry, Michael. I felt awful. I wanted to come back. I just couldn't."

He nodded then stared at a scuff on the wall just past her shoulder. "It was little things with my dad at first—forgetting a meeting or a client's name. But the disease progressed quickly. I sold my place in Kansas City and moved in with him. But I couldn't run the office and take care of him." He swallowed back the emotion and held tight to the neutral mask of indifference he had been hiding behind for the last five years.

"My dad said that, sometimes, he doesn't recognize you," Em added softly.

He let out an incredulous huff. "If you already knew about my dad, why the fuck did you ask?"

She met his gaze head-on. "I wanted to hear it from you."

He shifted his weight. "My turn. Quid pro quo, remember?"

"Go ahead," she said, lifting her chin.

"What were you doing at Sadie's Hollow?"

Her creamy cheeks bloomed crimson. "I was trying to remember. Trying to jog my memory."

"Why?"

She released the twisted cuff. "Because I need to know what happened that night at the hollow. Maybe it was just some stupid accident like everyone's always said, but something inside me knows there's more to it."

"Did you remember anything else?" he asked, his question barely a whisper.

He had gone over and over that night for years, trying to remember if he'd seen anything suspicious. But those thoughts always came to the same shameful conclusion: He'd been too busy playing music and wasting time with Tiffany Shelton to have noticed anything.

Her pained expression answered his question.

"My turn," she said, eyes flashing. "We're still playing the quid pro quo game, right?

He nodded. She would have made one ballbuster of an attorney.

"Is Zoe still in love with Sam?"

This caught him off guard. "Is Zoe, what?"

"Don't act like you never knew, Michael. I saw her at Park Tavern. I saw the way she was looking at him."

Fury shot through his system. "Are you jealous? Have you been pining away for Sam all this time?"

"Are you out of your mind?" she shot back. "Sam was like a big brother to me, for Christ's sake." The red bloom was back ripening her cheeks.

Michael turned toward the punching bag hanging in the opposite corner. The thought of Em with any guy nearly drove him to violence. Flashes of her dancing with that tool at the bar sent hot streaks of jealousy coursing through his veins. He needed to lace up his gloves and spend the next few hours pummeling the punching bag. Maybe then he'd be able to release the mountain of tension that was building inside him.

"I didn't come here to fight with you, Michael. I shut everything about Langley Park out for so long. Twelve years have passed. But to me, it's like I've stepped back in time."

He couldn't see her, but he could feel her. Her energy. Her spirit. He kept his gaze locked on the punching bag. Thoughts of her pressed up against her house calling to him to run through the rain and join her echoed through his mind. He felt that same pull now, that same urge to run through any obstacle to be by her side.

"Let me help you," he said.

"With what?" Em asked.

Michael turned to face her. "With remembering."

Em's fingers were back to twisting the hoodie's cuff. "I don't know how you could help. After you left me…"

Guilt and desire twisted inside his chest. Em didn't have to finish her sentence for him to know what she meant. After he left her, he never came back. He never went to find her.

But that didn't mean he couldn't help her now.

"You said it yourself, Em. You've been gone a long time. I can help you. We can search the area around the hollow, visit the nearby towns. Maybe you'll see something that will help you remember."

She parted her lips to speak, but nothing came out.

Michael pressed on, "I've always had this feeling that you must have been taken somewhere that night. I can't put together how you could have been injured so badly without somebody seeing or hearing something."

"I've thought the same thing." Her words were barely a whisper.

"Let me help you," he said and took a step closer.

She shook her head, but the furrow in her brow told him she was considering his offer.

"Maybe it's a stupid idea—a wild goose chase," she said. "I'm supposed to be helping my dad—"

"Sell the house," Michael said, finishing her thought. "I know your dad needs to sell the house to pay for the cottage at the Senior Living Campus."

Anger blazed in her eyes. "How do you know that?"

"Who do you think helped him get into the campus in the first place? Who do you think has handled all the legalities and paper-work? Who do you think made sure he had money set aside to update his Foursquare?"

Her fingers twisted the cuff of the hoodie.

"I'm not telling you this to hurt you, Em," he began as an idea came to him.

The fire in her eyes dialed down a fraction.

"You can work on the house during the week, and we can spend the weekends searching the area around Sadie's Hollow."

Em wasn't fiddling with the cuff anymore. She remained stock-still, the blue of her eyes now deceptively serene like the calm before the storm.

The attorney in him pressed on, eager to make his case. "I know your house needs some work done. I can put you in touch with an architect who knows the homes of Langley Park like the back of his hand. And, more importantly, you can't be speeding around the back roads of Kansas in your dad's old Mercedes coupe. That car was not made to traverse snow or ice-caked roads. You know how unpre-dictable the Midwest weather can be this time of year. We can take my old Range Rover. It can get through anything."

Em flicked her gaze to the Rover. "Quid pro quo?"

He nodded. He'd lost track of whose turn it was to ask a question. But at this point, it didn't matter. Em was close to accepting his help. He could feel it.

Her eyes traveled over the digital workstation. A keyboard, bass guitar and drum pad sat propped next to a pair of speakers. The screen was illuminated with a track he'd been mixing.

"Why didn't you study music in college?"

He looked at the instruments and released a breath. "Because I didn't. An accident may have derailed your life. Obligation derailed mine."

Michael met her gaze. It was like standing before a dam of memo-ries seconds before it was about to give way. He remembered the smile on her face and her sweet, bubbling laughter as he sprinted through the rain toward her. He remembered drifting off to sleep to the sound of her playing the violin late into the night as the music escaped through her open bedroom window and fluttered over him like whisper-soft kisses.

"I should go," she said. But she didn't move.

He knew she felt it, too. Their history filled the space between them. Memory after memory popped and cracked like fireworks on the Fourth of July.

He took her hand. "Em, let me help you."

She inhaled sharply. He was holding her left hand. He could feel the smooth, raised scar that ran along her ring finger—both a tactile and a visual reminder of the night she lost everything. A zigzagged scarlet letter proclaiming her greatest loss. He grazed his thumb across her wrist eliciting another sharp breath. Her hand relaxed, but she wouldn't meet his gaze.

"I know you don't trust me. But I promise, I'm not going to let you down again."

Her hand tensed, but she didn't pull away.

"I'll be at The Drip in the town center tomorrow morning at eight." She knew the place. He had watched her drive by his office each day this week holding a giant to-go cup from the local coffee house. "I'll park the Rover out in front. She'll be all gassed up and ready to go. We can leave from there and start looking anywhere you want."

"I don't think—" she whispered, but he didn't let her finish.

"You don't have to decide anything right now. You know where I'll be tomorrow. It's up to you, Mary Michelle."

13

E m locked the door to her childhood home and glanced over at Michael's house. The sun glinted off the second-floor windows like they were tossing her shiny, knowing winks.

"That's really Michael's house," she whispered, squinting her eyes as a far-off wind chime clanged in the breeze.

Of course, she remembered Michael's home. She remembered the entire town. But after all this time away, Langley Park had morphed into someplace almost make-believe.

But this place was no work of fiction.

The picturesque Tudors and bungalows lining the streets, the quaint town center thriving with mom-and-pop shops, the botanic gardens, serene with leaves littering the ground, were all as real as the sun shining from above.

She inhaled the morning air. The cold and sleet from yesterday were a distant memory. The sun met the day unencumbered by the heavy clouds that greeted most fall Kansas days.

She had pulled on a pair of jeans and a fitted T-shirt then finished off the outfit with a cropped leather jacket. Before leaving the house, she'd stopped in front of the mirror hanging in the foyer. She had scrubbed her face clean in the shower and neglected even to open her makeup bag. A smattering of freckles kissed the skin of her cheekbones. But it was her eyes that drew her attention. Without the heavy eyeliner, the color encasing her pupils burst like a field of deep blue hydrangea no longer shrouded in a dense fog.

She left the house and headed north on Foxglove Lane toward the town center. Was she really doing this? Was she really going to take Michael up on his offer? Michael, who had let her down. Michael, who had chosen Tiffany Shelton over her.

But things weren't so black and white anymore.

After she left Michael's carriage house last night, she had spent the rest of the evening tossing and turning. Her mind was bombarded with an endless list of pros and cons. Once she'd sorted through it all, there was only one choice. She had to learn what happened the night of her accident by whatever means possible. If that meant allowing Michael to help, then so be it.

She turned onto Mulberry Drive and continued toward The Drip Coffee Shop. Michael's old Range Rover was parked outside. Her heart rate picked up, and flashes of her hands clasped in his as his thumb glided over the pulse point on her wrist assaulted her senses. Her nipples tightened, and she pulled her jacket tight around her chest, trying to hide any evidence of her arousal.

Damn that childhood crush. Damn every synapse that sparked with excitement at the thought of his bare skin brushing against hers.

She stopped in front of the coffee shop and looked inside. Michael was sitting at a table with a map spread across the surface. He looked up and met her gaze through the glass. A palpable current passed between them like a ship returning to harbor.

She glanced at the table and shook her head. A pair of to-go cups sat side by side.

A man opened the door to go inside the shop and held it open for her. "You going in, miss?"

She gave the man a nod and went inside.

She walked up to Michael's table. "You must have been pretty sure I was going to show up."

He smiled his crooked smile, and his eyes crinkled at the corners.

His expression was so familiar, so comforting. She hadn't seen him smile like this since she had returned to Langley Park.

"I had a hunch you would show," he said, nodding toward an empty seat next to him.

She sat down then raised her eyebrows, demanding proof.

Michael laughed, and the crinkled eyes were back. "Cody told me."

"Are you feeling okay?" she asked, biting her lip to hold back the grin her heart was begging to give him.

"When I took Cody out for his morning walk, he nearly broke the leash trying to run over to your back door. I figured you were already up and in the kitchen—well, Cody did. I just put two and two together."

She studied him. She could still see the boy, but the set of his broad shoulders and the strong tendons in his hands were the not-so-subtle signs that Michael MacCarron was all man now. She thought back to Halloween night. She'd straddled him, pressed herself into him.

She knew firsthand he wasn't a boy anymore.

A wave of prickly shame passed over her. Why did she try and seduce him? It was a stupid, childish thing to think she could ever lump Michael in with her past trysts.

Trysts. The naked truth of the word twisted her gut. She'd never had a real relationship. The revelation hit her like a wrecking ball.

"I think I got your order right," he said, breaking through her spiraling thoughts.

She must have disappeared. Not physically, of course, but mentally. She used to do that when she played music. She would fade into the complexity of the notes, losing herself and becoming one with the composition.

Michael nudged the cup toward her. Em knew he had seen her blank out, but he didn't seem bothered by it. To the contrary, a warmth filled his gaze. She took a sip and hummed her approval. He did get her order right. She had been ordering flat white's all week. The steamed milk and rich espresso danced on her taste buds.

"How did you know my order?"

Michael gave her another crinkle-eyed smile, and it sent her pulse racing.

"I told the barista I was meeting the redhead who had been coming in here every morning this week. Between you, me, Sam, and a handful of five-years-olds, we make up the entire ginger population of Langley Park.

The hint of a smile pulled at the corner of her lips when a gust of air blew into the shop followed by the sound of excited chatter. Several women passed by carrying rolled yoga mats and formed a queue at the counter.

"Kathy Stein's yoga class next door must have just ended," Michael said, then a look of recognition crossed his face, and he stood.

A tall woman with a messy, blond bun stopped at their table. It was the Barbie doll from Halloween. Jennifer...Jeanie...something like that. Em watched them make small talk. A bitter surge of jealousy pulsed through her when the woman casually touched Michael's arm as they spoke.

She was about to abandon this whole stupid idea of letting Michael help her when the smiling blonde put a hand on her shoulder.

"Em, I'm not sure if you remember me. I'm Jenna Fisher. We met on Halloween. It's so nice to run into you."

The heated jealousy pumping through her veins dissipated when she met Jenna's warm gaze.

"Yes, I remember. Your little girl was dressed as Harry Potter."

"That's right," Jenna answered, then glanced down at the map of Kansas spread across the table. "Are you planning a trip?"

"Not really a trip," Em replied.

What was she supposed to say? They were looking for an old bridge and some tall men?

"We're going to visit some of the places kids used to hang out at back in high school. Maybe check out some of the old bridges in the area," Michael said, swooping in.

Old bridges? She was shocked he remembered her fragmented memories: tall men, old bridge, and the Paganini piece.

Before she could say another word, Jenna continued, "You know who you might want to talk to…"

The coffee shop's door opened, and Jenna's face broke into a wide grin, and she waved someone over.

Within the space of a breath, Em was staring up at Zoe Stein. Her dark hair was pulled into a high ponytail. She wore it longer now. Back in high school, the dyed pink tips of her hair used to brush her shoulders. She was dressed in yoga gear and had a rolled mat tucked under her arm. Zoe greeted her sister-in-law and Michael before meeting Em's gaze.

"Hey, Em," Zoe said. Her voice barely audible over the coffee shop chatter.

The group stilled.

"Hey," Em replied, hoping the smile she had managed to produce for Jenna was still in place. But the look on Zoe's face told her that her grin was long gone.

Jenna gestured to the empty chairs. "Can we sit with you?"

Em nodded. Jenna's warm smile was bewitching.

Jenna sat across from Michael, leaving Zoe the seat across from her. The energy radiating off the Zoe-Michael-Em triangle buzzed like a swarm of hornets. The whispers of all the things left unsaid popping and shifting the air.

Jenna turned to Zoe. "Before you got here, Em and Michael were telling me that they're setting off to find old bridges near the places you guys used to hang out as kids. Maybe you can help them?"

Zoe paled, and a wave of comprehension passed over her face. "Old bridges," Zoe said wide-eyed, parroting back her sister-in-law's words.

"Yes," Jenna said, seemingly unfazed by Zoe's response. "I know how good you are at tracking things down."

Jenna squeezed Zoe's hand.

Jenna returned her attention to Em. "You see, not so long ago, Zoe was able to track me down."

Zoe smiled, and the color returned to her cheeks. She drummed her fingertips on the table. "There's a bunch of websites that highlight old bridges. NPR even did a story about states that have whole pages set up to try and get people to adopt old bridges and take over their maintenance."

"Zoe works for Kansas Public Radio. She's a wiz at investigative reporting," Michael added.

Zoe's gaze dropped to the map. "I could put a list together. I think I know the area you're interested in."

Here it was. The olive branch. All Em had to do was reach out and take it. She knew Zoe wanted to help. She could see the plea in her old friend's hazel eyes. *Let me help you. Let me try and make this right.* Em shifted in her chair.

"It may be a good place to start," Jenna said. "I certainly can't see it hurting your search."

Who was this woman? She was like two parts Mary Poppins and one part homecoming queen.

Em nodded reluctantly. She needed to learn what happened. She was doing this for her father. The anger in her heart wanted to tell Zoe to fuck off, but the need to learn the truth was growing stronger, edging out the rage.

She met Zoe's gaze. "I'd appreciate your help."

"I'll get on it right away," Zoe said with glassy eyes.

"You can text or email anything you find to me," Michael said.

Zoe nodded as a little girl came zipping through the shop and landed in her lap.

"Little monster," Zoe said, kissing the top of the girl's head. "What did you do with your daddy and Grandma?"

"Oh, they're coming," the girl answered. "They're just super, banana slug slow."

"I remember you," Em said to the little girl. "You're Kate. You were Harry Potter for Halloween."

Kate stared at Em's hands. "Why did you do that?"

"Do what?" Em asked.

"You were talking and signing at the same time," Jenna chimed in.

Em clasped her hands. She hadn't even realized she had signed.

"I work at a school in Australia where all the children use sign language. I guess, when I'm talking to kids, it's like a default switch."

Kate nodded slowly, digesting the information. "Is your real name Emma? I've got three Emma's in my second-grade class: Emma King, Emma Vasquez, and Emma O'Malley. Oh, and there's one Emily. That could be your real name too, right?"

Em glanced at Michael. "Nope, my real name isn't Emma or Emily. It's Mary. Mary Michelle. I was named after both my grand-mothers."

Kate's face lit up. "Me, too! I'm Kathryn Elizabeth after my grand-mothers." Her brow furrowed. "So why do people call you Em if your real name is Mary Michelle?"

"That's my fault," Michael said. "When I was little, I couldn't pronounce Mary Michelle. All I could say was the "M" part. So, I called her Em, and then everyone else started calling her Em, too."

He was right. Before the accident, she had loved that story. By giving her a nickname, it was as if he had embedded himself into her very soul, and no amount of time or distance could change that. Em shifted in her seat. She needed to change the subject.

"Do you want me to show you how to sign, *Harry Potter*?"

Kate's face lit up. "Sure!"

Em raised her hand to her temple and, with her pointer and middle fingers extended, she made the quick motion of the lightning bolt scar.

Kate mimicked the sign. "Jenna, Michael, Auntie! I'm signing Harry Potter!"

"That's so cool, Kate," Jenna said, then directed her attention to Em. "I had no idea you were a teacher."

Her cheeks heated. "I'm not a teacher, just a teacher's aide."

"A teacher's aide is most certainly a teacher. I'm the reading specialist at Langley Park Elementary, and I don't know what our school would do without the support staff," Jenna countered.

Kate bounced in her Aunt's lap. "Now can you show me the sign for Jedi Knight? It's for my daddy. He loves *Star Wars*."

"Sure, it's kind of like you're pulling a hood over your head," Em said and demonstrated the sign.

Kate watched her closely then gasped and turned to Jenna. "Did you see what Em has on her finger?"

Em retracted her hands and clasped them in her lap. "I didn't mean to scare her."

"You haven't scared her," Jenna said with a reassuring smile. "The scar on your finger looks like Harry Potter's."

She never noticed. Em ran her index finger over the zigzag length of the scar.

Kate nodded, wide-eyed. "Did you get that scar from a bad person like Harry got his scar from Voldemort?"

Em met the little girl's gaze. "I'm not sure how I got this scar, Kate, but I'm hoping that soon, I'll find out."

14

"We better head out," Michael said, folding the map.

Em watched his hands fold the paper into perfect squares as Kate's question swirled in her mind. Had a bad person done this to her? Had someone *deliberately* hurt her? She had always thought someone else had to have known what happened that night. Seen something. Heard something. But the thought that someone may have set out to hurt her on purpose had never crossed her mind —until now.

"Em," Michael said, pulling her from her thoughts. "Do you want a refill before we leave?"

She shook her head and tucked away the revelation. "No, I'm good."

The group said their goodbyes, and she followed Michael out of the coffee shop.

"Are you okay?" he asked.

"Yes, it's just..."

"A lot to come home to?" Michael offered, finishing her thought.

That was the understatement of the century. But before she could answer, she heard someone calling out her name.

"Em! Oh, Em! It's so good to see you, sweetheart!"

She turned to see Zoe's mother, Kathy Stein, rushing toward her.

"Hi, Mrs. Stein," Em answered.

The woman enveloped her in a warm embrace. "None of this, 'Mrs. Stein' business. Call me Kathy."

She had loved this woman almost as much as she loved her own mother.

Em blinked back tears. "I don't know if I can. You've always been Mrs. Stein to me."

"You and Michael, both," Kathy answered. "I don't think you've ever called me Kathy either," she said, playfully eyeing Michael.

"Are you harassing people on the street again, Mom?" Ben Fisher walked up and joined the trio.

"Oh, Benjamin! I'm not harassing anyone. I'm just so happy to see our Em back in Langley Park."

"I'm glad I ran into you, Em," Ben said. "Did you want to schedule a time so I can take a look at your Foursquare?"

Em glanced from Ben to Michael. "Why would you look at my Foursquare?"

Michael held her gaze. "Remember when I mentioned knowing someone who could help with the house—you know, to help with any minor repairs?"

Em nodded. Between her encounter with Jenna Fisher, then Zoe, and now Kathy Stein and Ben Fisher, it was as if she was trapped on some kind of memory lane carousel spinning out of control.

"Ben's the architect I wanted to tell you about. He's the one who's renovated many of the homes in Langley Park," Michael added.

"Now, boys," Kathy broke in. "Em's got quite enough on her plate without worrying about house repairs at eight thirty on a Saturday morning."

Em gave the woman a grateful smile.

Ben reached into his pocket. "There's no rush. Here's my card. Give me a call whenever you're ready."

Em slid the card into her pocket. She could use Ben Fisher's help with the house. At a minimum, the house needed some sprucing up. The nicked cabinets and baseboards needed a new coat of paint, and the worn linoleum flooring probably had to go altogether.

"Thanks, Ben. I'll be in touch," she said, then turned to Kathy. "It was so nice running into you, Mrs. Stein."

"We'll have to have you over for dinner. Both of you," Kathy added, giving Michael's hand a squeeze.

"And don't forget the holiday party," Ben said.

Kathy's face lit up. "That's right! You must come to our holiday party—it's only a few weeks away. Michael, I'm putting you in charge of bringing Em."

"It's a plan, Mrs. Stein."

Em stared in wonder as her past life washed over her like a tsunami. It had been more than a decade since she'd had any contact with these people, and they still treated her with the same love and familiarity as they always had. She couldn't tell if the tightness in her chest was joy or heartache. Michael must have sensed her distress. He pressed his hand against her back, and his touch instantly set her nerves at ease.

"See you soon, dear. I'm so glad you're home," Kathy said, giving her one last embrace before following her son into the coffee shop.

Home.

The word sounded foreign to her ears. Home had never been a physical place. It never mattered if she was in Asia, Europe, or North America; home was the music. Anywhere she played the violin became her sanctuary, her safe place.

But she couldn't deny that something about Langley Park spoke to her soul—a connection that went beyond the brick and mortar of her house to her very DNA.

Could the sound of home be found whispering in the breeze, blowing wisps of her hair across her face? Could the sound of home be the chorus of families laughing and chatting as they strolled the streets of the Langley Park town center?

The creak of a car door drew her attention.

Michael held the Range Rover's door open. "We better get going."

Em took a step forward then froze. She could end this right now.

She could tell Michael she didn't need his help. Didn't want his help. She released a shaky breath. The roots of her anger no longer felt secure, like a weed in the rain-drenched soil, one swift pull could undo the days and months and years of festering growth in mere seconds.

"I can literally hear you thinking, Em," he said, leaving the car door open as he leaned against the side of the car.

She hated how badly she wanted to get into his car. It was so much easier to hate him with an ocean between them.

"What do you have to lose?" he asked and smiled that crooked, crinkle-eyed smile.

What do you have to lose?

What if her resolve slipped? What if the tight knot of anger that kept her together unraveled? Who would she be?

Michael's words echoed in her mind before the answer came clanging like church bells: Everything. She had everything to lose.

MICHAEL GLANCED OVER AT EM. They had driven nearly eighty miles southwest to Sadie's Hollow in silence. She had stared straight ahead, her gaze trained on the road. Expression blank and unreadable.

Em was in her head again. He knew this look well. He would watch her as a boy—crouched down low, his chin set on the windowsill as he gazed from his bedroom window into her room. She would stand as still as a statue, framed by the window, holding her violin for hours at a time. She was working something out in her mind. Em could not only hear the music in her head, but see it and feel it, and he could always tell the moment it clicked. Something in the air would change, and a ripple of anticipation would pass through him. She would pull the bow across the strings, and he'd be locked in that moment with her. A secret stowaway in her musical voyage.

He toyed with the idea of turning on the radio or popping a cassette into the old Range Rover's tape deck to try and distract her, but he knew it would be of no use. All he could do was wait until she worked out whatever was going on in her head. And it wasn't like he didn't have things to contemplate.

He needed to come up with a plan. There had to be more to the story of Em's injury. But as he turned off the interstate and headed down the country road toward Sadie's Hollow, a sense of dread passed over him. Even if there was a crime committed or foul play, it would have taken place more than a decade ago. The area around the hollow had remained relatively unchanged after all that time, but any evidence would surely be long gone.

His thoughts darkened. What if Em didn't remember anything new? What if this turned out to be some wild goose chase? What would that do to her? Would it reignite her anger? Would she vanish for another twelve years?

"Hey," she said, her gaze focused on the console between them.

He glanced down as his phone buzzed an incoming email. "Cell coverage is spotty out in the sticks. That may be an email from Zoe. Can you take a look?"

Em took the phone into her hands. "Your phone isn't password protected? That doesn't seem very lawyerly of you."

A muscle in his cheek twitched. He would gladly endure her teasing. "Never needed one. That phone is like my third appendage. I always have it with me."

"You shower with it?" she asked.

He held back a grin. "No."

"You sleep with it under your pillow?"

He kept his gaze locked on the road, but he could hear the smile in her voice.

"No," he answered, again. She really would have made one hell of a litigator.

She hummed her disapproval. "If I'm hearing you right, it sounds like your phone may not be an additional appendage."

"What does the email say, Mary Michelle?"

He glanced over as a pink flush colored her cheeks, and her teeth grazed her bottom lip. She had reacted this way the last time he had called her by her full name on Halloween night. The night he used every ounce of his resolve to resist her.

Every night since then, he had gone to bed with the memory of her tight, petite body wrapped around him. Her thighs pressed snug against his. Her breasts soft against his chest. The spicy scent of the whiskey still wet on her lips sent his thoughts into a dirty barrage of images. He had wanted to run his tongue along the seam of her lips and taste her, press his lips to hers and kiss her until the call of her body was too much to deny. He could have had her right there on the piano bench. His hands flexed against the steering wheel, remembering the way her ass fit in his grip.

He had taken a shitload of cold showers since that night.

Em sat forward. "It is from Zoe. She sent a list of bridges. Some have pictures attached."

"Does anything look familiar?"

"There must be twenty of them—and these are just the ones near the hollow."

He heard a hint of hopelessness in her voice.

"It's a start, Em. We'll take it one step at a time."

"But I don't have..." she trailed off, but he knew what she was thinking. She didn't have much time. She had to sell the house as soon as possible to allow her father to finalize the purchase of the Senior Living Campus cottage.

He pulled up in front of the old cemetery as a pang of annoyance shot through his chest. They weren't the only ones paying a visit to Sadie's Hollow this morning.

"Is that Kyle Benson?" Em asked.

Michael cut the ignition, threw off his seatbelt, and opened the car door. "Stay here," he said, his eyes flashing anger as he got out of the car.

Michael strode over to where Kyle was taking a picture of an old tombstone. The men shook hands, but their posture looked anything but friendly.

Em opened the car door and shook her head. Nobody, not even Michael MacCarron, told her what to do.

The ground was still damp from yesterday's icy rain, making the blades of dried out grass twinkle and shine in the morning light. Barely a day had passed, but the hollow seemed like a different place. With the dark skies gone, every twig and branch stood out against the big, blue Kansas sky.

Kyle held a camera in one hand and blocked the sun from his eyes with the other. "Hi, Em."

"Hey, Kyle. What are you doing all the way out here?" she asked.

"Just work," he said, glancing over at Michael. "I was telling Michael about the project I was working on for the Kansas historical society. I'm photographing some of the old cemeteries around the state."

"I see. Must be interesting work," she answered. She couldn't figure out why Michael looked ready to pounce.

"Are you here to try and remember more about the night you were injured?" Kyle asked.

"It's really none of your business why we're here," Michael barked.

"It's okay. I already told Kyle I was going to try to learn more about the night I was injured," Em answered.

Michael pinned her with his gaze. "You told *him*?"

"We talked about it a little the night I drove her home," Kyle answered.

"You didn't quite get her all the way home, did you, Benson?" Michael threw back.

Em's gaze bounced between the men. "Hey, it's all good. And yeah, we are here to see if I can remember more about that night."

Kyle looped the camera strap around his neck. "Has anything come back to you?"

She shook her head and glanced at Michael. What was his problem? She knew he was never crazy about Kyle, but he was still someone who was at the hollow that night. He could be helpful.

A thought popped into her mind. "Kyle, are you familiar with this area—I mean from your work?"

"Somewhat, why do you ask?"

Michael's jaw twitched like he was grinding his molars into dust.

"You see," she began, "I remember a bridge. I can't remember what it looks like, only what it felt like to cross over it. I was wondering if you knew of any old, possibly wooden bridges in the area."

Kyle scratched the back of his head. "I think you'd have more luck north of here. I can't think of many bridges around here."

"We've got a list of more than twenty bridges in the area," Michael countered.

Kyle put his hands up. "Sorry, counselor! I'm no *expert witness* when it comes to finding old bridges. You may want to talk to Tiffany Shelton. She might remember something about that night. I bet you could track her down, Michael. Last I heard, she hadn't moved too far from Langley Park."

At the mention of Tiffany Shelton, Em's pulse kicked up in a fight or flight rush. Her fingertips tingled, and the bloom of anger heated her skin.

"I better be off," Kyle said, reaching for his camera bag.

She watched his truck disappear down the road then turned to Michael. He'd shoved his hands into his pockets.

"Why do you dislike Kyle so much? What did he ever do to you?"

"I don't like the way he looks at you. Never have," Michael replied, keeping his gaze trained on his shoes.

"That's really messed up," she shot back.

He looked up, fire burning in his green eyes. "Messed up?"

"You gave up any right to judge guys on my behalf when you chose—"

He cut her off. "I'm so fucking sorry I abandoned you for Tiffany Shelton!"

He closed the distance between them. Before she knew it, his hands were cupping her face.

"I don't know what else I can say, Em. I will fucking apologize to you every day for the rest of my life if that's what it takes."

His fingertips pressed the nape of her neck, and the delicious pressure begged her to melt into his grip. His scent stirred her senses as flashes of his lips brushing against hers jumbled her thoughts. Michael's breath was coming in shallow pants, dancing and teasing her freckle-kissed skin. She raised her hands and rested them on top of his.

Her fingers twitched as they rested on top of his. Instinct was taking over. She wanted to twine her fingers with his. She wanted to guide them into her hair. She wanted him to wrap her auburn locks around his fist and pull. She wanted to hover on the cusp of pleasure and pain as he devoured her mouth with kisses. But she stopped herself.

She swallowed hard. "Have you ever considered that your problem isn't with Kyle Benson?"

Michael frowned. "What's that supposed to mean?"

"You're not angry with him. You're angry with yourself," she said.

He closed his eyes and pressed his forehead to hers. "You don't know what you're talking about."

She exhaled a shaky breath. "You're wrong. I know everything about misplaced anger and even more about living with gut-wrenching guilt."

Michael pulled back and dropped his hands. "We're wasting time. Let's focus on what we came out here to do."

15

E m stirred her spoon in the bowl of tomato soup which was growing colder by the minute. It was three o'clock in the afternoon, and she and Michael had stopped at a diner in Garrett, Kansas, a few miles north of Sadie's Hollow for a late lunch, though neither was doing much more than picking at their food.

After their run-in with Kyle Benson, they had walked the perimeter of the hollow countless times and visited three bridges on Zoe's list.

And what did she remember?

Nothing.

This was her sixth trip to the hollow in as many days. She had driven the almost eighty miles, down and back, every day that week hoping something would trigger her memory.

The bridges from Zoe's list were nothing to write home about. Yes, they were old and in need of repair, but none of them were made of wood. But that didn't keep her from making Michael drive back and forth over each bridge as she closed her eyes and willed her body to remember.

Now they sat across from each other as a banged up radio

propped against the cash register rattled a twangy country tune. Michael had gone into lawyer mode after their tense conversation. Engaged, yet politely reserved, he had kept his distance. Once they arrived at the diner, he'd taken the map out and worked methodically, marking the remaining locations of the bridges from Zoe's list.

"Anybody need a refill?"

A waitress with a long gray ponytail and a name tag with "Peggy" written by hand in curly lettering smiled down at her. The deep lines etched on her face spoke of a long life full of hard work. She leaned in to refill Michael's water, but he raised his hand and waved her off.

"No, thank you. We're ready for the check."

He glanced up, and Em gave him a slight nod. They had been dancing around each other with pleasantries all day.

The waitress fussed with a pocket in her apron, pulled out their bill, and placed it on the table. She offered them a kind smile. "I wanted to ask if you folks wanted to donate to the 4-H Club. We always take up a collection during the year and donate all the money on Tina's birthday."

The woman gestured toward the cash register where, along with the radio, a jar sat crammed tight with coins and bills. A framed photograph of a young woman in a graduation cap and gown next to the jar. Her dark hair was fashioned into two braids that rested near her collarbone.

"Who's Tina?" Em asked, unable to pull her gaze from the photograph. The girl, so lovely and vibrant, smiled as if she believed everything good was ahead of her.

The waitress fingered the cross she wore on a delicate chain around her neck. "Tina Fowler. She was from LaRoe just a few miles away from Garrett. She used to waitress here all through high school. She was such a good girl. Even got herself a full-ride scholarship to college. She wanted to be a veterinarian. She was always raising chickens and rabbits. That's why we like to donate to the 4-H Club. Such a loss."

"What happened to her?" Em asked.

"Goodness! It must be going on twelve years now. Sweet Jesus, how time passes. Tina was riding her bike in to help me open the diner. We open at five in the morning, so Tina was on the road real early. Her family had a place out near LaRoe about five miles west of Garrett. The police said it was a hit and run."

"That's awful! I'm so sorry," Em said, glancing over at Michael who remained silent.

The waitress released the cross. "Police never did find the bastard who hit her and left her to die alone. Tina was killed a week before she was supposed to leave for college. It hit this town hard. She was like a ray of sunlight, I'll tell ya. But the community came together just like we did all those years ago when the cement plant went bust and so many folks were without work. All you can do is stick together and try to take care of each other. The good Lord decides the rest."

"For Tina," Michael said, startling Em and the waitress.

She was so entranced with Tina Fowler's story, she had almost forgotten he was there.

Michael handed the waitress two crisp hundred dollar bills.

The waitress pressed the bills to her chest. "Thank you, sir."

Michael placed a few more bills next to the check, and his gaze darted to the photograph of the forever young, Tina Fowler. "Let's hit the road, Em."

EM GLANCED AT HER PHONE. It was nearly a quarter to five, and the sun hung low in the sky as the Senior Living Campus security guard waved and buzzed her through the gate. She had seen this security guard a few times, and he gave her an easy smile as she passed by. Thankfully, she hadn't encountered the smug guard from her first visit.

She walked up the drive toward the main building. She took out her phone and paused to scroll through her emails. Tom Lancaster had sent her all the times and dates she would be needed to play "dinner music" while the residents enjoyed their Saturday meal.

She glanced at the playlist, and a scintillating tingle ran through her body. Despite the anxiety churning in her belly, she was excited to play the piano again. She thought back to last night, and how she had helped calm Noland by playing "Come Thou Fount of Every Blessing."

She opened the door to the main building and nearly crashed into Tom's wife, Mindy Lancaster.

The startled look on Mindy's face highlighted her sharp features. "I wasn't sure if you were going to show up."

Em pasted a smile to her lips. She had never cared for Mindy Lancaster. While Tom was gentle and encouraging, his wife was stiff and serious. When she was just a girl, Mrs. Lancaster used to remind her of a rigid headmistress—and nothing had changed in the last twelve years to alter that perception.

Em held up her phone and displayed Tom's email. "Tom said arriving by a quarter to five should give me plenty of time before the residents show up for dinner."

"And the playlist?" Mindy continued. "Do you think you'll be able to play all the songs? I brought the sheet music just in case. I wasn't sure how long it's been since you've played." She let the last few words dangle in the air like rotting pieces of fruit.

Em scanned the email. Beethoven's *Fur Elise*, Mozart's *Greensleeves*, and Debussy's *Clair de Lune* topped the list. It was like being reunited with old friends. Tom must have remembered that these were some of her favorite pieces.

"Do you need the music?" Mindy asked again, holding the sheets with her good hand while she waved her other, encased in a bright pink cast.

A thread of hesitation wove its way through her chest. *What if she couldn't do it? What if her fingers had forgotten what was once second nature?* She met Mindy's gaze and saw a glimmer of triumph flash in the woman's eyes. Mindy was an accomplished pianist, but she had never risen to even a fraction of what Em had achieved as a musician.

A confidence Em hadn't known in years surged through her veins. She thought back to her earliest piano competitions. The competitors, twice, sometimes three times her age, sneered or even laughed as she took the stage, all pigtails and plaid skirt. But the jeering ended the moment her fingers pressed upon the ivory keys.

Em lifted her chin. "I'll do fine without the sheet music, Mrs. Lancaster. I guess you don't remember, but I mastered these pieces by my fourth birthday—maybe it was my fifth, but who's counting?"

Mindy tightened her grip on the sheet music. The paper collapsed inward like the tightening of a noose. "Have it your way. You can leave after dinner. A deejay will come and play music for the dancing portion that follows the meal. Any questions?"

"I've performed for the Queen of England. I think I can handle this," Em shot back.

She wasn't going to take any more crap from Mindy Lancaster. She may have let her father down. She may have let this whole damn town down. But the anger that kept her away from music, away from the memories that threatened to tear her apart with guilt and grief, was transforming. This new anger needed to learn the truth. This new anger had a fire behind it fueled by a dogged determination.

The door opened, bringing with it a gust of cold air, and Bill MacCaslin entered the building.

"Hi, kiddo," Bill said. He planted a kiss on his daughter's cheek. "Mindy, it's so good to see you."

Mindy's sourpuss expression vanished and was replaced with a saccharine smile. "Always good to see you, Dr. MacCaslin. How are you feeling?"

"I won't be running a marathon anytime soon," he said, gesturing to his portable oxygen, "but, all things considered, I'm doing much better."

Mindy toyed self-consciously with the plaster on her cast. "I'm glad to hear that."

"And, I get to hear my little girl play the piano tonight so I'd say I'm a pretty lucky man."

Em clasped her hands together and traced the length of her scar with her index finger. Mindy's pointed gaze followed her finger's movements.

She dropped her hands to her sides. "I better go warm up, Dad," she said, then turned to Mindy. "Thank you for your help, Mrs. Lancaster. I can take it from here."

MICHAEL ENTERED the lobby of the campus's main building. The usually bustling space was eerily quiet. The only inhabitants were two nurses sitting at the information desk, and even they seemed oblivious to his presence. One of them had been knitting. She had the needles in her hands but stopped mid-stitch. The other nurse sat with her eyes closed.

What the hell was going on here?

Michael was about to ask that very question when the slow, dreamy first notes of Chopin's Nocturne No. 20 in C-Sharp Minor floated through the air.

Now he understood the nurses' behavior. It was Em. She was playing the piano. He would know the sound of her fingers on the keys anywhere.

He walked past the nurses and toward the ballroom like a moth powerless to resist the flame. The ballroom was packed with people. He had been deejaying at the campus for a few years now. Mindy Lancaster usually played the piano while the residents enjoyed dinner, and then he would come and throw a few songs on for the dancing portion of the evening. Many residents attended, but he had never seen the ballroom packed with nurses, doctors, and the house-keeping and facility management staff.

It was as if every living soul who heard Em play was lured into the ballroom. Even the waitstaff stood motionless holding trays, frozen in place.

He leaned against the wall. Em's body swayed and dipped as her fingers glided across the keys with the ease of a bird in flight. Her eyes were glassy, and she blinked slowly. He knew this look. She was caught somewhere between this world and the next, hovering in a place where only harmony and melody existed. The thought of her cutting herself off from music for over a decade nearly made him weep. But here she was, playing as if the accident had never happened.

A shiver traveled the length of his spine. Maybe her gift hadn't been taken away that fateful night at the hollow?

The piece came to a close and Em's hands hovered above the keys. Every person in the ballroom seemed to hold their breath, watching her hands rise and then fall to her lap. She wasn't back from that in-between place yet. Her eyes remained vacant until the burst of applause snapped her back into this world.

He glanced toward the doors as Mindy Lancaster slipped out of the ballroom. In all her years of playing for the residents, she had never received this kind of response. The ballroom echoed with cheers and clapping, and all thoughts of Mindy Lancaster were forgotten when he looked across the ballroom and met Em's gaze.

It wasn't like Halloween when she had seen him after she'd played violin on stage. That night, her eyes were filled with hate and resentment. But tonight, they were full of wonder as if she could barely believe what she had done.

Michael walked toward her as the spell that had taken over the ballroom faded away into the noisy clamor of waiters removing plates and residents picking up their conversations. Em's father was the first to reach her with a spring in his step that Michael hadn't seen in years.

Bill MacCaslin beamed with pride. "Kiddo, that was..."

"Incredible," Michael offered, nodding to Dr. MacCaslin before turning to Em.

She was wearing makeup, but it wasn't the heavy, dark eyeliner that made her look so foreboding and dangerous. No, tonight she was luminous. Rosy lips and the hint of a shimmering eyeshadow made her blue eyes sparkle. The loose waves of her auburn hair were tucked behind her ear, and as a lock came free, he reached out, grazing his fingertips against the soft skin of her neck and smoothed it back into place.

Em's hand went to her hair, and a blush crept up her neck. "I didn't know you were the deejay," she said, eyeing the headphones hanging out of the equipment bag slung over his shoulder. "You didn't mention anything about it today."

"Today?" Bill asked.

Em tensed. "Michael and I took a drive."

"I took Em to some of our old stomping grounds," Michael added.

Em's expression relaxed.

"That's wonderful! I'm glad you kids are getting some time together. There was a time when we could barely pull you two apart. Better together, that's what your father and I used to say, Michael," Bill said, putting a hand on his shoulder.

Michael forced a smile. He didn't know what hurt more, thinking about the time when his father remembered him, or now, when he didn't.

"Dad, would you mind asking if there's anything left for dinner? I haven't eaten since lunch, and I'm pretty famished."

"I'm sure one of the waitstaff could help us out. I'll be right back," Bill said and disappeared into the crowd.

The same lock of Em's hair fell forward again and brushed past her cheek. A beat of silence passed between them. *Did she want him to tuck it back into place again?*

A rosy blush bloomed on her cheeks as she secured the smooth strands behind her ear. But her hand lingered on the spot where he had touched her when he'd tucked back the errant lock. She dropped her hands.

"I was hoping I'd get to see your dad tonight."

Michael shifted his stance. "The residents from the memory care center don't usually attend these events. We were trying something new the night you..." He stopped. Thoughts of his father's outburst caused his body to stiffen, the physical manifestation of his heart hardening as his father slipped further and further away.

Em ran her finger down the strap of his bag and let it linger on his headphones. "You *do* get to be a deejay."

She was giving him an out, and he was grateful to end any talk of his father.

"Yeah, the good people of Langley Park don't seem to mind their attorney mixing music if it's for a bunch of old people."

Em's eyes held a mischievous spark. "Well, Mr. Deejay, what do you have for us tonight?"

"I hate to disappoint you, but I don't think you're going to be too impressed. Over the years, I've learned that a steady stream of Lionel Ritchie interspersed with some Bee Gees is what gets this crowd going."

She laughed, and the sound washed over him like a warm summer breeze.

"Oh, yes," he continued. "Once you hit your seventies, expect to enjoy a good slow jam."

"Maybe I'll stick around," she said with a hint of a smile. "It's been a while since I've heard 'Three Times a Lady.' "

"A classic," he added, holding her gaze.

EM'S FACE GLOWED. She had only taken a few bites of the pasta her father managed to wrangle from the kitchen before every male inhabitant of the Langley Park Senior Living Center requested a dance. Michael watched her gift each man a genuine smile, but she declined every invitation.

He cued up the next song, took off his headphones, and walked over to Em's table.

"The last song is up next," he said, offering her his hand.

"I don't dance," Em replied.

"Oh, come on, kiddo! It's Michael! We used to bathe you two together. Surely, you could give him one dance."

Em shook her head as a sweet pink blush inched up her creamy neck. "Dad, we're not toddlers anymore!"

"One dance, Em," Michael said.

"If it stops my father from discussing our days of joint bathing, then yes, I'll dance with you."

"You sure know how to make a guy feel special," he said, taking her hand and leading her onto the dance floor.

The Bee Gee's classic, "How Deep is Your Love," ended and Lionel Ritchie's iconic voice filled the ballroom.

Em's eyes widened. "Is this..."

"Yep," he answered, placing his hand on the small of her back and taking her hand in his. "If you want to be technical, it's the Commodores. But, yes, that's good ole Lionel on vocals."

He started to move to the music, but Em tensed.

"Michael, wait. I can't..."

"Can't what?"

She bit her lip. "It's not like I ever went to prom or anything."

"What are you talking about, Em?"

"I've never danced with anyone... sober."

His memory flooded with images of her grinding against that tool in the bar on Halloween. His jaw clenched but quickly relaxed. A flush crept up her neck, and he could tell she was genuinely nervous.

He softened his expression. "Lucky for you, I'm an excellent dancer," he said, guiding her into an exaggerated dip. He lifted her up slowly and gathered her into his arms.

The ballroom sported a disco ball. He hated disco balls. How fucking cheesy could you get? But as he looked down at Em's face, his opinion on disco balls completely reversed. The light caught the auburn in her hair and glowed red-gold like the comforting flame of a campfire on a cold night.

He swayed to the beat, and Em relaxed in his arms. She shifted her fingers and laced them with his, and instantly he imagined her in his bed—her hair fanned out across the sheets. Her hands raised above her head, laced with his, as his cock drove into her, over and over again.

"Hey," Em said, catching him mid-imaginary thrust. "I wanted to ask you about Tina Fowler."

This put an immediate end to his fantasy.

"What do you mean?"

"You were a little weird at the diner when the waitress was talking to us about her. Did you know her?"

Michael shook his head. "No, but I thought I remembered something about her. Probably just something I saw on the news or in the paper."

Her brow creased.

"What is it, Em?"

"I wondered..." But she stopped speaking as an odd expression crossed her face.

16

W*ho was that woman?*

Em's expression changed from confused to curious. Michael stopped dancing and craned his neck to see.

"Oh, Christ," he chuckled. "It's Eunice Teller. She must have slipped past the nurses. She's like Houdini. Get ready for a walk down memory lane."

"Mary Michelle MacCaslin!" the woman exclaimed.

Em searched the woman's face then turned to Michael. He was doing his best not to laugh. Irritation flooded her system. *Why was he getting such a kick out of this?*

Mrs. Teller gave her such a look of adoration, Em couldn't help but return the woman's smile with one of her own.

"Six pounds and seven ounces," the woman said, eyes shining with emotion.

"Do I..." Em began, but Michael broke in.

"Mrs. Teller was our labor and delivery nurse," he said, still holding back a laugh.

"Our what?"

"I helped deliver you both and bring you into this glorious

world," Mrs. Teller answered, then turned to Michael. "And you, young man, were…"

"I know. I know, Mrs. Teller. Nine pounds and three ounces."

"Oh, your poor mother!" The older woman smiled. "My two, beautiful little redheaded babies born only minutes apart."

Now it made sense. It had been years since she had seen Mrs. Teller, and the woman seemed ancient even back then.

"Oh, what a night that was. We were short-staffed, and I kept running back-and-forth between rooms. Thank goodness Michael was such a polite baby. Had he not waited five minutes, you'd both not only have the same birthday but would have been born at the exact same time."

"Mrs. Teller," Michael said gently, "would you like me to walk you back to your room?"

"My room?" she echoed and turned her head from side to side like a lost child.

The music stopped, and the chandeliers bathed the room in bright light.

A flush-faced Anita Benson headed toward them.

"I've been looking for you everywhere, Mrs. Teller."

"But I heard the music and saw all the people dancing," the older woman replied.

Michael released her hand but kept his palm pressed to the small of her back. A move that didn't go unnoticed by Anita Benson as the nurse glanced their way.

Em's heart twisted. Only moments ago, Mrs. Teller was bubbling with life and enthusiasm. Now, her eyes were filled with confusion.

Michael stepped forward. "It's all right, Mrs. Benson. I can escort Mrs. Teller back to the Memory Care Center."

"See," Mrs. Teller said, "always such a polite young man. You remind me of my Rodney. We met back in high school at Garrett Senior High. He was the star quarterback, and I was the head cheerleader. The perfect small town love story."

"Yes, yes, Mrs. Teller," Anita said with a tight smile.

"That's where you met your Bobby, right Anita?" the woman

continued. "Such a shame what happened in LaRoe." Mrs. Teller's face brightened. "I've seen his younger sister here. She was always so good at—"

"Mrs. Teller," Anita said, placing her hand on the woman's arm. "I think you're confused, dear. Let's get you back to your room."

"No, I'm not confused. I remember. I can still remember," Mrs. Teller said as streaks of panic laced her words.

"Mrs. Teller," Michael said, offering the woman his arm, "I'd be honored to walk you back."

The older woman stared at him blankly, but the chivalrous gesture seemed to ease her confusion. She linked her frail arm with his. "Anita is right. I do get a bit confused these days."

Michael walked a few steps with Mrs. Teller, then turned back. "I'll catch up with you later, Em."

"Of course," she replied, catching Anita Benson watching their exchange with a pointed gaze.

EM WOUND her damp hair into a messy bun. She stared at her reflection in the bedroom mirror. She had cleaned the room and made it inhabitable. The ribbons, trophies, and photographs once littering the floor, now sat in neat piles on her dresser. She pulled a tank top over her head and reached for Michael's hoodie. Inhaling deeply, she took in the spearmint lemongrass scent.

After Michael left to take Mrs. Teller back to the Memory Care Center, she said goodnight to her father and walked the short distance home to Foxglove Lane.

She flexed her fingers and traced the zigzagged scar. She was playing music again. Warmth bloomed in her chest, but a little voice in her head stamped out her excitement.

Langley Park's music prodigy threw away her talent years ago.

What makes you think you're anything more than mediocre? You haven't even played anything difficult.

You'll never be as good as you were.

She glanced over at the violin case on her desk, shoved her hands into the hoodie's pockets, and headed down to the kitchen. She set the kettle to boil and leaned against the kitchen counter.

In one day, she had seen Zoe, Ben, Kathy, Kate, and Jenna. She had run into Kyle Benson at Sadie's Hollow, and she'd played the piano for the residents at the Senior Living Campus.

And then there was Michael.

Michael holding her in his arms. Michael smoothing back her hair. His fingertips grazing against her neck made her body want things it shouldn't.

The kettle whistled, and Em poured the boiling water into a mug. Dunking a teabag, she surveyed the peeling paint on the kitchen cabinets. Maybe it was a good thing she had run into Ben Fisher. She would need his help to get the house ready to sell.

Ready to sell.

That was the reason for coming home, right? She needed to help her father sell the house, but then what? Go back to Australia? Sure, she loved working at the Renwick Centre and being close to her mother. But her life didn't feel so black and white anymore. The anger that used to sustain her wasn't enough.

She sipped the tea and looked out the window. Her carriage house sat dark, but there was a light on inside of Michael's. The square windows glowed yellow-orange like a beacon in the darkness.

She slipped on her old rain boots and caught her reflection in the window. Messy bun. Oversized hoodie. Tiny sleep shorts and old rain boots. She looked like the definition of a train wreck. But her appearance didn't matter. She was only going to Michael's carriage house to ask after Mrs. Teller.

She opened the back door and gripped the hot mug. An icy breeze rustled the tree branches, and she doubled her pace as her breaths came in short excited gasps.

There was no reason to get worked up, but her heart disagreed. Of course, she wanted to ask Michael about Mrs. Teller. That was enough reason to be trudging across her backyard half-dressed, wasn't it?

Before she could stop herself, she knocked on the side door.

Michael opened it, and all thoughts of Mrs. Teller disappeared. Every time she looked at him, fire and ice coursed through her veins, and her heart beat like a pendulum swinging wildly between extremes.

Focus.

"Can I come in?"

Michael took a step back. "Sure, I was just..." He gestured to his laptop. It was connected to an electric piano keyboard.

Em surveyed the space. The Range Rover sat parked in the first stall. Michael's computer along with the keyboard and a large computer monitor were situated on an L-shaped desk in the corner. An old futon sagged along the back wall, and a well-used punching bag hung in the far corner next to it. A space heater plugged in next to the door glowed red and was doing a pretty good job of keeping the room warm.

"Why don't you do this in the house?" she asked, walking to the far corner and giving the punching bag a nudge.

Michael ran his hand along his jaw. "My dad never let me keep any of my equipment in the house. He never approved of it. He thought it was a distraction."

"I get that. But now he's..."

"Gone? Pretty much a vegetable?"

"No, Michael, you know that's not what I meant."

He nodded, and the tension in his shoulders relaxed.

Em went to the desk, set down her mug, and examined the screen. It looked more like something you would see in the hospital with wavy lines akin to a heart rate monitor. Her gaze was drawn to a piece of paper taped to the corner. It read: Chopin Nocturne 20 remix.

"Are you doing something with Nocturne?" she asked, knowing Michael heard her play the piece tonight.

"It's nothing," he said and reached to close his laptop, but Em placed her hand on top of his.

"Wait a second. Tell me what all those lines are," she said, leaving her hand in place.

Michael opened his laptop, and the lines came to life.

"Sit," he said, pulling out the chair. He slid the earphones over her ears then leaned over and gestured to the screen. "This is the EQ or equalization. It helps shape the frequencies of the sound." He pointed to the next line. "This is compression. It controls the dynamics. The last line is reverb. It gives the sound space and can make something that was recorded in a small studio sound like it's in a concert hall."

He moved his finger across the laptop's touchpad, and the music came to life inside the headphones. It was Chopin's piece, but Michael had mixed in electronic and industrial sounds that added a depth of emotion she wasn't prepared to hear.

The song ended, and she slipped the headphones down to hang around her neck. "Michael, that was incredible. You did that to Nocturne 20?"

He nodded but kept his eyes on the screen. "I've been playing with the idea of taking classical pieces and adding an electronic, modern element to them."

"It's like nothing I've ever heard." It broke her heart that he felt he had to keep this part of himself hidden.

Michael bent down, and they were nose to nose. He closed his eyes and pressed his forehead to hers.

"Em," he breathed. "You have to know. You haven't lost any of your talent. You've still got it."

She shook her head. "It's not the same. I haven't played anything technically difficult in over a decade. Anyone could have knocked out the pieces I performed tonight."

"No," Michael said, opening his eyes and cupping her face in his hands. "I know you. I've listened to you play the piano and the violin my entire life. I hear your music in my dreams. I'm telling you, you haven't lost anything. I'd know. I'd be the one who would know if you did."

Tears pricked her eyes. "I still need to know what happened."

"I know," he breathed and pressed his lips to hers. "Me, too."

Her breaths were coming faster. Michael's fingers traced the length of her jaw and settled on the headphones resting around her neck. He pulled back a fraction. Em craned her neck forward to try and reach him, but before she could move another inch, Michael gripped the headphones and pressed the ear pieces together. The pressure around her neck forced her to gasp, and he pressed his lips against her open mouth as their tongues met in a hot clash of desire, each kiss stoking the heat growing in her core.

Michael released the headphones, pushed them aside, and wrapped his bare hands around her neck. The exquisite pressure had her chest heaving as she gasped for air. This should have terrified her. For her, sex was about control. It hinged on manipulation and conquest. But right now, all she could think about was Michael twisting her pearl necklace the night he kissed her at Sadie's Hollow.

No one else had ever touched her this way.

His tongue traced the seam of her lips. "You like this, don't you," he breathed.

"Yes," she gasped, the delicious pressure forcing her to work for each breath.

He kept one hand on her neck and with the other, he unzipped the hoodie. His hand found her breast, and she arched into him as he kneaded the delicate flesh, and her nipples tightened into sharp peaks.

Michael pulled away, his hands releasing her neck and breast. He picked up the headphones and let them dangle from his index finger. "Put these on," he said, then licked his lips.

Sweet Jesus, he was sexy when he was telling her what to do.

Em took the headphones and slid them over her ears. Michael pressed a button on his laptop, and his techno version of Chopin's piece came streaming through. It filled her lust-infused mind with pulsing beats and the Nocturne's haunting melody.

Em kept her gaze locked with Michael's, and when he mouthed, "Stand up," she followed his command.

He swiveled the chair and sat down. She was about to protest his stealing her seat, but Michael pulled her into his lap, her back against his broad chest. Her ass pressed against the hard bulge of his cock straining against his pants.

She gripped the arms of the chair and let her legs fall open. Michael's hand wrapped gently around her neck while the other traced a line from her sternum, down past her stomach, and slipped inside her pajama shorts. The thin fabric stretched as he cupped her sex. He dropped his hand from her neck and planted hot kisses on the delicate skin where his fingertips had pressed and teased her flesh.

Em rolled her head back, allowing it to fall against Michael's chest. Her hips moved back and forth, rubbing against his length. Michael massaged her in a steady beat that matched the pulsing rhythm.

Her senses on overload, Em surrendered. She surrendered to the spearmint-lemongrass scent filling her nostrils. She surrendered to his mouth, hot and wet, nipping at the delicate skin below her earlobe. She surrendered to his touch as he worked her sweet bud. Reaching back and entwining her fingers into Michael's auburn hair, she surrendered to it all, writhing with lust and grinding her ass against him like a bitch in heat.

Her orgasm tore through her like a crescendo. Like a thunderclap. Like a symphony's grand finale. Every sound, every note, working in perfect harmony. She called out, and her words were a tangle of moans woven in with his name.

"Michael! Michael! Michael!"

He pulled the headphones off and tossed them on the floor. With one swift motion, he lifted her off his lap and had her teetering on the edge of the desk. Em grabbed onto Michael's shirt. Had she been stronger, she would have ripped the damn thing off. But he read her mind and wrenched it off with one quick pull. Shirt discarded, Em let her fingers glide down the plane of his stomach, feeling each hard bump of muscle.

He cupped her face. "I nearly came in my fucking pants hearing you call out my name." His mouth crashed onto hers as he gripped her ass and pulled her body flush with his.

"Why are you still wearing pants?" she panted against his lips.

"Fuck, Em. I always knew it would be like this," he growled and unbuttoned his fly.

But just as the button came loose, a loud chime filled the air.

Michael froze, and the chime came again. He pulled away and picked up the cell phone sitting next to his laptop.

Em searched his face. "Who is it?"

Michael stared at the screen. His flushed skin paled into a ghostly white. "It's my dad. Something's wrong. They only call this late if it's an emergency."

17

"I'm coming with you," Em said, tucking disheveled strands of hair behind her ears.

Michael pulled his T-shirt over his head and slid his cell phone into his pocket. "No, you're not."

She grabbed on to the hem of his shirt. "Give me a minute to run inside and put on some pants."

"Em, you don't want to see this." Michael closed his eyes. "Christ, I don't want to see this."

"See what? Is your dad hurt?"

"I've directed the nursing staff to call me whenever he has an aggressive episode."

Images of Noland punching Michael in the jaw during the children's music recital flashed before her eyes.

"Please, Michael. I want to go with you. I might be able to help."

His green eyes darkened. "My father has Stage Six Alzheimer's. Do you know what that means?"

She didn't answer.

"It means severe fucking decline. It means he can't remember the people he sees every day. People he's known his entire life. He has delusions. He thinks we're all out to get him."

Em lifted her chin. "You can either wait for me, or I'm driving to the campus myself. Either way, I'm going with you."

"Jesus, Mary Michelle!" He dropped his head and closed his eyes. "Fine. I'll pull up in front of your house. We'll take the Audi."

"Tony," Michael said in a clipped tone. "Thank you for calling."

"Sure thing, Michael," the man replied. "Your dad is having a rough night. I've put in a call to his doctor. I'd like to give him something to help him calm down and get some rest. We should hear back any minute."

Michael nodded. "Is it all right if Em MacCaslin joins me? She's a friend of the family."

Em's lips cracked into a weak smile. Between her concern for Noland and Michael describing her as "a friend of the family," she knew her expression looked far from friendly.

"Sign in, right here, Ms. MacCaslin," the nurse said, eyeing the duffle bag hanging at her side, then handed her a name tag. "We ask that everyone wears one of these. Visual reminders are helpful to our residents. Once we head inside, you'll notice that everything is labeled with words and pictures." His gaze was back on the bag. "You don't have any food, liquids or medications in there, do you?"

Em shook her head then glanced over at Michael. He shifted his stance and checked his watch.

The nurse scanned the form. "Okay, looks like everything's in order. Let's go back."

The Memory Care Center was housed in the Senior Living Campus's main building. The nurse led them through two sets of secured doors before coming into the main room. It looked more like a preschool than a nursing home. The room was divided into centers. There was an area with gardening tools, an area that resembled a child's nursery with baby dolls and cribs, an office area with papers and calculators, and an area with easels, paints and other arts and crafts supplies.

"It's not what you expected, is it?" Tony asked. He was an

imposing man, almost as tall as Michael. But when he smiled, he went from intimidating to looking as gentle as a lamb.

"No," Em replied. "It's not what I expected at all."

"There's some pretty solid research that shows individuals with Alzheimer's and dementia benefit from an environment that's familiar. These centers allow our residents to act out the parts of their life that they remember." Tony gestured to the cribs and then the office area. "Caring for their children and going into work are all activities many of our residents can relate to. They experience less anxiety when they're engaged in behaviors that are comfortable and routine."

Em glanced over at Michael who stared straight ahead like a soldier going into battle. She turned back to Tony. "That makes a lot of sense."

The nurse led them down a corridor, and a man's angry voice echoed through the hall.

"Dammit, I've told you people a million times, I need to get to my office. I've got meetings all morning, and I'm expected in court this afternoon."

Michael released an audible breath. "How long has he been like this?"

They stopped outside Noland's door. "Not long, about half an hour. I called you after he refused to take his evening meds."

Michael nodded. He was wearing his lawyer mask. Indifferent. Blank. Detached. A band of ravenous wolves could be closing in on him, and he wouldn't have even batted an eye.

"You know, Mr. MacCarron," Tony said, lowering his voice, "we're equipped to handle this. Don't get me wrong; you have every right to be notified about your father's care. But you don't need to come each time he has an episode."

Mask still in place, Michael crossed his arms. "He's my father."

The nurse nodded. "Okay. Carmen and Anita are in with him now. I'll let them know you're here, and I'll let you know when the doc sends the orders for that sedative."

"Thank you, Tony," Michael said as robotically as the Tin Man himself.

Em clutched her duffle bag and followed Michael into the room.

It was a good-sized room, but Em's gaze was drawn to the bedsheets strewn across the floor. Blank papers covered in scribbles lay scattered across every surface like a mad scientist's laboratory. In a chair in the center of the room, sat E. Noland MacCarron, red-faced and eyes wild.

"Who is this son of a bitch," Noland snarled as they entered the room.

Noland swung his gaze from his son and let it fall on her face. He smiled. She was about to return his grin with one of her own when Noland's expression faded into a hard line.

He crossed his arms. "Miss, I don't mean to offend you with this coarse language. We're in the middle of negotiations here. Why don't you call my office? We'll set up an appointment for another time."

"Are you her husband?" Noland asked, directing the question to Michael, but pressed on without waiting for an answer. "Like I told your wife, call the office, and we can set up a time to meet next week."

Michael crouched down. "Dad, it's me. It's your son, Michael."

Noland barked out a laugh. "What the hell are you playing at? My son is seven years old."

Michael and his father were near spitting images of each other. Could Noland not see that the man looking him square in the eye was his own son?

Anita Benson and the other nurse, Carmen, took a step back. The room fell into a thick silence as all eyes fell on Noland and Michael.

"Dad, it's me. Michael. Remember, I'm all grown up now."

Noland blinked a few times then stared at his son. Seconds hung heavy in the air as they waited to see if Noland recognized Michael.

The older man leaned forward. "You're not my son, you lying bastard."

Em unzipped the duffle bag and her body vibrated with the shock of adrenaline. She pulled out her violin case, and, hands trembling, she released the latches and opened the lid.

Polly. Her Polly. Her beautiful Paul Bailly violin.

Her breath came in short gasps as she inhaled the scent of Swiss chalet pine. Like a parent reunited with a lost child, she lifted the instrument from the case. She had broken every trophy and torn up each certificate. She had ripped photos and butchered all the reminders of her life as a musician. But she hadn't destroyed Polly.

She gulped a breath and fumbled with the small compartment that held the rosin. She placed the violin on the ground, slid the bow from the case, and ran the small golden-orange cake of sticky amber residue back and forth over the bow's strings. She glanced up at Noland. Red angry blotches mired his neck. She took another breath and rubbed the rosin on her bow in smooth, steady strokes. She didn't have time to tune the instrument, but without applying rosin to her bow, there would be no sound at all.

Em stood and held the violin in position. She ran the bow across the E-string. A little flat. She would have to live with it.

Noland reared back, but this time, Michael was ready for his father's right hook and dodged the punch.

Em drew the bow across the strings, and the first notes of "Come Thou Fount of Every Blessing" filled the room.

Em's fingers pressed the familiar strings, and Noland stilled. She met his gaze, but his eyes weren't full of the recognition she had seen last time she played this song for him. Not even close. His eyes narrowed into angry slits and the blush that crept up his neck now engulfed his face, red and hot.

Noland lunged toward her and knocked his chair to the ground. "Who are you?" he growled. "Stop that! Knock that shit off!"

Michael sprang to his feet and positioned himself in front of her. "Dad!" he said, holding his father's shoulders. "It's Em. It's our Mary Michelle. She's trying to help."

Noland's eyes darted back and forth like a trapped animal. "Everyone here wants me dead!"

The door opened, and Tony came in holding a syringe.

"Mr. MacCarron, I'm Tony, a nurse here at the Memory Care Center. It's going to be all right. This is medicine to help you rest."

Michael held his father while Tony administered the sedative. Noland blinked as if each movement took expert concentration. His fierce expression melted like a child's ice cream left out in the summer sun. Em met his glassy-eyed gaze. At that moment, she would have sworn he had recognized her. But before he could say another word, his body went limp, and E. Noland MacCarron hung like a rag doll in his son's arms.

EM LEANED against the wall outside Noland's room clutching her violin. The rush of adrenaline still popped in her veins, and she nearly jumped out of her skin when the door to Noland's room clicked open.

"It's just me," Anita Benson said. She handed her the empty duffle bag and violin case.

Em took the items, crouched on the floor, and secured the instrument in its case. She placed the case in the duffle and willed her hands to stop shaking.

"I know you're going to tell me I made it worse for Noland. But last time I played for him, it worked. Last time I played for him, he recognized me. He came back to himself. You were there, Mrs. Benson. You saw it."

Anita's pinched expression relaxed. "The brain is a complicated organ. Throw in an Alzheimer's diagnosis, and the complexity is magnified." She took a step closer. "I didn't come out here to scold you, Em. I think what you tried to do for Mr. MacCarron was very kind. But Alzheimer's is an unpredictable disease. What helps a patient one day, may not work the next."

"Oh," was all she could muster in response as she stared wide-eyed at the woman who had judged her so harshly in the past.

"Why don't we sit down?" Anita gestured to a cluster of chairs in the main area. "Noland's asleep, but Michael is still speaking with the nurses. They shouldn't be much longer."

Em swiped at her face. She hadn't even noticed the warm tears making slick trails down her cheeks. *Christ!* She did *not* want to cry in front of Anita Benson.

"I know what you saw can be quite jarring," Anita said, patting her shoulder. "But what happened tonight is a product of his disease."

Em stared at the scuffs on the linoleum floor. "I only wanted to help."

"Of course, you did." Anita gestured for her to sit. "Nobody doubts that."

Em met her gaze, and the woman smiled. In all the years she had known Anita Benson, this was the first time she had seen her smile.

Anita glanced toward Noland's room, then settled into a chair. "Kyle mentioned seeing you near Garrett this morning out by Sadie's Hollow."

Was that just this morning?

"Yes, we ran into him while we were...while I was trying to..." Em broke off.

But Anita was quick to fill the void. "Kyle also mentioned you don't remember anything from the night you..." She pursed her lips. "The night of your injury."

Em would rather have her toenails pulled out with pliers than discuss her injury with Anita Benson, but the woman seemed sincere. Em searched her face for some shred of disgust or resentment but couldn't find any.

"No, I don't remember much. Just flashes of images and sensations that don't make any sense."

Anita's brow furrowed. "I'm sure that's frustrating." She leaned forward. "But you've got so much on your plate right now, dear. Your father needs help getting settled in the assisted living cottage, and you've been tasked with getting his house ready to sell. Are you sure you've got time to be taking trips to Sadie's Hollow?"

Em's mouth went dry. Everything Anita Benson said was true.

A door opened and closed. Em and Anita stood, expecting to see Michael and the nurses, but it was Mrs. Teller. She was wearing a pink bathrobe and a child's plastic tiara.

"Did I hear music?" the woman said, her arms in a mock dance pose.

"No, no, Mrs. Teller," Anita answered. "It was just Em MacCaslin playing the violin for Mr. MacCarron. It's late," she added, checking her watch. "Let me help get you back to your room."

Mrs. Teller clutched Em's hand. "Did you graduate from Garrett High?" she asked with an innocent twinkle in her eye as the birdlike bones of her fingers tightened their grip.

Em took in the woman's frilly get-up and smiled. "No, Mrs. Teller, I didn't."

"Are you sure?" Mrs. Teller released her hold. "The other young lady who comes to play the piano for us did. I'm sure of it."

Anita patted the woman's arm. "Mrs. Teller was Garrett High's Homecoming queen. Isn't that right, dear?"

"Oh, yes! And my Rodney was the Homecoming king. I still have my crown," she said, pushing the play tiara askew.

Anita lowered her voice. "Mrs. Teller thinks we're all from Garrett. It's a product of her dementia."

Em nodded.

Mrs. Teller waltzed across the floor, embracing an invisible partner.

A trio of voices echoed through the hall. Em caught Michael's eye as the group entered the main room.

"I'm going to help Mrs. Teller back to her room. Take care, dear," Anita said, gifting her with another smile.

Michael took hold of her elbow and led her toward the exit.

Em tried to meet his gaze, but Michael wouldn't make eye contact.

"I'm sorry. I thought I could help—like I did last time."

Michael stopped walking but kept his hand wrapped around her arm. She searched his face. The anguish in his eyes churned like a dark, angry sea.

"Oh, Michael! I'm so sorry," she whispered.

He squeezed her arm like a child holding tight to a treasured blanket.

"I know this is hard for you," she said, searching for the right words.

She hadn't chosen wisely.

Michael's eyes widened as if she had slapped him. The raw emotion disappeared, and the mask was back. Blank. Detached.

He released her arm. "It's late, Em. Let's go."

18

"Michael, talk to me. Please, say something."

Em stood across from him, standing on her driveway. He faced her, standing on his. He looked down at the strip of dry grass separating the MacCaslin property from the MacCarron's. A foot, maybe fourteen inches, but it might as well have been the Kansas River.

He hadn't spoken a word during the drive home. Em's pleas slid off him like Teflon. It took everything he had to hold it together—to keep all that pain locked inside.

But there was one thing he knew for sure: He didn't have time for her pity.

He had a law firm to run. His clients expected him to provide the same diligent service just as his father had done for the last forty years. In addition to living up to the legacy of E. Noland MacCarron, he also had to stay on top of his father's condition. A job that was taking up more and more of his time and energy every day.

He couldn't give in to a moment of weakness. But Christ, he wanted to.

He wanted to drop his head into Em's lap and have her stroke his cheek. He wanted to let it all out. The frustration. The guilt. The pretending. The monotony of living a life he didn't choose.

He stuffed his hands into his pockets and let his eyes travel up the length of her body. The hint of a smile played on his lips. She was still wearing his hoodie. She shivered and pulled the extra fabric tight across her chest. A few hours ago, that body was writhing and panting in his lap. She hadn't been wearing panties, just those tiny pajama shorts. And she was wet. So wet. His hand flexed inside his pocket, itching to feel the slick slide of heat between her thighs.

"Michael, I know this is hard."

His eyes focused. He'd gotten so lost in his fantasy he'd almost forgotten his father.

Em watched him like a hawk, chin raised. He searched her eyes and saw it. *Pity. Motherfucking, pity.*

"Let me help you," she tried again.

"Aren't you the pot calling the kettle black," he said, words laced with disgust.

Em took a step back as if he'd slapped her across the face.

"What is that supposed to mean?"

He barked out a laugh. "*You* didn't want any help. You had over a decade—twelve fucking years to answer my letters. I would have done anything to help you. Now you're back, and you're barely letting me lift a finger. I'm basically your glorified chauffeur."

"You know that's not true. It's complicated. Everything is so complicated." She took a step closer. "Your dad, Michael. I had no idea. I really didn't."

"Enough about my father for Christ's sake! Yes, it sucks. Yes, it breaks my fucking heart. But it's my cross to bear."

"It doesn't have to be," she whispered.

Her words cut him like shards of broken glass. He wanted to believe her. But not like this. Not if all she felt for him was pity. The thought made his insides twist.

"It's been a long night, Em. We're both tired. Go inside and get some rest."

She crossed her arms. "I don't pity you. I know that's what you're thinking. But you're wrong." She picked up the duffle and took a step toward him. "If what you think you see in my eyes is pity," she said and took a shaky breath, "then you don't know me at all. And you never did."

Her eyes glassed over, but she blinked away the emotion. Without another word, she turned on her heel and left. He stared hard at the gravel driveway, listening to the squeak of the front door open and the angry crash when it slammed shut. The same angry crash he had heard on Halloween.

That crash had turned his world upside down.

He closed his eyes and ran a hand down his face. He hated to admit it, but he was glad she was with him tonight. Her presence, her willingness to do whatever she could to help—it brought him comfort.

She had played her violin tonight. Her Polly. Christ, that couldn't have been easy for her. He wasn't even sure Polly had survived when she tore apart her room after her injury. He had peeked into her room when he helped her father move. The layers of time and dust had accumulated on every disheveled, broken treasure, and the violin case sat like an ancient tomb that no one dared open. He was sure Dr. MacCaslin hadn't touched it either. Knowing she had destroyed Polly would have been too much for him.

Michael stared at the side of Em's house. Images of her smiling in the rain filled him with a longing that seeped into his bones. He closed his eyes and let the image expand into the empty corners of his soul. They were better together. No matter where she was on this planet—France, Japan, Australia, something in his heart always called out to hers.

But he'd let her down. Guilt clutched at his heart, sharp and heavy. He closed his eyes as the gentle notes of Chopin's Nocturne 20 in C-Sharp Minor drifted through the air and danced in the night breeze.

He let out an exasperated breath. Now he was delusional. Maybe he wasn't too far behind his father in losing his fucking marbles. But when he looked up, Em was there, standing in front of her bedroom window. Golden light encased her like a treasure preserved in amber.

He stared at the window. She was playing for him. She always played for him. He could hear her voice calling out to him in every note, in every vibration of her fingertips pressed upon the delicate strings. He burst through her front door and raced up the stairs to her room. His heart always knew how to find her. He could have been blindfolded. He would still have made it to her without a scratch.

She laid the violin to rest in its case and stood in front of him. She pushed up on her tiptoes and cupped his face in her hands.

"What do you see?" she asked, forcing him to meet her gaze. "What do you really see, Michael?"

The room was quiet, but he could still hear the music. She was the music.

"I see everything, Em." He slid his hands down her back and lifted her into his arms. "You're my everything."

She had taken off her jeans and was back in those sweet little pajama shorts. Her bare legs wrapped around his waist as his fingers pressed into her buttocks through the thin fabric. She wasn't wearing panties. His cock turned to steel, and Em released a breathy moan.

She felt it too. Their connection was more than just carnal lust. It was layer upon layer of smiles and laughter. An infinite loop of memories and music.

He carried her over to the bed and sat down with her legs still wrapped around him. She slid onto her knees but kept her core pressed flush against him. The golden glow of the small lamp lit her features, and he resisted the urge to pull out his cock, rip off those pajama shorts, and drive into her.

He sucked in a ragged breath and dropped soft kisses on the sprinkling of freckles that dusted the bridge of her nose. He let his lips explore her neck and earlobe.

Em traced her fingers down the length of his jaw. Her touch was like a match pulled across the striker strip. It set his body on fire. She clawed at his shirt, but he finished the job, pulling it over his head and throwing it onto the floor.

Em shifted in his lap, grinding into him. He unzipped the hoodie and peeled off the garment, allowing his fingers to linger along the ivory skin of her delicate collarbone. She wasn't wearing her tank top anymore, and her naked breasts heaved with each breath.

"Christ, Em! You're perfect," he said, taking her breast into his hand and circling his thumb around the peak of her nipple.

He shifted his body farther onto the bed but stilled when something pressed into his thigh. He reached down and pulled out a string of pearls. "Are these the pearls?" He held them under the golden lamplight. The clasp was missing, and thin lengths of twisted thread hung limply on each side where a few pearls should have rested.

"Yes," she answered, gathering her hair up on top of her head.

Em craned her neck to the side, and Michael knew exactly what she wanted him to do. He draped the pearls around her neck, twisted his fingers around the cool, tiny spheres, and tightened the fit. Em gasped, and he growled as his lips crashed into hers.

He couldn't hold back now. Images and sensations of their first kiss at Sadie's Hollow flooded his mind. Those pearls, cool and smooth against her skin, sent his need to have her into overdrive.

Michael loosened the pearls and let the strand fall into his palm. He wound the necklace around his fingers and palmed her breast. He let the pearls pass over the peak of her left breast, then her right. Em's head fell back, and she closed her eyes, arching into his touch as she gripped his thighs. She looked like a wanton goddess soaking in each touch, each delicious sensation.

She tilted her head forward and opened her eyes. Pools of endless blue flooded his lust-filled mind. He dropped the pearls and captured her mouth, pressing a kiss to each corner. He moved lower kissing her jaw, her neck. The soft light illuminated the delicate round indentations made by the pearls. He kissed each mark and allowed his tongue to glide over her skin. It tasted of oranges and sunlight and Sunday mornings spent wrapped around each other in bed.

Em weaved her fingers into the hair at the nape of his neck. "Michael," she breathed, "make love to me."

He searched her face. He knew each freckle, each eyelash. He had memorized all her smiles. Her face had haunted his dreams for years.

"I just want to look at you for a minute."

Her lips curved, and she smiled her shy smile.

He ran his thumb across her bottom lip. "We're better together, Em."

Her shy smile bloomed, and he knew that easy grin, sticky with cherry popsicle running down her chin. He cupped her face. "I need to know you believe that, too," he said, leaning in and taking her bottom lip gently between his teeth.

She shuddered, her hot breath mingling with his. He released her lip and found her earlobe.

"Tell me, Mary Michelle."

Now it was her pulling back and cupping his face. Her eyes darkened with lust. "You and me." She pressed her lips to his. "It's always been the two of us."

"Say it," he mouthed against her lips.

"We're better together. Always."

She'd barely breathed the words before Michael had her flat on her back. He pulled off her sleep shorts and sank down to hover above her naked body, kissing a trail past her navel and down to her sweet center. Her knees fell to the sides, and, unashamed and unguarded, she opened herself to him. He licked a line across her delicate folds as she lifted her hips to meet his tongue.

His gaze turned upward, and he followed the line of her body. She was sprawled on the bed, just like in his fantasy, auburn hair spilling across the pillow, hands resting above her head. He noticed a flash of white tangled between her fingers. The pearls. A fresh jolt of lust shot to his cock. He gripped her hips and worked her swollen bud with his tongue.

Her skin heated beneath his touch as her core grew hot and wet. She writhed and twisted. Her gasps coupled with sweet moans sounded more beautiful than any piece of music he had ever heard. Her hips bucked under his touch in a steady beat only the two of them could hear. She cried out, ecstasy ripping through her as her thighs tightened around him, and she rode out each wave of bliss.

Em met his gaze with half-focused eyes and gifted him with a lazy cherry popsicle grin. But this time, he was the one with something sweet and wet on his lips. He undid his fly with one hand and had his pants and boxer shorts off in one swift motion.

He licked his lips and prowled up the length of her body. "I love the way you taste," he growled. His cock hung heavy and twitched as it grazed Em's inner thigh. He stilled a moment and met her gaze. "Do we need to use protection?"

She shook her head and gifted him with a sexy grin. "I'm on the pill."

He trailed his hand along the side of her stomach and entwined his fingers with hers. With the pearl necklace clasped between their fingers, he thrust inside her.

Her body welcomed his cock and gripped him with a delicious heat. He pulled back and thrust again, feeling that sweet slide, as he buried himself to the hilt inside of her.

He stilled, worry creasing his brow. "Is this okay? I don't want to hurt you, Em."

Her lust-filled gaze softened. "You won't hurt me, Michael. I trust you."

He could almost hear the clank of the chain breaking loose as the bonds of guilt, regret, and shame fell away. Drunk with this new freedom, adrenaline surged through his body.

She squeezed his hand, and the pearls dug into his palm. A hot current of pleasure teetering on the cusp of pain shot through his hand and went straight to his cock.

He rocked his hips back like a slingshot pulled taut, ready for release and met her gaze. "I'm going to fuck you until you can't remember your name."

"Which one, Em or Mary Michelle?" she asked with a naughty grin.

"Both," he growled.

He squeezed her hand and drove inside her. Em arched her hips, taking his cock deeper.

Holy Fuck.

Michael captured her other hand and held it above her head. He let go of all his inhibitions. He fucked her like a well-oiled machine. Pressure building, his body ached for the perfect release he could only find with her. A thin sheen of sweat coated their skin, amplifying the clap and slide of their bodies as Em met his thrusts in perfect harmony.

Their climax came in bursts of sound and breath and motion. He released her hands and kissed her, cupping her face and tasting her cries and gasps as he spilled into her with a primal growl.

19

E m held her breath. The late afternoon sun streamed through the front window like a spotlight highlighting each key on the Steinway. Her gaze trained on her injured finger, she played scale after scale, trying to discern if Michael was right.

What if she hadn't lost everything that night at Sadie's Hollow?

What if her talent wasn't gone?

What would that even mean?

Sure, she had played the piano and the violin since she'd returned home to Langley Park, but she hadn't played anything technically difficult. The real test would be Paganini. A chill crept up her spine at the thought. She wasn't ready to try *Nel cor più non mi sento.* Not yet.

The floorboards squeaked above her, and Michael's heavy footfalls echoed through the house. A delicious shiver ran down her spine. She had spent the night curled into him in her tiny bed. He had wrapped his arms around her, and she'd fallen asleep surrounded by his strength and intoxicating scent of lemongrass and spearmint.

She didn't have to turn around to know he was behind her.

Michael ran a finger across her back and gathered her hair into his hand.

She continued playing the piano, switching from scales to a four-octave arpeggio. Michael nudged her forward and lowered himself behind her on the bench. She arched into his solid strength as her fingers worked their way up and down the keys.

He kissed the sensitive skin behind her ear. "I thought I was dreaming when I heard the piano."

Em craned her head back, and Michael captured her mouth in a lazy kiss. His powerful legs tightened around her. He dropped his hands to her thighs and dragged his fingertips from her knees to the space between her legs. He caressed her inner thigh, making slow circles with his thumbs.

"These pajama shorts are going to be the death of me," he said, voice low and husky from sleep.

She wriggled forward but was unable to keep the smile out of her voice. "You're ruining my form."

He straightened up. "That's right," he answered. "Feet firmly on the ground. Wrists up. Don't let the elbows bounce."

He exaggerated each movement with a mock-serious expression.

"You remember," she said, squealing as he gathered her into his lap.

He kissed the scar on her ring finger. "I remember everything. And I meant what I said, Em. I don't think the accident took your gift away."

She searched his face. "Even if I can still play like I used to—and I'm not saying I can. I still need to know what happened that night. I need to know for my dad. I need to know for myself. I need everyone in Langley Park to know I didn't mean to let them down."

Michael's brow furrowed. "You didn't let anyone down. And any person that gives you shit for leaving never cared about you to begin with."

She rested her head in the crook of his neck. She knew he was right, but a nagging voice inside her head needed the world to know she didn't purposefully throw away her future.

He pressed a kiss to her temple. "We're going to figure this out. I promise. Even if it's the last thing I do on this earth, we're going to get some answers.

Michael cradled her in his arms. He took her hand and laced his fingers with hers. She gazed down at the jagged mark and released an audible sigh. It almost seemed hard to believe a tiny bit of scar tissue had dictated the last twelve years of her life.

Michael ran his thumb across the raised skin. "I have an idea," he said, releasing her hand and helping her to her feet. "But you have to keep those shorts on."

Em plopped down on the futon in Michael's carriage house. "This is not what I thought you were alluding to."

Michael opened his laptop and pressed a few keys. "I think you're going to like this," he said tossing her a wry grin.

His remix of Chopin's Nocturne 20 streamed out of two small speakers on his desk. Her gaze traveled to the headphones. Her body ignited with desire remembering how she came in his lap, his music pumping in her ears, brightening every dark corner of her mind.

She leaned into the futon and closed her eyes. She smiled when she smelled Michael's lemongrass spearmint scent. He planted whisper soft kisses to each corner of her mouth.

"You always smell so good," she sighed. "What is that?"

He laughed and tangled his hand in her hair, wrapping the long auburn strands through his fingers. "It's my mom."

Em opened her eyes. "Your mom?"

He chuckled, and something sentimental warmed his expression. "She loved this scent. She always bought the organic lemongrass spearmint clothes detergent and the shampoo from Pete's Organic Grocery in the town center."

Em closed her eyes and inhaled. Thoughts of a pre-teen Michael sitting on her bedroom floor, all long legs and elbows, tapping out a melody as she practiced violin filled her mind. His easy presence and familiar scent added a layer of familiarity to her music, a peaceful texture that coated each note.

She pressed her lips to his but froze when he set something solid in her lap. She opened her eyes and narrowed her gaze. It was a violin. But not a traditional violin like her Polly. This thing looked like something out of a science fiction movie. Like a regular violin, it had four strings, a chin rest and pegs at the top for tuning. But this violin was completely clear with little sockets on the side and an on and off switch.

Em held up the odd-looking instrument.

"It's an electric violin," Michael said with a wide grin.

"I figured that much," she answered, looking the instrument up and down. If Cinderella needed a violin to match her glass slippers, this was it.

"It's made of acrylic, and it's got LED lights built in."

Michael plucked a string, and a flurry of lights flickered inside the instrument.

It was hard not to get excited when Michael emanated such raw joy.

"What are you doing with it?" she asked.

"I've been messing around with it, playing with different sounds. There are lots of artists playing electric violins—especially ones that are crossing over into techno."

She lifted the instrument into position. Despite it looking more like an ice carving of a violin than an actual instrument, the chin rest felt sturdy and her fingers relaxed against the strings.

He slid the headphones over her ears and plugged them into the jack in the side of the violin. He met her gaze with smiling eyes. "Try it. You might be surprised."

Em wrinkled her nose. "I don't know," she answered, staring down at the alien instrument. She was a classically trained violinist, and this glowing mass of clear acrylic looked like something from a Sci-Fi flick.

Michael held out the bow. "Come on, Em. What would it hurt?"

She took the bow, and her lips curved into a smirk. "At least the bow doesn't light up."

Michael returned her smirk and tilted his head toward the violin like a challenge.

She closed her eyes and drew the bow across the strings. "Oh my gosh," she exclaimed, her eyes popping open.

"Not bad, right?" Michael said.

"It's different, but no, not bad at all."

He removed her headphones and plugged the violin into a speaker. "Play something simple. I want to show you something."

"Simple, huh," Em said, narrowing her eyes.

"Twinkle, Twinkle, Little Star" burst from the speakers.

Michael laughed and shook his head. "What do you think of this?" he asked, pressing a few keys on his laptop.

Em gasped as the music amplified. It sounded like there were twenty other violins playing along with her. She repeated the child's tune over and over, enchanted with the glowing instrument as Michael manipulated the sound with different effects.

She had lost count of how many times she'd played the tune when Michael turned to her. His playful tone was gone, and his green eyes darkened to a smoky sage. "Play something real. Play Chopin's Nocturne 20 for me." He pressed a few keys on his laptop and his electronic version of the song burst from the speakers.

Em listened to the dreamy composition grow in complexity as the techno elements complemented Chopin's haunting tune. Her mind emptied of thoughts and worries. Her father, the impending sale of her childhood home, her injury, and her pain all evaporated like drops of rain kissed by sunlight.

She drew the bow across the strings, but what came out wasn't what Chopin composed. Like a silversmith turning precious metals into works of art, she played the tune, bending and shaping it into something new.

Then the music stopped. Em blinked once, then twice. She had drifted to that place where her mind hovered between this world and the next.

"Were you recording that?"

His green eyes shined with wonder and adoration. "Yeah," he replied.

A pang of anxiety surged through her chest. "It's just for us, okay. I don't want anyone else hearing that."

"I wouldn't share it with anyone without checking with you," he said, taking the violin out of her hands and setting it on the desk. "Do you want me to play it back for you?"

She nodded. She didn't trust her voice. As a musician, she had never deviated from the notes written on the page. Like a trained soldier, she followed every marking, every notation. She had spent all of her childhood playing the piano and the violin exactly as the arrangement demanded. She had never even dreamed of putting her mark on something as timeless as Chopin's piece.

Michael sat down at the desk and focused on his laptop. The screen was filled with jagged and arcing lines, and his fingers moved rapidly between the keys and the mousepad. "I'm just messing with the reverb and compression."

He tapped one last key and swiveled the chair around. The remix filled the air as her violin riff twisted and turned its way through the explosion of sound like live wires leaping and sparking.

She met Michael's gaze. She needed the connection, needed to keep herself grounded in this moment.

"This is you, Em," he said.

She closed her eyes. The music was everywhere, in her, around her. Michael's warm hands cupped her face, and she inhaled his scent. Only two things existed in her world: Michael and music. He kissed her, and the contact sent pulsing heat to her core.

She grabbed his shirt and wrapped the soft cotton around her fingers. The hard bumps of chiseled abs pressed against her knuckles. She released the fabric and pressed her hands against his bare skin.

Michael pulled off his T-shirt, revealing a hard torso cut with clean, muscular lines. A dusting of dark auburn hair trailed from his navel down to a thick bulge in his pants. Em pulled back a fraction, her greedy gaze devouring each inch of his chiseled body. It was no wonder the punching bag in the corner looked beat to hell. She pictured Michael, sweat-slick, punching and jabbing until his muscles reached the edge of exhaustion. She ran her fingers down his torso, memorizing each inch of muscle wrapped in taut, smooth skin.

Michael pressed her hand to his heart. "I never let you go, Em. You've always been here. You'll always be here." His grip tightened and his heartbeat quickened beneath her touch, syncing with the thrum of the music.

She swallowed hard. He had lived in her heart, too. She'd tried to cut him out, tried to chain off the part of her that would always be his. But it was always there, no matter how hard she tried to fight it. Her whirling winds of anger and resentment couldn't destroy the place where Michael had always lived in her heart.

He released her hands and lifted her into his arms. He dropped back into the chair, and she straddled him like she had on Halloween. But she didn't want to control him, and she didn't want to use him. Now her body ached for his touch. It whimpered with want when he lifted his lips from her skin for even a fraction of a second.

The music bathed them in sound and vibration, and Em pressed her core against him. Animal arousal coursed through her veins, and Michael released a low, raw growl.

"We're better together," she whispered, leaning back and twisting out of her tank top.

He finished the job, pulling off her pajama shorts. "Fuck, yes we are."

Michael shifted in the chair and yanked down his pants in one swift move, exposing his cock, heavy and glistening with the seed of his desire. She sank on to him, and her wet heat welcomed his hard shaft. He stretched her, inch by delicious inch, and she released a ragged gasp.

"Do you feel it?" he breathed, gripping the smooth flesh of her ass, guiding her body in strong, measured thrusts.

She felt everything: the demanding pulse of the music, her body surging with desire, his hard length filling her completely. The chair creaked and moaned as she gripped his shoulders and allowed his body to set a punishing pace. Sweat trailed down the space between her breasts, and he licked the moisture. She watched his tongue, mesmerized and drunk on lust.

He massaged her swollen clit in perfect rhythmic circles. Em threw her head back, lost in a tidal wave of sensation. He gripped her ass with a lion's ferocity and pressed a deft finger between her buttocks, massaging the sensitive place no man had ever touched before.

He worked her body, harder and deeper. His ragged breaths came in hot beats between kisses. "Mary Michelle, you are so fucking sweet and so fucking tight."

Her name, dripping off his lips, sounded so hot and so dirty. She couldn't hold back and met her release, eyelids fluttering, her body no longer her own.

She belonged to Michael. She belonged to the music. Their music. The notes poured through her like a dam breaking loose. He joined her within seconds, squeezing her ass with a carnal force that would surely leave a mark.

Em dropped her head to Michael's shoulder. Tremors of her orgasm rippled through her body like warm rain, leaving her loose and sated. He released his grip on her ass and the tender flesh ached with a delicious burn teetering on the tantalizing precipice of where pleasure met pain.

"Em," Michael breathed into her ear as his fingertips painted mindless shapes on the small of her back. "I missed you. I missed you so much."

She met his gaze. He must have seen the truth in her eyes because the crooked smile he gave her sent sparks ricocheting the length of her spine.

He leaned in. "Listen. Just listen."

The remix had been playing on a nonstop loop. The song

sounded so familiar now that she couldn't picture a time where this music wasn't a part of her soul.

"This is good, Em. It's not like anything I've ever heard. We could do this. We could make music together."

She closed her eyes, letting the idea take root when a rush of frigid air washed over her naked body in an icy gust.

20

E m gasped and arched into Michael as something cold and wet
nudged her thigh. She looked down and let out a relieved sigh.
"Cody, boy! Did you get lonely?" she asked, greeting the canine
intruder and scratching between his ears.

Michael chuckled. "I can promise you, Cody MacCarron is the
least lonely dog in Langley Park. Kate Fisher walks him almost every
day. And she brings you treats, doesn't she old boy?" He patted the
dog's protruding belly.

Em and Michael untangled their bodies, and Cody pranced
around the room. Michael adjusted his pants and looked at his watch.
"Christ, it's past six o'clock. Let me put Cody back in the house. Kate
must have left his dog door open."

Em finished dressing. "I'll go with you. I haven't been inside your
house once since I got back."

Michael's shoulders tensed as he pulled his T-shirt over his head.
"What is it?"

"The house isn't in great shape."

She took his hand. "You know I don't care about that."

Sensing it was time to go, Cody scurried through the carriage house doggy door and bolted toward the main house. Michael tightened his grip on her hand as they neared the front door.

Michael's American Foursquare was nearly a carbon copy of hers except instead of red brick, his was a muted lemon yellow color. As a girl, she had known it like the back of her hand. Mrs. MacCarron always kept sweets hidden away in a drawer under the dishtowels. She and Michael would tiptoe their way into the kitchen, slide the drawer open, and swipe the treats like cat burglars on a big-time heist. She smiled as the memory grew warm in her chest. Mrs. MacCarron must have known what they were up to. Knowing her, she probably left the sweets there on purpose.

She entered the foyer and stopped in her tracks. Just like in her home, the staircase was situated directly in front of the foyer. Except, the staircase in the MacCarron house was wrecked. The handrail was missing, and slats of espresso-stained wood that once served as the steps sat in a pile. Someone must have come through and tried to fix the missing stairs, but they'd used regular plywood giving the structure a misshapen quality like a child's art project.

"What happened to the staircase? Did you do this?" Em asked, spotting the espresso posts resting against the wall.

"No, this was all my dad."

"Why did he do this? Was he trying to repair something?"

Michael didn't answer. He walked past her and into the kitchen. A low mechanical hum pulsed for a few seconds, and Cody let out a high-pitched whine. Doggy dinnertime.

Em crouched down and took a closer look at the slats. The boards were sharp and ragged as if someone used a crowbar to yank them out of place.

Michael came out of the kitchen and crossed his arms. "I told you the place was a mess."

"This isn't a mess. This is..."

"Insanity?" he offered.

She met his gaze but didn't take the bait. She remained quiet, giving him space to talk.

"Want to sit?" Michael asked and tilted his head toward the living room.

She followed him to the love seat.

"I knew something was off with my dad after my mom passed away. He'd forget little things, a meeting here, a filing deadline there. I told him he needed to hire a legal secretary. But you know my dad, he liked doing it all himself. He prided himself on being self-sufficient."

Michael wrapped his arm around her and pulled her in close. She rested her head against his chest, feeling his throat constrict as he swallowed.

"He didn't come into the office one day. I called the house, but he didn't pick up. I had to cover all of his meetings as well as my own. So, I wasn't able to stop by the house until late. When I got here, I walked into this," he said, his gaze locked on the staircase.

"What was he doing?"

Michael's embrace tightened. "He was looking for my mom. He thought she was trapped under the stairs. I walked in, and he looked so relieved to see me. He said, 'Michael, we have to help mom. She's been calling out to me all day. She's stuck under the staircase.'"

Em laced her fingers with his. "What did you say?"

"I tried to tell him mom was dead, but he just stared at me like I was crazy. He became belligerent, started ripping off the railing, hitting the posts with an ax like a lunatic. I watched him for the better part of an hour." Michael let out a weary breath. "Finally, I decided to help him. I figured, if I helped, I could try and take the stairs apart without completely damaging them. So that's what we did until my dad ran out of steam and passed out on the sofa. I moved back in with him two days later."

Em squeezed his hand. She had been so wrapped up in her anger, she never once asked her father about Michael; and, when her father had made even the briefest comment about Langley Park, she would change the subject.

A sickening lump ripe with shame and guilt weighed heavy in her chest. "I'm sorry I never reached out to you, Michael."

He rested his chin on her head. "It wouldn't have mattered. You know my dad's reputation. He was a legend. People loved him. People trusted him with everything: their money, their dreams, their secrets. I wasn't about to let anyone know that E. Noland MacCarron had fucking lost his marbles."

"What did you do? I mean, you had to know that he couldn't work?"

"I took it all on. It was a slow decline. At first, it was just these crazy episodes. He would come into the office and seem like his normal self, then I'd look at whatever he was working on, and it would be gibberish. I started giving him pretend clients so he could feel like he was working."

"Oh, Michael," she said, pulling back from his embrace to meet his gaze.

He gestured to the dining room table stacked with papers. "Today was the first time I've slept past five in the morning in years. I've been working my ass off, first to keep my father's condition a secret, and now, to keep the firm going. My dad doesn't even recognize me, but I don't want to let him down. Law was never my dream, but I'll be damned if I let the MacCarron reputation go to shit."

Em understood. She was just about to tell him that when a framed photograph on the coffee table caught her attention. She stared at two young women reclining side by side in Adirondack chairs on the MacCarron's porch. Each woman was holding a tiny bundle. The words *Better Together* were written in her father's hand-writing across the top of the photo.

Em picked up the photo. Her mother had a copy of it sitting on a shelf in her study half a world away. Years ago, Em had moved the pictures around, obscuring this photo behind books and knick-knacks, so she didn't have to look at it. But she always knew it was there.

Michael traced his mother's smiling face with his fingertip. "I'm glad you're back, Em."

"Me, too," she answered as a tremor of disbelief passed through her because it was true. She was glad to be home, glad to be with

Michael. All her jagged edges smoothed out when she was in his arms.

He cupped her face in his hands and pressed a kiss to her forehead. "This is the happiest I've been in a long time."

Em closed her eyes. His words washed over her in a wave of spearmint lemongrass bliss, but her empty stomach replied before she could. The loud lurch of sound emanating from her stomach made her gasp with embarrassment. They had spent most of the day in the carriage house without breaking to eat. Her belly wasn't pleased.

Michael laughed an easy laugh and gathered her back in his arms. "Let's get some dinner. We can't let Langley Park's Wunderkind starve."

She broke free of Michael's hold and tried to give him her best "screw you" stare, but they both broke out into giddy laughter when her stomach growled again. This time, the sound was even louder. Em wrapped her hands around her stomach.

Michael lifted her off the couch and threw her over his shoulder. "Come on, growly bear. It looks like you can't survive on sex alone. Let's get some food into you."

She pounded his back and laughed as her stomach let out another chorus of growls.

"MacCarron! We need you to break a tie."

Em and Michael hadn't even passed through the threshold of Park Tavern before someone was calling out to Michael. She scanned the restaurant. A few patrons sat at the bar while a group of men sat at a high-top table. She recognized Zoe's brother, Ben Fisher, and Sam Sinclair, but she didn't know the other two men.

Michael leaned down and whispered in her ear, "Looks like we walked in on the weekly meeting of the *Star Wars* Rebel Legion."

"The rebel what?" Em asked, but Ben was quick to break in.

"MacCarron, you know very well we're not part of The Rebel Legion."

Michael chuckled and shook his head. "The Rebel Legion is a group of *Star Wars* super fans who like to dress up and creep people out."

Ben threw Michael a mock incredulous glare, then met her gaze. "Michael's got it all wrong, Em. From time to time, we get together and talk *Star Wars*."

"Or Jenna kicked Ben out of the house for making her ears bleed listening to all of his *Star Wars* theories," Sam said, laughing and flinching as Ben gave him a playful punch to the arm.

Sam wrapped her in a bear hug. "It's good to see you, Em. I was wondering when you'd come to say hello."

Em's chest tightened as she stared up at the gentle giant who had been like a big brother to her with his unruly auburn locks and warm smile.

"And I see you've dragged my good-for-nothing little cousin away from work. Way to go," Sam added and slapped Michael on the back.

"Your ugly mug couldn't do that, that's for damn sure," Michael shot back with a cheeky grin.

Sam gestured to the table. "Let me introduce you to the other non-members of the Rebel Legion." He nodded toward a man with short cropped hair. "This is our Peace Officer, Detective Clayton Stevens."

"Just Clay will do," the man said, shaking her hand.

"And our resident Amelia Earhart, Nick Kincade," Sam added, slapping the back of a man who looked more like a movie star than a pilot.

"Are you the Nick that Sam met the summer he built schools in Honduras?" Em asked.

"That would be me," Nick answered. "It's a pleasure to meet you, Em."

"Captain Nick flies airplanes for UPS. So, if one of your packages gets lost in transit, it's probably this guy's fault."

Nick shook his head. "You wouldn't believe the shit I take from this guy. If it weren't for all the free beer, I'd be..."

"You'd be where, Kincade?" Sam asked, eyes dancing. "Over at The Scoop grabbing a soft serve with six-year-olds?"

Nick glanced out the window, weighing the option. "You know, a triple scoop doesn't sound too bad."

Sam shook his head. "Well, if you go, bring me back a pint of mint chip. In the meantime, I'm going to steal little Miss Mary Michelle."

Michael met her gaze. "Not for too long," he said, his green eyes darkening.

"I'll bring her back in one piece," Sam said over his shoulder as he led Em over to the bar.

"This place is gorgeous," she said, admiring the gleaming Cherrywood bar and the rows of spirits glowing gold and amber under the bar's warm lights.

Sam stepped behind the counter and wiped at a spot with a dishtowel. "It's a labor of love," he replied, but his voice had lost its teasing edge.

Sam leaned his forearms on the bar. "I hear you've been making trips to Sadie's Hollow?"

"Zoe told you?" Em shot back.

"Don't get angry. She cares about you, Em. I know she would do anything to help you."

"I know. I know you're right, Sam. It's just…"

"It's just that it's hard to let go of the anger, the disappointment, the loss?" Sam offered.

She nodded. There was no use denying it. "I need to know what happened to me that night."

"And Michael's helping you figure that out?"

"Yes."

Sam stared at the tattoos peeking out from under his rolled-up sleeves. "That's good. He needs this. All he does is work his ass off and care for his father. That is not a life."

Em glanced away, unsure of what to say.

"He needs you, Em. He always has. And I'm pretty sure you need him, too. You two are the great hope of the ginger race," he added with a wry smile.

"Gingers conspiring to rule the world," Zoe said, walking toward them.

Sam popped the top off a Boulevard Pale Ale and handed it to Zoe. "Hiding out in the bathroom again?"

Zoe released an exasperated breath. "I love *Star Wars*. Don't get me wrong. I mean, I was freaking Princess Leia for Halloween for like five years in a row when I was a kid. But I cannot handle another debate over which order you're supposed to watch the episodes."

Ben's voice carried through the tavern. "You've got to watch episodes four through six, first."

"And then watch one through three," Nick chimed in. "Otherwise, you miss the big reveal of Luke being Vader's son."

Ben and Nick clinked glasses like they'd solved global warming.

"Ben has Star-dar. He can sense a *Star Wars* discussion anywhere in a five-mile radius," Zoe said, blowing her big brother an exaggerated kiss.

Sam left the bar and headed for the men's table. "Dudes! No way! Chronological is the way to go. It's the natural order. Stevens, MacCarron, back me up, guys."

Zoe leaned in toward Em. They watched as the table erupted into a heated debate.

"Don't even mention that Jar Jar whatever—you'll be stuck here for days," Zoe said with a shaky laugh.

Em knew that awkward laugh. Her heart twisted knowing that her old friend was nervous.

Zoe pressed on. "Did Sam introduce you to the guys?"

"Yeah, the police detective, Clay, and the pilot, Nick."

Zoe leaned in. "Did Sam tell you that Nick used to date Ben's wife?"

"No, he didn't mention anything like that. I knew Nick was Sam's friend from a long time ago, but nothing about Ben's wife. Jenna, right?"

"Yep, that's her. And, yeah, it's a crazy coincidence."

"And they get along?" Em asked.

"Not at first, but, it turns out, Nick is as big a *Star Wars* geek as

Ben. You know guys, within seconds of learning they both camped out to buy the first ticket for the last *Star Wars* movie, they became buds for life."

"So," Em asked, shifting the conversation, "are you and Sam..."

Zoe's smile fell a fraction, but she pasted it back in place. "We're great. We're great friends."

That wasn't the whole truth, but Em nodded. She'd seen the way Zoe had been watching Sam on Halloween night. In that brief moment, she knew Zoe's feelings for Sam went far deeper than just *great friends*.

A waitress walked up carrying a grilled cheese sandwich. It was toasted to perfection and oozing with melted cheese. She set the plate on the bar along with a chocolate milk. "The guy over there thought you might be hungry. He ordered you this."

Em looked over at the guy's table and met Michael's gaze. He watched her with a wide grin. She shook her head and mouthed, "Thank you."

Zoe swiped a french fry from her plate. "He remembered your favorite meal. Chocolate milk and all."

A warm blush heated her cheeks.

Zoe didn't seem to notice and took a long pull from her beer. "I'm glad I ran into you tonight. I wanted to see how the bridge hunt was going. Anything jog your memory?"

Zoe wanted to help her. She could see the need shining in her old friend's eyes. "No, we visited a few bridges, but nothing clicked. Something weird did happen, though. Two things, actually."

Zoe leaned in. "Something you remembered?"

"No, we saw Kyle Benson. He was taking pictures of some of the old gravestones at the little cemetery near Sadie's Hollow. He said it was for some historic society thing."

Zoe nodded and swiped another fry. "Now that he's sort of being groomed to run for state office, I've noticed him taking on more *Kansas-centered* community projects—probably trying to pad his résumé. But, I've got to tell you, I don't know if he really wants to run for anything. The guy's pretty content with just taking pictures. It does seem pretty important to his mom. She'll tell anyone who will listen. You remember her, Nurse Ratched."

Em chuckled. Her old friend's blunt humor was bubbling back up to the surface. "Yes, we've had a few rocky run-ins since I returned. But she was kind to me the other day. And I know she's been good to my dad."

"I'm glad," Zoe said. "Maybe she's mellowed out. And the second thing?"

Em gave Zoe a confused look.

"You said two weird things happened when you visited the hollow."

"Yeah," Em said, taking a bite of her sandwich. "Do you know the name, Tina Fowler?"

Zoe's eyes widened. "I do. We did a story about her for Kansas Public Radio a few years ago for the ten-year anniversary of her death. If I remember right, she died in a hit and run accident, and they never caught the perpetrator. The little town she was from still raises money for the local 4-H Club. It didn't make the Kansas City papers when it happened. The town's done so much to keep her memory alive—that's what attracted KPR to the story."

Em's thoughts drifted. Something about Tina Fowler's death scratched in the back of her mind.

"What made you ask about the Fowler hit and run?" Zoe asked.

"Michael and I stopped at a diner in Garrett," Em replied. "We met a waitress who knew the girl."

"That area has been hit hard. They used to have a cement plant that employed literally everyone who wasn't a farmer out there. The plant went bankrupt or got closed down. I can't remember. It happened years ago. Anyway, then this Tina Fowler was killed. She was some kind of golden girl to the community. Her picture is still up in most of the little shops and restaurants."

"Yeah," Em said. "You should have heard the waitress talk about her."

The nagging sensation in her mind had turned into a buzzing

hum. Something was there, but she couldn't harness the thought long enough to process it.

Zoe drummed her fingers on the bar.

"What is it?" Em asked.

"I'd have to double check to be absolutely sure, but I think Tina Fowler may have died the same night you got injured at Sadie's Hollow."

21

E m's head buzzed with a heady thrum. "That can't be right, Zoe. The waitress at the diner said Tina was killed heading in to work in the early hours, like four in the morning."

Zoe leaned in. "Michael and I didn't find you until, Christ, I don't know? Eight or eight thirty in the morning."

The buzzing sound intensified and spread into every corner of her mind.

"We got to the hollow around ten thirty that night," Zoe continued. "Remember, you had a performance that evening, so we left late."

Em nodded. She had to focus, but something in the back of her mind itched to be revealed. "It was probably close to midnight when Michael left me to start deejaying the party."

"That leaves a window of at least eight hours, Em. Eight hours you don't remember, and eight hours nobody remembers seeing you."

"Hey," Michael said, startling them. "Did you get enough to eat? I only ask because Clay just mentioned Jar Jar Binks. We either leave now, or we're stuck here for at least another two hours."

"We'll talk later, Zoe," Em said, processing this new revelation.

"Okay. I'll look into this more." Zoe pulled out her phone and scrolled down her list of contacts. "I can check with the reporter who covered the story."

Em put a hand on Zoe's forearm, and Zoe met her gaze. A look filled with whispered secrets, shared plates of chocolate chip cookies, and days spent peddling bicycles side by side passed between them.

"Thanks, Z."

Zoe nodded and blinked back tears. "I'll let you know what I find out."

MICHAEL SQUEEZED Em's hand as they left Park Tavern. "I was able to pull Ben away from the *Star Wars* debate long enough to discuss your Foursquare. He wanted me to tell you that he'll be over this week to help you figure out what needs to be done before you put the house on the market."

A shiver passed through him, but it wasn't from the cold. He would do everything in his power to help Dr. MacCaslin pay for his cottage in the Senior Living Campus, but the thought of someone else living in Em's Foursquare hit like a punch to the gut.

Em didn't reply. From the corner of his eye, he watched her nod. But her mind was somewhere else.

He squeezed her hand. "Are you okay?"

"Can we walk a bit before we head home?" she asked. Her voice sounded far-off.

"Of course, let's walk through the gardens."

They headed east on Bellflower Street and passed by the town square. Em released his hand and linked her arm with his. They walked at a comfortable pace as she leaned into him.

It was a cool evening, but not cold. The warm lights crisscrossing the town square were their only company. The ice cream parlor across from Park Tavern had closed up shop for the evening, and the families of Langley Park were safe at home, tucking children into bed and planning for the week ahead.

"What's on your mind, Em?" he asked as they crossed the street and entered the Langley Park Botanic Gardens. The trees were strung with lights in preparation for the holidays, and the gardens glowed in tones of red, green, blue, and white.

Em tightened her grip on his arm. "Remember Tina Fowler? The girl who died in that hit and run."

"Of course. It's a tragic story."

"I'd mentioned it to Zoe, and she knew all about it because Kansas Public Radio did a story about the ten-year anniversary of her death a couple of years ago."

"Okay. I'm not sure where you're going with this."

"Zoe thinks my accident may have happened around the same time Tina Fowler was killed."

Michael thought back to the interaction with the waitress. "But Tina died early in the morning on her way to help open the diner for breakfast."

"Right. But you and Zoe didn't find me until eight in the morning, and you left me at about midnight to go deejay."

Michael's heart clenched at the memory. "Yeah, I wasn't looking at a clock, but midnight sounds about right."

"There's almost eight hours where I can't account for what happened. It only makes sense that I was injured somewhere between midnight and eight in the morning."

Michael let the timeline sink in. Christ, she was right. But that didn't automatically mean the events were connected.

"Em, the diner is at least a good ten minutes drive from Sadie's Hollow. What are the chances that you strayed that far?"

"I don't know. I know it doesn't make a lot of sense, but it is a pretty strange coincidence, right? I mean, how many hit and runs do you think happen in a town of that size? It can't be many."

"I agree. It is a strange coincidence, but I don't see how the events are connected. You had scrapes on your knees, and you were covered in some sort of chalky dust. But the only real injury was to your hand. It doesn't appear that anyone tried to do something to you as extreme as what happened to poor Tina Fowler. And we don't even know…"

Em released a long breath. "We don't even know if there was a *somebody* in my situation. It could have gone down like everyone in Langley Park thinks, and I really am that reckless girl who got drunk and high and injured herself. Maybe I'm grasping at straws, at anything that proves I didn't do this to myself on purpose. I don't have much time to figure this all out."

He led her over to a bench. "We're going to figure this out. We'll find the answers. I just don't know if Tina Fowler is part of the equation."

Christ, he wished he had a fucking crystal ball that would give them the answer. He wished he could snap his fingers and Em wouldn't have to leave, wouldn't have to sell the Foursquare. His heart sank. They were meant to be together.

He closed his eyes and leaned his forehead against hers. He tried to be positive. *One thing at a time, MacCarron. She's not leaving tomorrow. There's time.* He repeated the mantra like a prayer.

"Do you hear that?" Em tilted her head. "It's music."

He heard it, too. The one-two-three beat of Johann Strauss' "Vienna Waltz" whispered in the night air.

He shook his head and chuckled. "I think I know what that is. Come on."

Michael led Em toward the pavilion that overlooked Lake Boley. Tonight, the usually open pavilion was fitted with white tent flaps.

The outlines of people dancing inside reminded him of when he and Em would lay on his bedroom floor with a flashlight as their fingers created barking dogs and soaring butterflies on the ceiling.

"It's the high school cotillion kids."

"Cotillion?" Em asked.

"Yeah, you learn table manners and how not to break wind in public. It's like Etiquette 101, and a teenager's worst nightmare."

Em laughed. "And the waltz?"

"That's the worst part," he said as they watched the shadows move in awkward pairs. "You have to dance with some girl while the adult chaperones watch over."

"At least they get to listen to a beautiful piece of music," Em said, swaying to the beat.

"I can tell you from experience, that's the last thing those kids are thinking about," Michael added with a smirk.

Em closed her eyes and leaned into him.

He had an idea. He raised their joined hands and rested his palm against her back.

Em's eyes fluttered open. "What are you doing?"

"Waltzing. You know, the box step. But I can't remember if I'm at the top of the box, or you're supposed to be at the top of the box."

Em relaxed in his arms. "I don't know anything about boxes. Plus, you're asking the wrong girl. The closest I've ever gotten to a dance was setting up for the dances at the school I worked at in Australia."

"But don't you work at a school for deaf kids?" He abandoned the waltz and reverted to swaying from side to side.

Em's face lit up. "Just because they can't hear, doesn't mean they don't enjoy music and dancing. They totally feel the beat, especially with drums. People are developing these really cool installations that turn sound waves into lights and vibrations. The deaf community has really embraced it."

"You're happy in Australia?" The words escaped before he could stop them.

Em glanced away, but just when he thought she wasn't going to answer, she met his gaze.

"I needed Australia. I needed to get away after I was injured. I was so lost."

"I'm so sorry—" he began, but she cut him off.

"Please don't. Don't apologize again. I was angry. So angry, Michael. But I know you and Zoe never wanted me to get hurt. I think I always knew that. I just had nothing to hold onto anymore. Music was gone. I felt like life as I'd known it was over. I turned all that rage into blaming you and Zoe."

Her blue eyes deepened with emotion.

"The first year was rough. I wanted to stay in bed all day. But my mom and grandma were firm believers in work being good for the soul. If I wasn't at the Centre helping my mom, I was with my Grandma Mary. So, I spent the majority of my day in silence communicating through sign language. I could only sign with my right hand for a while, which was annoying, but, as time passed, my left hand got stronger."

"I was sad to hear your grandma passed. I wish I could have met her."

Em's eyes shined. "I didn't handle her death well. I'd only been back in Australia for a couple of years, and then she was gone. I started going out, drinking, wearing all that makeup. That's when I started remembering more of what happened to me."

"I didn't think you remembered more than those few things."

"Tall men, a bumpy bridge, and the Paganini piece," Em offered.

Michael nodded. "Yeah, is there more?"

Em shook her head. "No, but sometimes when I was reckless, like really out of control with alcohol or sex, I'd feel like I was standing on this edge, like the answers were somewhere trapped in my head, but just out of reach. The more reckless I was, the closer I felt to remembering the truth." She looked away. "I'm not proud of the person I've become."

"Em, you did what you had to do to survive. I'm not judging you. I'd never think less of you."

Her lips curved into the ghost of a smile. "Well, you know my mom. She wasn't going to put up with me staying out all night. She gave me an ultimatum: pull it together and get a real job as a teacher's assistant at the Centre's school or move out. My gran left me a little money after she passed, but I was only granted access to it after I turned twenty-one. So, I was pretty much broke. I took the job, and it was the best thing for me at the time. It gave me a buffer from music. You know, up until a couple of years ago, I couldn't even handle hearing someone whistling on the street. And the kids made it easy to forget. The eight hours I spent at school each day were like a refuge from all that anger raging through me."

Strauss' waltz ended and Shostakovich's Jazz Suite No. 2 filled the air like a jaunty soundtrack for a flying trapeze act.

"You didn't answer my question, Em. Are you happy in Australia?"

They swayed together in the moonlight surrounded by trees cast in twinkling lights. It was the kind of night that inspired enchanted tales of brave knights and dreamy damsels. With her hair hanging in loose waves and the soft light warming her features, Em looked like a fairy-tale princess, ageless in beauty and grace.

She had only been home a little more than a week. But that week had seemed like a lifetime. He'd gone from living each day, counting the hours, and waiting for the next crisis with his father to counting the seconds until he could run his hands through her hair and make her tremble with his touch.

She met his gaze, and he nearly drowned in the endless pools of blue.

"This is the happiest I've been in twelve years." She bit her lip. "No, that's not right."

Uncertainty shot through him. He tried to speak, but she silenced him by pressing her index finger to his lips.

"I have never been happier than I am, right now, here with you."

He cupped her face. "We're better together," he whispered, relief and hope lacing his words.

Em pushed up on her toes and pressed her lips against his. Something beyond this world passed between them. A silent contract that didn't require lawyers or notaries. A connection that went soul deep.

Michael gathered her into his arms and carried her to a private spot behind the tented pavilion. The sound of laughter and clinking glasses hummed over the music drifting from beneath the tent flaps like smoke signals calling them back to a place only the two of them knew how to find. The dancing portion of the cotillion event had ended, and the string of waltzes faded as Chopin's Nocturne 20 in C Sharp Minor streamed from the tent like rays of warm sunlight.

That song. Their song.

He lifted her against the side of the pavilion, and their breath grew more urgent, more ragged. With one hand supporting her ass, Michael reached between her thighs.

"How much do you like these tights?" he growled, feeling the thin fabric that separated her sex from his touch.

He caressed her through the thin barrier.

"Not much," she breathed.

"Good," he said and ripped the material to shreds. She wasn't wearing any panties. "Jesus, Mary Michelle! First, those fucking pajama bottoms and now these tights. As far as I'm concerned, I never want you wearing underwear again."

She giggled into his ear, but he silenced her by undoing his trousers, freeing his cock, and sliding deep inside of her. The rush of the cold night air and the heat of their union sparked an inferno where their bodies met and became one. The need to claim her surged through him like a storm raging on the open sea. Waves crashed and snarled in nature's battle between chaos and harmony.

Michael gripped Em's ass and guided her body up and down in steady strokes. "I never want to lose you again," he said, doubling his pace.

She answered him with puffs of breath tangled with soft cries of pleasure. She tensed her muscles and entwined her fingers into his hair. He could feel the tight tremor of her core as she neared release. He met her mouth with a fierce kiss, stifling her cries as her body shuddered around his thrusting cock.

He found the perfect rhythm, and the muscles in his arms flexed and contracted. Unable to hold back, he joined her, flying over the edge. Her breath, her cries, and the slide of her body against his produced the sexiest trio of sound he had ever heard.

Em exhaled a satisfied little hum, and Michael inhaled the faint orange scent of her shampoo. They would always be better together. She belonged in Langley Park. She belonged with him. He didn't have much time, but he would use every minute he had to prove it to her.

22

Em leaned against the counter in her Foursquare's kitchen and handed a mug of coffee to Ben Fisher. "The house is really coming together. Your guys do amazing work."

The past few weeks had flown by in a flurry of craftsmen working to update and repair the old house. A fresh coat of paint had ushered out the last traces of tobacco smoke, and her childhood home was transforming from a space trapped in the 1950s to a sophisticated, move-in ready home.

"It's looking good." Ben inspected the newly installed espresso-stained hardwood flooring in the Foursquare's kitchen where well-worn linoleum once rested. "Is Michael around?"

She smiled. She and Michael had fallen into a comfortable rhythm over the last three weeks. Monday through Friday, she would visit her father and oversee the renovations while Michael put in long hours at the office. On Saturdays, they would visit bridges near Sadie's Hollow. And, while nothing substantive had come to light, they were steadily making their way through the list Zoe had put together.

Sundays were spent in bed finding new uses for grandma's pearls, and every moment they weren't a tangle of writhing, sweat-slicked bodies, they were in the carriage house composing, mixing, and making music together.

Em took a sip of coffee. "No, he had to go meet with a client. People seem to love to change their wills over the holidays."

"But today's Thanksgiving?"

"Michael says people get a little *tit for tat* this time of year. A nephew choosing to go to Cabo over the holidays instead of coming home to pay homage to Great Aunt Whatever could see himself written out of an inheritance."

"Ah, the life of being Langley Park's most trusted attorney," Ben said and headed toward the front door.

Em smiled at the comment and grabbed her coat as they passed through the foyer.

"Do you need me to drop you off somewhere?" Ben asked, looping a scarf around his neck.

"No thanks. I feel like a walk. I wanted to pick up a strudel for my dad from that little bakery in the town center before everything shuts down this afternoon for Thanksgiving."

"Are you and Michael going to the Senior Living Campus today?"

"Yeah, Michael says they put on a pretty nice spread for Thanksgiving. Plus, we can both be with our fathers that way."

"How is Noland?"

"He has good and bad days. They've adjusted his meds, and he hasn't had any violent episodes recently."

"That's good to hear," Ben said. He clicked his key fob and unlocked his car. "Send my regards to your father and Mr. MacCarron. And don't forget, my parents' holiday party is just a few weeks away. My mother is adamant that you and Michael join us this year."

"We wouldn't miss it."

Ben's car disappeared down Foxglove Lane. Em tightened the belt of her trench coat and set off toward the town center. As she walked, she started going over all the things that still needed to be done with the house. Ben was making it easier by connecting her with reputable contractors, but she still had to pick a realtor and have professional photos taken.

Was she really going to sell this house? There was no choice. She had to. Her father needed the revenue from the sale of the Foursquare to afford his assisted living cottage. It was as simple as that.

She took out her phone and scanned through a listing of local realtors. A few looked promising. She kept scrolling down when she careened into a body on the sidewalk.

"Pardon me. I'm completely guilty of distracted walking," she said.

"This may just be the way we greet each other," Kyle replied and adjusted his camera bag.

"Hey, Kyle! I'm so glad I ran into you." She glanced at the bag. "I need to hire a photographer to take some pictures of my Foursquare. Have you ever photographed houses?"

"I have." Kyle shifted from side to side. "I've done quite a bit of work photographing old homes for several historical societies in Kansas and Missouri."

"Can I see some samples of your work? Do you have a website?"

He glanced away and shook his head. "None of that work is online. I do have the printed photographs at my place."

Em looked at her watch. It was a little past ten. She had at least a couple of hours before she was due to meet Michael at the Senior Living Campus.

"I have some time right now," she offered. "You still live in Langley Park, right?"

He nodded and shifted his stance again. "Yeah, I do."

"Do you live near your mom's place? Wasn't she on the west side of Langley Park?"

His smile wobbled. "I live in my mom's carriage house. I've got a studio apartment on the second floor. Sounds kind of pathetic, doesn't it?"

Em met his nervous smile with a reassuring one. "Kyle, I've lived with my mother for the last twelve years. I'm the last person who would judge you for living in your mom's carriage house."

"Home sweet home," Kyle said, opening the side door of his carriage house.

The first-floor garage portion of the carriage house contained what looked like a car under a thick canvas. The remaining space was crammed tight with boxes.

Em lifted the edge of the canvas. "This isn't your truck, is it?

"No, no," Kyle answered, smoothing the canvas back in place. "Just the old beater I used to drive in high school."

"Michael kept his Range Rover from high school. What is it with guys and their first cars?"

Kyle gestured to the staircase leading to the second floor. "It's not always easy saying goodbye to the past."

She met Kyle's gaze. "Yeah, I know what you mean."

She climbed the stairs and listened to Kyle's heavy footfalls on the steps behind her.

"Have you had any luck figuring out what happened that night at Sadie's Hollow?" he asked.

She entered the carriage house apartment. The rectangular space was divided into a kitchen and living and dining area. A large table at the far end was cluttered with photos and photography equipment.

"No, Michael and I have visited several bridges in the area, but nothing's clicked yet.

Kyle flipped on a few lamps and pawed through a stack of photographs. "I'm sorry to hear that. Let me grab some of those house photos for you. As you can tell, my organizational skills aren't top notch."

While Kyle flipped through photos, Em studied his bookcase. He had several framed pastoral scenes, a few well-worn classics by Steinbeck and Dickens, and a violin sat dormant under a layer of dust.

"Not playing much violin anymore?"

"No," he answered sifting through another pile. "I quit playing after high school."

A fresh paperback copy of Tocqueville's *Democracy in America* sat on the shelf. Its spine was smooth and void of any creases or cracks.

Em held up the book. "Is this to help with the whole state senate thing?"

Kyle looked up from the pile of photos. "My mom picked that up for me. But nothing's written in stone yet. The guy who holds the seat now got busted with his nineteen-year-old mistress and has a past littered with sexual misconduct. The paper did a whole exposé on him. A few local activists I met through my work with the Historical Society have shown some interest in having me run for the seat, but it's still early in the process."

"I'm sure they want someone without any skeletons in their closet after something like that," Em said and returned the book to the shelf.

Kyle gave her a tight smile. "I'm going to see if there are some more house pics in my bedroom."

Em paged through the worn copy of *Grapes of Wrath* as the sound of drawers opening and closing filled the small apartment. She flipped through a few pages of the book and discovered a photograph of a woman holding a baby. She recognized her. The woman was a younger, happier looking Anita Benson. There was a man, nearly the spitting image of Kyle, standing to her left with his arm wrapped around her hip. A girl, possibly in her early teens, stood to Anita's right. The young girl looked familiar with her mousy-brown hair hanging in limp strands.

Mindy Lancaster?

Em stared at the photo. She dropped it when she felt a tap on her shoulder.

"I didn't mean to scare you," Kyle said, retrieving the picture.

Em focused in on the girl. "Is that Mindy Lancaster?"

Kyle nodded. "Yeah, that's my Aunt Mindy."

"Aunt Mindy?" Em repeated. "I didn't know you were related to the Lancasters?"

"My father was Mindy's older brother. She was a lot younger than my dad, like fifteen years younger. My dad died shortly after that picture was taken." Kyle propped the photo on the shelf. "It's the only picture I have of him. A fire destroyed all of the photos and keepsakes from when I was a baby."

"I'm so sorry, Kyle. Do you remember much about him?"

"No, not really."

"And Mindy? Are the two of you close?"

"No," Kyle answered. His expression had gone from friendly to blank. "Here are the house photos."

Em took the stack of pictures. "Kyle, I'm sorry. I didn't mean to pry into your life. I was just skimming through the book and—"

"Not a big deal, Em," he said. His smile was back in place. "You can take the pictures with you. Just let me know if and when you'd like me to photograph your place."

A clock on the wall ticked like an irritated librarian drumming her nails. An awkward silence spread out between them. She wanted to ask Kyle more about his connection to Mindy Lancaster, but he was already heading toward the door.

Their impromptu meeting was over.

EM OPENED the door to the Senior Living Campus' Arts and Crafts room. "The nurses said I'd find you back here. Do you want me to help you—"

Michael leaned down and stopped her question with a kiss. He buried his hands in her hair, turning her soft waves into a disheveled mess. He pushed her up against the door. His cock strained against his trousers and pressed into her belly. She let out a delicious moan. That magnificent cock had been buried deep inside her this morning.

"I've missed you," he said between kisses.

"Michael," she breathed. "We're inside a retirement community's arts and crafts room."

"Yeah," he answered, planting a line of hot kisses along her jaw. "Not much gets past you, Em."

"What if someone comes in here? That wouldn't be good."

He palmed her breast. "What's not good is the fact that you're still wearing a bra."

His hand abandoned her hair and gripped her ass. "Sweet Christ, I love it when you wear tights."

She was wearing another skirt, tights, boots combo. She closed her eyes and surrendered to his touch. Michael had ripped the crotch out of at least four pairs of tights since their night behind the pavilion.

Her eyes flicked open. "There's no way I'm sitting through Thanksgiving dinner with your father and my father with a gaping hole in my tights."

He made a sound between a whimper and a groan. "To be continued?"

She met his gaze and palmed his cock. "Do you even have to ask?"

His gaze went to her hand. "A little less of that or else I don't think I'll be able to make it through dinner."

She released her grip. "What are you doing in here?"

"They needed more centerpieces," he said, adjusting his fly. "Come on, Mary Michelle, you can help me carry them to the ballroom."

Michael handed her a gold and white cornucopia-looking thing. She gazed down at the odd centerpiece.

"I had the weirdest thing happen with Kyle Benson today," she said, shifting the centerpiece under her arm as Michael handed her a second.

"Isn't every run-in with Kyle Benson weird?"

She ignored his comment. He'd never been fond of Kyle.

"Kyle Benson is Mindy Lancaster's nephew. Mindy is Kyle's late father's sister. Did you know that?"

"No, but lots of people are related in some way or another around here."

"He says they aren't close," she continued. "I wonder why?"

Michael balanced a third cornucopia on top of the two he already had in his arms. "If there's one thing I know, especially after spending a good part of the day disinheriting a truckload of nieces and nephews, is that all families have their fair share of quirks and drama."

"Sage words of wisdom from Langley Park's hottest attorney," she said with a naughty grin.

A mischievous glint sparked in his eye. "I like that. I may have that printed on my business cards."

He bent down with his hands full and pressed a kiss to her lips. She dropped a cornucopia as the one balanced precariously in his arms followed it to the ground. They laughed and kissed as the remaining centerpieces crashed to the floor when the door to the Arts and Crafts room swung open.

"Everything all right in here?"

23

E m pulled back from Michael's kiss. "Oh, my goodness!"
Mindy and Tom Lancaster stood in the doorway. Tom worked to hide an amused grin while Mindy's cheeks bloomed crimson, and her eyes nearly popped out of their sockets.

"This is a nursing home," Mindy gasped. Her gaze bounced between the centerpieces, strewn in a heap of gold and white on the floor, and Michael, who was working to remove his hand from where it had started to inch up the front of her blouse.

"I think retirement community is more politically correct," Tom countered gently, pulling Mindy's attention away from Em and Michael.

"Of course," Mindy replied as the flush on her cheeks began to fade.

"This is a popular spot today," Michael remarked and shook Tom's hand. "What brings you two to the Arts and Crafts room?"

His question caused Mindy's cheeks to dial back up to hot pink.

"The staff was wondering what was taking you so long to retrieve the centerpieces," Mindy answered. "I guess now we know."

"Give them a break, Min." Tom placed his hand on his wife's back. "You remember what young love felt like?"

"Well, never in an Arts and Crafts room," she answered.

"Are you playing tonight, Tom?" Em asked, desperate to change the subject.

"I am. A few of us from the symphony put on a little performance before dinner is served. We've been doing it every Thanksgiving for the last few years." Tom's face lit up. "Em, you should join us."

"I'm sure Em is here to enjoy Thanksgiving with her father, honey," Mindy said to her husband.

"I don't even have my violin," Em answered, watching from the corner of her eye as Mindy fiddled with the pink cast still encasing her wrist.

"Another time," Tom offered with an easy smile. "And from what I've heard, you might be even better now than you were as a girl."

Em smiled. She had spent years studying the violin under Tom's gentle guidance. He still had that way of making her feel like she could do anything. "Thank you, Tom."

Mindy crouched down and tried to pick up all the cornucopias. "These centerpieces aren't going to find their own way to the ballroom."

Tom shook his head with good-natured ease, shared one last smile with Em, then bent down to help his wife.

"I DON'T THINK I can eat one more bite," Bill MacCaslin said and patted his stomach.

Michael cut a slice of pie for his father. "They do a great job every year."

Noland MacCarron remained quiet throughout the meal. Every so often, he'd ask about his wife or share some tradition they had taken part in while she was still alive. While his comments were disjointed, he didn't seem to be agitated or mind Michael's presence.

"You've barely touched your food," Mrs. Teller said. "I hope you're not on one of those diets. A gal needs to be strong and healthy. That's what my Rodney always says."

"My stomach's just a touch sour. I'm sure I'll be fine," Em said, patting the woman's hand.

The Tellers never had any children, and when Eunice had entered the ballroom alone, Michael insisted she sit with them, which turned out to be a godsend. When Noland would say something offbeat or nonsensical, Mrs. Teller would roll with it and compliment Noland on his quick wit or excellent sense of humor.

"Are you sure you're okay, Em?" Michael asked, putting his arm around her chair. "Mrs. Teller's right. You've hardly had anything."

"Isn't that sweet," Mrs. Teller said to Noland and Bill. "Michael is just as attentive as my Rodney." The woman smiled and turned her attention to Michael and Em. "Did I ever tell you young people about my first date with Rodney?"

They smiled politely. Mrs. Teller could barely go half an hour before mentioning her beloved deceased husband.

Mrs. Teller let out a contented breath. "It was very scandalous for the time." The skin of her paper-thin cheeks blushed a muted crimson. "I climbed out of my bedroom window. Rodney was waiting in his father's Buick Skylark. Oh, what a car that was! Rodney's father was a big-wig at the plant and that Skylark was his prized possession. Well, we both snuck out, and Rodney drove us to Sadie's Hollow."

Em's ears pricked up at the mention of the hollow.

"He had an entire picnic basket filled with all my favorite things. We laid out a blanket under the stars and talked and talked for hours. It was chilly that night, and he had given me his letterman's jacket to wear." Eunice Teller's eyes flashed with nostalgia and the glassy look that often lit her gaze cleared like a windshield wiper casting away heavy beads of rain. "I insisted Rodney be buried in that little cemetery next to the hollow. We used to have so many friends in that area. Years ago, the townsfolk of LaRoe, Garrett, and Lyleville always came together to support each other. It only seemed right for that to be Rodney's resting place."

Em didn't realize her hands were shaking until Michael reached into her lap and gave them a reassuring squeeze.

"Mrs. Teller," Em asked, "growing up, do you remember any bridges, any old wooden bridges in the area around Sadie's Hollow?"

"Goodness, the oldest bridges would be out in LaRoe. But it's been two or three decades since anyone's lived there. It's a ghost town now."

"Are there any wooden bridges you can think of in Lyleville or Garrett?" Em asked, trying to capitalize on the woman's moment of clarity.

Mrs. Teller pressed her lips together, pondering the question. Her face lit up. "You can ask the young Mrs. Hale. She would know."

"I don't know a Mrs. Hale," Em said, watching the woman's eyes cloud over.

"She's right there," Mrs. Teller said and waved to Anita Benson.

Anita approached the table and greeted the group. "I was looking for you, Mrs. Teller."

"Mrs. Hale, can you think of any old wooden bridges near Garrett? That's where you met your Bobby."

Anita's face went blank.

Mrs. Teller pressed on. "Have I ever told you that's where I met my Rodney? I was the Homecoming Queen, and he was the Homecoming King at Garrett High School."

"Mrs. Teller, dear," Anita began, "it's been an eventful afternoon. Let's get you back to your room for a little rest."

"I'll join you," Michael said. "I think my dad could use some rest as well."

"But, Mrs. Hale," Mrs. Teller continued, "you surely remember your Bobby?"

Anita gifted Mrs. Teller with a tight smile. "Dear, it's been an exciting day. I think you're a little confused. I'm not Mrs. Hale. I'm Anita Benson, one of your nurses at the Memory Care Center."

"Memory Care Center?" Mrs. Teller echoed back, her voice small and confused.

Bill MacCaslin stood. "I'll join you. It would be my privilege to escort you back to your room, Mrs. Teller."

The older woman smiled.

Bill pressed a hand to Noland's shoulder. "I can also help your father get back to his room, Michael."

"Are you sure, Dr. MacCaslin? I'm happy to do it."

Bill gave him a wink. "Don't you and Em have somewhere to be? Plus, it would do my old bones good to stretch my legs a bit before I head back to the cottage." He came to his feet and strapped on his portable oxygen backpack. He unlocked Noland's wheelchair and angled it toward the door.

Em's gaze bounced between her father and Michael. Something was going on with the two of them. But she couldn't stop thinking about what Mrs. Teller had said.

Anita Benson tapped her shoulder. "I hope Mrs. Teller didn't upset you. You know she often thinks we're all somebody from her high school days."

"Yes, I remember you telling me that," Em said. But she was convinced that at least part of what Mrs. Teller had told her was real. A wave of dizziness swept over her accompanied by a disorienting buzzing sound.

"Ready to go, Em?" Michael asked.

His words cut through the clutter of noise, and she took his hand.

"I hope you two enjoy the rest of your Thanksgiving," Anita said, following behind her father who was pushing Noland's wheelchair.

"Young lady," Mrs. Teller called to Em.

"Yes, Mrs. Teller?"

"I can't find my tiara. Have you seen it?"

Em's face fell.

Anita glanced back at Em then patted the older woman's arm. "I think your tiara is in your room, dear. I'll help you look for it when we get back."

"I THOUGHT we could take a walk through the botanic gardens before we went home," Michael said.

They walked hand and hand down the main drive of the Senior Living Campus. The street lamps lining the road cast warm pools of

light as the last breaths of daylight succumbed to the growing darkness of the evening sky. The temperature was mild for late November,
and a gentle breeze played toss with the last few stray leaves scattered
across the lawn.

"I could use a walk," Em answered, inhaling the fresh air.

The buzzing in her head had quieted, and the nausea that had
plagued her during dinner had passed. She was trying to untangle
what Mrs. Teller had told her. Parsing out what was real from what
was just a product of the woman's dementia was proving to be a fool's
errand.

They passed through the garden's main gate. Michael was more
quiet than usual, his thumb tracing nervous circles on her palm.

"What did you make of Mrs. Teller?" Em asked.

"What do you mean? The Sadie's Hollow connection?"

"Yes, the hollow connection. You don't think that's odd?"

"Em, there's not a whole lot going on in southeast Kansas. Anyone
from the area would know about the hollow. Kids have been partying
there for ages. Hell, we knew about it, and we live more than an
hour's drive away."

"What about when she called Anita, Mrs. Hale. You don't think
that's strange?"

He squeezed her hand. "She also asked for her missing tiara."

Em blew out a breath. "I know. I know."

"I think it's best to take everything Mrs. Teller says with a grain
of salt. She's got pretty severe dementia." Michael raised their joined
hands and kissed her knuckles. "I want you to do something
for me."

"What are you up to?" Em asked, catching him with a goofy smile.

He tossed her a wink. "Why do I have to be up to anything?"

"That's not an answer, and something's going on between you and
my dad. Did you think I didn't notice?" she rallied back.

"Just close your eyes."

She shut them halfway. "They're closed."

"Liar! Do it for real."

Em shrugged her shoulders. "Okay, they're closed for real."

Eyes closed, she took his arm, and they walked farther into the gardens.

"Open your eyes, Mary Michelle."

She blinked a few times adjusting to the light. He had led her to the pavilion. The tenting from the other night when they came upon the cotillion dance was gone. In its place were hanging strings of white lights.

"It's beautiful, but why are we here?"

"Why?" he parroted back, smiling. "Because you never got to go to prom or homecoming and nobody forced you to endure cotillion waltz torture."

Her tears blurred the twinkling lights.

"I wanted to give you the whole experience," he began, leading her up the steps and into the center of the pavilion. "First, I took you to dinner."

She brushed a tear away and cocked her head. "Thanksgiving at a nursing home counts as dinner?"

Michael smiled. "Classy, huh?"

"What if it was snowing or freezing outside?"

A self-assured expression crossed his face. "I had a backup plan."

"Oh yeah?"

"Oh, yeah." He twirled her in a slow circle. "You remember Tony, one of my dad's nurses?"

Em nodded with a wry grin. "I remember Tony."

"He said he would throw some lights up in the arts and crafts room if I gave him a nod during dinner."

"The arts and crafts room?" she laughed.

Michael gathered her into his arms. "Seemed to work for you this afternoon."

She met his gaze. "Okay, you've got the location covered. I'm no expert, but isn't there supposed to be music?"

Michael's green eyes sparkled. He reached into his pocket and handed her an earbud. "I'd never forget the music."

She placed the bud into her ear, and he did the same. Their Chopin remix began to play. She listened to the original melody blend seamlessly with the techno beats. She closed her eyes and inhaled his scent.

"This is perfect, Michael. All this, it's better than I could have ever imagined—and the music. I never thought I'd get it back."

"You could do this, Em. We could do this together. I mean, in just a few weeks we've already created four tracks. And they're good. They're really good."

They had taken popular classical pieces and added a techno twist. Em played the electric violin on each track, subtly modifying the melody and creating a sound that was both familiar and completely unique.

"What about your work at the law firm? What about your reputation?"

"Em, I'm a better lawyer when I'm making music with you. Running the practice these last few weeks hasn't felt like a chore or an obligation. Everything flows. There's a balance I haven't known in years, and it's you. It's having you back in my life. We're…"

"Better together," she said.

He smiled that crooked smile. "Don't go back to Australia, Em. Stay with me."

She wanted to scream yes, but something was holding her back. "What about my mom?"

"We'll visit for every holiday. We'll spend as much time there as you like. But Langley Park is your home. It's our home."

He was right. She loved Australia. Australia had been the shelter she needed after her injury, but Australia wasn't her home. It was her hiding place. Langley Park was in her bones. The ebb and flow of the town was the soundtrack that never stopped calling her home.

And then there was Michael.

Michael was in every note she had ever played. Every melody she'd ever hummed. His crooked smile. His spearmint lemongrass scent. His green eyes filled with wonder as he sat cross-legged on her bedroom floor.

He tilted her face up. "I have loved you my entire life. I loved you before I even knew what love was. I couldn't separate myself from you if I tried. You're not in my heart, Mary Michelle. You are my heart. Please, stay with me."

She met his gaze. Two pools of deep sage green reflected her past, her present, and her future.

She smiled up at him. "I need you to take me somewhere."

24

"Why did you want to come here, Em?"

Michael pulled the Range Rover off to the side of the road but kept the lights on. It was pitch black outside. The closest street lamp was a speck of light in the distance. They had driven eighty miles in complete silence.

Was the pavilion too much? Had he scared her? Had he pressed her to stay too soon?

The only comfort during the drive was that Em had held his hand, her smooth fingers laced with his, for the entire trip.

"This is the place where I thought everything ended," she said, breaking the bubble of silence.

The light of the dashboard illuminated her face. She was staring straight ahead into the dark recess of Sadie's Hollow.

She released his hand. "Come on."

Em hopped out of the car and walked into the inky black night. Clouds had rolled in, and the moon was obscured behind a thick swath of heavy cloud cover. He grabbed the flashlight he kept in the Rover and hurried to catch up. Flicking it on, he pointed the stream of light ahead of him to where Em was heading toward the cemetery and The Steps to Hell.

"Em! Don't!" he called out, ashamed he still believed in that silly superstition.

This place held horrors for him, too. He didn't dare close his eyes. If he did, he knew what he would see. Em, unconscious and covered in a gray powder. Auburn hair fanned out in dusty, sweat-caked waves over the steps. And her hand. Christ, that angry gash on her finger, caked with dried blood and bits of glass and earth.

She took his hand. "I wanted to answer you here. I'm not letting this place control my life. I'm not angry about what happened to me anymore. I only want to know the truth."

He joined her on the first step. His eyes adjusted to the dark, and he peered down the steps. Just steps. He didn't see Em's listless body lying helpless on the limestone stairs.

"What do you say, Em?"

She met his gaze in the inky darkness. "I want to make music with you. It's like I've been living on bread and water these last twelve years. And now, every day is some magical feast of harmonies and melodies. But I'm not ready to share this with anyone. Not yet. No posting on the web or sending demos out or whatever those internet musicians do these days."

He smiled. "I can agree to those terms."

The wind kicked up, and wisps of Em's hair blew across her face. He released her hand and tucked the locks behind her ear. His fingertips lingered, and he traced a line down her jaw.

She took his hand and pressed it to her heart. "This has always belonged to you."

Her heart beat a steady song of life and love against his palm. But if this was going to be their fresh start, he had to tell her everything.

He swallowed hard. "I need to tell you something."

She nodded, giving him space to speak.

"I used to tell myself that I didn't go back and find you that night because I was young and stupid. The truth is, that night, you were just so much. So much beauty. So much talent. So much life. You deserved the world and everything it was begging to offer you. It was easier to submit to Tiffany, to everyone complimenting me on my music, because I knew this was it for me. This was the high point in my life. But you, you were going to conquer the world."

Warm tears trailed off her cheek and onto his hand. He tilted her face up and kissed each tear.

"I swear on my life. I will never be reckless with your heart ever again. I will always keep it safe. I have loved you all my life. I know all your smiles. I've memorized every freckle. I will never, never let you down again, Em."

She parted her lips, and he captured her mouth, kissing her deeply. He pulled back and drew his tongue across her bottom lip.

"Say yes. Say you'll stay," he breathed.

"Yes," she replied. "I'll stay. I'm home. You are my home."

He slid his hands into her hair and twisted handfuls of soft auburn. She let out a sigh, sounding of relief and love and desire all weaved into one gasp of breath. The air was charged all around them as if nature herself had been waiting for Em to agree to stay. The sky flashed like the Fourth of July, and a deep rumble vibrated through the hollow. They shielded their eyes as heavy sheets of sleet poured from the sky.

"Thundersnow," he said, as another quick flash of light cracked through the air. "Come on." Michael grabbed her hand, and they ran back to the safety of the Rover.

Em twisted her damp hair into a messy bun. "I haven't experienced thundersnow since I was a little girl."

He turned on the car and cranked up the heat. Through the glow of the headlights, they watched the soupy air fill with thick streams of ice and water. The patter of the sleet against the car faded into the background and was punctuated with the occasional burst of light and grumble of thunder.

Em leaned over the console and snuggled her head into the crook of his neck. "I've always loved thundersnow."

He wrapped an arm around her. "Me, too."

The mix of rain and ice morphed into fat flakes of snow, and she pressed a kiss to his neck. "Let's go home."

He shifted the car into drive, and they traversed the dark country road. Her lips traveled from his neck and nipped at his earlobe. She'd balanced herself by holding on to his thigh. Her hand slid up his leg, and it was now dangerously close to his hardening shaft. He gripped the steering wheel tighter as her hand made a slow pass over his cock.

He turned onto some country road. He wasn't sure which one, and he didn't care. She palmed him hard, coaxing his cock to grow hot and thick.

"You're putting my driving skills to the test," he hissed through grated teeth.

Em's hand stroked a steady rhythm, and he made another mindless turn onto another random country road. He was pretty sure he was seconds away from ripping the steering wheel from the steering column.

"We're going to get lost in the middle of Bumble-fuck Nowhere if you keep that up."

She answered him by unbuttoning his fly.

"I thought you said your Rover could get through anything."

"It may have met its match with you," he groaned.

She leaned over and took his cock into her mouth. His head lolled back, and he pulled the car over and slammed it into park.

"Fuck, Em. People should write ballads about your mouth."

He slid his hands into her hair, twisting the locks around his fingers as she worked magic with her glorious mouth. He could spend all eternity with her lips sliding up and down his cock, but he wanted more.

"Slow down," he groaned.

She turned her head and met his gaze. A dirty smile graced her lips, and she licked the head of his penis like she was taking the cherry off an ice cream sundae.

"Fucking, Christ," he growled and pulled her over the console.

She straddled him and licked her lips.

"Are you trying to make me lose my shit in thirty seconds?" he breathed.

She took his cock into her hand. "Maybe? This seems to be working for you."

He reached between her thighs and massaged her through yet another pair of tights.

"Go ahead," she said, reading his mind as she traced her thumb over the head of his penis.

He gripped the nylon and pulled, ripping possibly the twentieth pair of tights she owned.

"At least I know what to get you for Christmas," he said.

She laughed and pressed her lips to his. "I love you, Michael Edward MacCarron."

He shifted in the seat and slid his pants down past his hips. She gave him a sexy smile and bit her lip. An electric jolt traveled straight to his rock-hard cock. He palmed her ass and guided her onto his shaft.

"It's pretty fucking hot when you say that. Say it again."

Her lips parted, and she moaned as he filled her.

"Say it," he whispered into her ear, thrusting in slow, delicious strokes.

"I, I…"

He took it as a compliment when she couldn't answer. Her hair had fallen free of the makeshift bun, and the waves of auburn glowed a hazy blue in the light coming from the dashboard. She looked like some mythical creature bobbing and swaying in the light.

He pumped inside her, ripping more of the nylon tights to grip her bare ass. He was close to letting go, but there was no way in hell he was going to come before she found her release. He rolled his hips and altered the angle of penetration. It was just what she needed. Em dug her nails into his shoulders. Her body shuddered and contracted around his cock with an iron grip.

"Fuck, yes," he breathed.

He ripped her blouse open and pressed his lips to her collarbone, kissing and biting the delicate skin as he found his release deep inside of her core.

Em cupped his face in her hands. She was breathing hard, trying to catch her breath. "I love you, Michael."

He drew sleepy circles on the small of her back. "See, that wasn't so hard to say, was it?"

She tilted her head to the side and gave him her sweetest cherry popsicle grin. He gazed into her eyes, but something was different. She was no longer bathed in only the blue light from the dashboard. He blinked as the hum of a car engine accompanied the burst of high beam lights that now fully illuminated her face.

"Oh my gosh! It's a car!" Em said, scrambling off his lap.

His heartbeat kicked up. There was a good chance it was some poor deputy from Garrett sent to patrol the quiet county roads on Thanksgiving evening. Michael pulled up his pants and worked to secure his fly. If some cop asked him to exit the vehicle, evidence of their escapade would be all over the front of his trousers.

Em patted her hair and zipped her coat up, but it did little to hide the shredded tights. He eyed her and let out a chuckle.

She bit her lip. "I've got to at least try and look presentable."

He tucked a wild auburn lock behind her ear. "I think we're well past presentable."

The car was nearly upon them. White light filled the inside of the Rover. Michael reached for the glovebox. He wanted to have his insurance card ready for the officer. But before he could even look up, the car sped past them. All he saw were its taillights disappearing into the snowy darkness.

"I guess it wasn't a cop." He tossed his insurance card back into the glovebox. "It's probably some farmer."

He was about to put the car in gear when Em opened the car door, triggering the bright interior lights.

Michael shielded his eyes. "What are you doing, Em?"

"I saw something when that car went by."

"Em, wait a second," he said, eyes blurring from the light, but she was already out of the car, jogging into the darkness.

"Bring the flashlight," she called back.

"I know we're in the middle of nowhere, but it still isn't safe to be out here."

Michael switched on the flashlight and swept the side of the road with the thin beam of light. Em was crouched on the side of the road in front of some sort of object.

"What is it, Em?"

"You've got to see this," she answered.

He jogged over to find her brushing fresh flakes of snow off a wooden cross. The smiling image of a girl in cap and gown was affixed to the top. Someone had carved the name Tina Fowler below the picture.

Em ran her finger over the photograph encased in plastic. "It's Tina. This must be where she was killed."

A chill washed over him. Tina Fowler had died alone in this very spot. He swung the flashlight back and forth. To the naked eye, there was nothing remarkable about this stretch of country road, but that didn't stop a bitter, coppery taste from invading his mouth.

"Look," Em said, fingering a small bouquet of drooping, wilted flowers. "Somebody must maintain this. I thought the waitress said Tina's family left the area."

"Yeah, I think you're right about her family. But the folks in this area have been raising money in her name for a long time. The waitress from the diner could be the one keeping it up."

Em pressed her finger to the cross and traced each letter in Tina's name.

He crouched down. "Em, we should go. I'm not even sure where we are, and this snow doesn't look like it's going to let up anytime soon."

She let her finger linger as flakes of snow replaced the ones she had just brushed away. She met his gaze. "I think I've been here before."

He knew she was desperate to find out what happened the night she was injured. It didn't even matter that she was still able to play the piano and violin. That night, that injury had transformed her entire world and stolen twelve years from her. But what if she was grasping at straws, looking for any connection to that night to try to explain what had happened?

He dusted the snow off her shoulders. "We're pretty far from the hollow. I don't know how you could have gotten here."

"Someone could have taken me here," she shot back.

"Possibly, Em, but why? Why would anyone take you anywhere?"

"I don't know, but I want to go back to the diner in Garrett and talk to that waitress."

He took her hand and helped her to her feet. "Nothing is open now. We can come back in a couple of days. I just don't—"

"Don't what?" she asked.

"I don't want you to attach all your hopes on Tina Fowler. I think it's smarter to focus on what you remember: the bridge, tall men. It's more concrete."

She nodded. "I know what you're saying. I just have this feeling that my injury and her death may have something in common."

"I agree. Both events happened around the same time, but that doesn't have to mean that they're connected."

She shivered and crossed her arms. "Do you always have to go into lawyer mode?"

"We need to look at all possibilities from every angle." He let out a sigh. "You're freezing. I'm freezing. Let's find our way out of wherever the hell we are and get back to Langley Park. We're going to look into this. I know you want answers, I want them, too. But there's nothing more we can do tonight."

25

E m sat stock-still and gripped the dashboard.

"Breathe, Em," Michael said. He squeezed her knee and cut the ignition.

After returning home late Thanksgiving evening, they had used a map and the navigation app on Michael's phone to determine Tina Fowler's roadside memorial was located on the outskirts of the abandoned town of LaRoe.

The country road looked different in the daylight. The late fall mood swings of Mother Nature meant a blustery night could be followed by a sunny morning. The snow from Thanksgiving had vanished, leaving the tall grass to sway crispy dry and muted yellow in the Saturday morning breeze.

Em released her breath. She had been keyed up since their trip to the hollow. Everything was moving so fast and at the same time, so slowly.

In a matter of weeks, she had found her way back to music and back to Michael. That in itself should have been enough, but the clawing need to learn what happened that night at Sadie's Hollow wouldn't go away. The images and sensations she remembered taunted her like a prize dangling just out of reach.

She stared at the small wooden cross. It was easy to see Tina's name carved into the wood without the veil of snowy darkness. Her gaze trailed down to the vase secured to the bottom of the roadside memorial where a fresh bouquet of sunflowers welcomed the morning.

"Those are new," she said, opening the car door.

"The flowers?" Michael asked, following her over to the cross.

"Yeah, when we were here on Thanksgiving, the flowers were wilted. And I think they were roses. It was hard to tell. But they weren't sunflowers. I know that for sure."

Michael fingered a fresh petal. "You're right. Whatever was here got switched out."

"What do you think that means?"

"It could just be some local. Maybe someone in town for Thanksgiving who knew the Fowlers."

Em stared into the field of dried prairie grass, but an old bur oak reaching bare limbs into the sky, thick with age, caught her eye. Someone had come along and nailed strips of wood to the trunk, creating a makeshift ladder leading up to the branches. The wood looked almost as old as the tree. It was bleached gray from countless days weathering the Kansas wind and sun, and the nails used to secure the slats had rusted to a burnt red that bled into the surrounding wood.

"This must have been someone's climbing tree," Michael said. He pulled on one of the rungs. "It's still pretty solid."

Em ran her hand across one of the lower rungs. Instantly, her body felt sticky with sweat. Her skin itched. Her vision doubled, then tripled like a kaleidoscope, and nausea washed over her in thick, hot waves.

"Em, are you okay?"

She leaned against Michael and clutched his jacket. She took a few shaky breaths, and her vision evened out.

"You're white as a ghost," he said, scooping her up into his arms.

She blinked slowly. "I'm all right. Put me down. I need to touch that tree again."

"Hell, no," he answered. "Maybe you picked something up. You weren't feeling good during Thanksgiving dinner. You could have a virus or something."

"No, it doesn't feel like that." The strange buzzing in her head was back. "Please, Michael. Set me down. I'm okay."

He didn't look convinced.

She stroked his cheek. "Really, I'm okay. I just got this bizarre flash when I ran my hand over that weird piece of wood."

He set her down. "If you go all woozy again we're heading to the nearest hospital."

She gave him a nod then ran her hands down the tree, feeling the rough bump of bark and then the lift and fall of her fingertips as they moved up and down and passed over the makeshift ladder.

She made another pass at half the speed. "I've felt this before."

"Are you sure?" Michael asked.

"I think so. Are there any trees with wooden slats nailed on like this in Langley Park? Could I be mistaking this tree for one we climbed as kids?"

Michael ran his hand down the tree trunk. "Not that I can think of."

She took a step back and surveyed the tree in its entirety. "What do you think this means?"

"I don't know, Em. This tree is old and the wooden rungs nailed into the trunk could be ten, twenty, maybe even thirty years old or older. It's possible, if you were somehow here the night you were injured, that this tree could have looked and felt just like this."

He was right. The tree looked like it had withstood the test of time. Kansas was prone to wild storms and catastrophic tornados—neither of which had uprooted this majestic oak.

She met Michael's gaze. He wasn't playing devil's advocate with her premonitions today. Maybe he could feel it, too. Tina Fowler may have died here. But there was more to it than just a tragic early morning hit and run. She knew it, and she could sense Michael coming on board.

He put an arm around her shoulder. "I think we need to go to the diner."

THE MAIN DRAG THROUGH GARRETT, Kansas, was bustling with activity Saturday morning. Families cooped up indoors over the Thanksgiving holiday were out in force enjoying the shops and sunshine.

They entered the diner, and Em stared at the photograph of Tina.

"A few seats are open at the counter by the register," Michael said.

Em spied the seats, but her gaze was pulled to the oddly familiar glass jars of what looked like homemade jam sitting in neat rows near the picture of Tina Fowler.

Were those jars there the last time they'd visited the diner? She couldn't remember.

She took the seat next to Michael and scanned the room, hoping the waitress they'd met a few weeks ago was working today. What was the woman's name? Was it Pamela? Patty? All she could remember was the curlicue design of the letter "P" on her name tag.

"Can I start you two off with some coffee?"

Em swung around on the stool and saw the curly lettering on the waitress' apron.

Peggy.

"Sure, that would be great," Michael answered.

"Do you remember us?" Em asked. "We were in a few weeks ago."

The waitress finished pouring their coffee and looked up. "I do. I do. You donated quite a bit to our collection for Tina. How are you folks doing?"

"We're good," Em answered. Her heartbeat kicked up a notch. "We were driving through the area and saw Tina Fowler's roadside memorial. Does someone in town keep it up?"

Peggy leaned against the counter. "That is a bit of a mystery. I don't know who keeps it up. I've asked around plenty, but I've never figured out who it is. It's a kind gesture, for sure."

"How long has it been there?" Michael asked.

"Goodness!" Peggy drummed her fingers. "It's been there for as long as I can remember. Why do you ask?"

"We noticed that the flowers were switched out," Em answered.

Peggy nodded. "I don't get out that way much. Nothing much out there but a few farms, these days. It's nice to know someone's still honoring Tina's memory."

"Do you think the farmers are maintaining the memorial?" Michael asked.

"I don't think so. Like I said, I've been asking for years. I think I've asked every soul in the area. Nobody's copped to it yet. I like to think it's a guardian angel," Peggy said as her gaze swung toward the door and the sound of jingling bells. The deep creases around her eyes crinkled as she smiled. "Well, look what the cat dragged in."

"Hi, Peggy! Is my jam order ready?"

Em recognized that voice. She turned to see Mindy Lancaster. Mindy met her gaze, and a stunned expression passed over her mousy features.

"Do you all know each other?" Peggy asked.

"We do," Em answered.

"Nice to see you, Mindy," Michael said, offering her his seat, but she waved him off.

Peggy loaded several jars of jam into a cardboard box. "We are so proud of our Mindy. She won all sorts of awards for playing the piano as a girl. Earned a scholarship to a fancy school in Boston."

Mindy's posture stiffened. "That was a long time ago, Peg."

"Mindy's husband, Tom, was my violin teacher," Em said, hoping this nugget of information would keep Peggy talking.

Peggy clapped her hands. "What a small world! Tom is one of my favorites. He brought our Mindy back to Kansas. Is he still with the symphony?"

Mindy gave a sharp nod. "He is."

"Tom always loved my jam," Peggy said, directing the comment to nobody in particular.

Then it clicked. Em had seen those distinctive jams before. The Lancasters gave them out to their students as holiday gifts.

"What brings you to Garrett?" Mindy asked, but Peggy intervened.

"They were in a few weeks ago for lunch and contributed to Tina's 4-H collection. They came across her memorial and were wondering who kept it up."

Mindy glanced at Tina's photo. "Such a loss."

Peggy closed the box and slid it toward Mindy.

Michael placed a few bills on the counter, then picked up the box. "It was nice to see you again, Peggy." He shifted his gaze to Mindy. "Let me carry this out for you."

Mindy fingered the cast still encasing her wrist and gave Michael a polite nod.

They followed Mindy out to her car, and Michael set the box in her trunk. He went to close it, but Mindy motioned for him to stop.

"Here," she opened the box and handed them each a jar of jam. "Tom and I wanted to thank you both for helping out with the music at the Senior Living Campus." She smiled, and her features softened. "Em, your mother always used to tell me how much she enjoyed this jam. Would you like another jar to bring back with you to Australia? I imagine you're eager to get back."

Em tried to read the woman. Mindy Lancaster had never warmed to her. She wasn't the kind of person that took a shine to anyone —except Tom.

Em shared a glance with Michael. "I'm not going back to Australia, but I'd be happy to ship the jam to my mom. I do remember her liking it."

Mindy pursed her lips. "I don't want to overstep myself, but your dad told Tom that he was going to be selling your house."

"Em's going to stay with me," Michael said.

A saccharine smile graced Mindy's lips. "Isn't that sweet. The boy next door ends up with the girl next door. I'll be sure to let Tom know. He'll be thrilled you're staying." She glanced at her car. "Well, I better be getting back. I don't want to miss Tom's performance this afternoon."

Mindy turned to leave, but Em caught her by the arm. "Is it hard?"

Mindy frowned. "Is what hard?"

Em met her gaze. When she was a little girl, the Lancasters had seemed so much older. But Mindy couldn't be more than fifty now. Their age difference, which couldn't be more than twenty years at the most, didn't seem like such a gulf. "I never thought about it until now, but you moved back to Kansas for Tom, so that he could play with the symphony, didn't you?"

A blush bloomed crimson on Mindy's pale cheeks as she turned to close the trunk. "Crazier things have been done for love."

EM TWISTED the bottom of her sleeve.

"What are you thinking?" Michael asked.

They were more than halfway home, and she had been turning over the events of the morning in her head. "I'm trying to put it all together in a way that makes sense."

Michael nodded but kept his gaze on the road. "The one thing we know for sure is that your injury occurred at or around the same time Tina Fowler was killed."

"Right," Em said, mentally ticking this off in her head.

"And something about that tree near the roadside memorial felt familiar to you."

"Yeah, I can't put my finger on it. But it did seem familiar."

They lapsed into a pocket of silence. The pieces were there. She just wasn't seeing the whole picture.

Em tried to lay it out. "Mindy Lancaster is Kyle's aunt. But Mindy and Kyle's mom aren't close. At least that's what Kyle told me the other day."

"Yeah, but remember, Em, families are complex. When Anita's husband died, there could have been a family dispute about money or property. That kind of stuff happens in families every day. It's unfortunate, but not uncommon for family members to be estranged."

She rubbed the back of her neck. "What about everything Mrs. Teller mentioned?"

Michael started to say something, but she stopped him. "I know, I know, Mrs. Teller suffers from dementia and thinks we're all in the Garrett High School homecoming parade with her ninety percent of the time. But it really seemed like she knew Anita Benson from another time. Remember, she called her the 'young Mrs. Hale.'"

"You've got a point. I never knew Anita, and I guess Kyle, too, were from this area. There's not much in Lyleville—just Sadie's Hollow, the cemetery, and a handful of shops and houses. It sounds like LaRoe's been a ghost town for years. There's a chance Mrs. Teller is right, and Anita Benson is from Garrett or somewhere in this area, too. But these things might just be coincidences."

Em pressed her fingertips to her eyes. "Maybe you're right. Maybe I'm jumping at anyone and anything that has even the slimmest connection to this place."

He took her hand and brought it to his lips. "I think you're trying to take everything into account and look at every option. That's not a bad thing."

The tension in her neck and shoulders released a fraction. She stared at Michael's profile. His hair had always been a shade darker than hers, and the light streaming in through the windshield highlighted glints of copper like a shiny penny in the sun. She studied the curve of his cheek, the cut of his jaw, the dark auburn scruff. She knew his face as well as she knew her own. Even during her years studying music abroad, the image of him calling out to her was always the last thought to drift through her mind before falling asleep.

She had loved him her whole life, even when she wanted to hate him.

He glanced her way and gave her a wry grin. "Thinking about how handsome I am?" He lifted her hand to his lips and pressed another kiss to her knuckles.

"No, I'm thinking about how lucky I am," she said, surprised when her voice cracked.

"Hey," he said, a gentle lilt to his voice.

They had driven past the hospital, and Lake Boley came into view, calm and serene like a sheet of blue-gray glass. He pulled the car over, and Em focused on the pavilion at the water's edge.

She shook her head and tried to will away the tears in her eyes. "I don't know why I can't let it go. I'm home. I'm with you. Music is back in my life, and once I sell the house, my dad will be able to finalize the purchase of the cottage. Shouldn't that be enough?"

He cupped her face in his hands, and she melted into the warmth of his touch.

"There's nothing crazy or selfish about wanting to know what happened the night you were injured. Not a day's gone by where I haven't wanted to know the exact same thing." He ran his thumb across her bottom lip. "We're better together, right?"

Em closed her eyes and let the heat of his touch warm her face.

He pressed a kiss to her forehead. "We're going to figure this out."

She opened her eyes and met Michael's sage green gaze. "Thank you."

The corner of his mouth raised into a crooked smile. "I love you, Em. There's nothing I wouldn't do for you."

She knew he meant it.

He leaned over the console and pressed a whisper-soft kiss to her lips, her cheeks, her chin. Something between them vibrated once, twice. It quieted for a moment then buzzed again.

"I think that's you," Michael said, retrieving her phone from the center console.

"Kathy Stein is texting me."

"What does the text say?" Michael asked.

Em looked at the screen. "She says there's an emergency. She needs me to come to the yoga studio." Em held out the phone for Michael to see. "Looks like Zoe and another number are included in the text."

Michael pulled the car back into traffic. "Text her back, and tell her we're on our way."

THEY PULLED up in front of the yoga studio in the heart of the Langley

Park town center and jumped out of the Rover as Zoe and Jenna Fisher came jogging down Mulberry Drive.

"I saw my mom texted you, too," Zoe said. "Have you gone inside the studio yet?"

"No," Em answered. "We just arrived."

Michael shared a concerned look with Jenna. "I hope it's not her ankle."

"She twisted her ankle badly about six months ago," Jenna said, filling her in.

Michael opened the door and ushered the women inside.

The tranquil studio was lit with candles. Four mats were fanned out in a circular pattern around a small statue of Buddha. Several other statues of Buddha sitting cross-legged were scattered around the space. Em found a few more peeking out from behind a rack of mats like enlightened garden gnomes.

"Mom!" Zoe called out. "Mom, where are you?"

Kathy Stein emerged from behind a door on the far side of the yoga studio holding yet another Buddha statue. "I was in the back." She surveyed the harried expressions of the group. "Did something happen?"

"Mom, you sent us all a text saying there was an emergency and to get to the yoga studio ASAP. Did something happen?"

Kathy nodded. "Absolutely, something's happened. And it's been happening for more than a week."

"Mrs. Stein," Michael began, "is it your ankle? Are you in pain?"

Kathy laughed. "Oh, no, my ankle is completely healed."

Em, Michael, Zoe, and Jenna stared at Kathy, confusion and worry etched on their faces.

Kathy placed the Buddha on the floor then raised her hands and pressed them together in a prayer pose. "Mercury is in retrograde," she said like a doctor breaking bad news to a patient.

A pocket of silence swallowed the studio.

"The planet, Mercury?" Jenna asked.

Kathy's eyes widened. "Yes, when Mercury's in retrograde, it appears to be moving in the opposite direction compared to the other planets."

Zoe raised her hand like a kindergartener. "And how is this an emergency, Mom?"

"When Mercury's in retrograde, anything that *can* go wrong often *will* go wrong."

"So, you're not hurt, Mrs. Stein?" Michael asked and eyed the sea of Buddhas.

"No, I texted Jenna, Zoe, and Em so we could rebalance our chakras during this turbulent time," Kathy answered.

"Do I have to stay for this?" Michael asked.

"You're always welcome to stay, dear. But I called the girls here to harness the power of female energy."

Michael's eyes nearly popped out of his head, and he met Em's gaze with a deer in the headlights expression.

She bit back a laugh. "Why don't you head home," she said. The poor man looked terrified. "I'll catch up with you later."

In the span of five seconds, Michael moved at a speed men are only capable of when fleeing garden parties, baby showers, and women's book club discussions.

The door slammed behind him, and the women exploded into laughter.

"You should have told him we were going to synchronize our menstrual cycles," Zoe said, wiping a tear from her cheek.

"I've never seen him move so fast," Jenna added.

Em was laughing so hard, she could barely speak. Zoe caught her eye, and they were back to the special place you make with your dearest girlfriend. Back to nights spent sharing secrets and dreams. Back to lazy summer days dipping their toes into Lake Boley.

Kathy positioned herself at the top of her yoga mat. "All right, girls. Let's carry this joyful energy into our practice today."

From the looks of it, Jenna and Zoe had just finished an outdoor run and were pretty much dressed to practice yoga. She, on the other hand, was wearing boots, leggings, and a tunic.

"I don't think I have on the right clothes for yoga, Mrs. Stein."

"Just take off your boots and socks, dear. The poses we'll be doing today won't require any special clothing," Kathy replied.

"So, this is happening?" Zoe asked to no one in particular.

"I could do with a chakra cleansing," Jenna said and took her place on a yoga mat. "It should probably be a requirement for anyone working in elementary schools, especially during the holidays."

"I agree," Em said, coming to stand on the mat between Jenna and Zoe. "The same thing would happen at the school I worked at in Australia. Something in the air or the water made the kids extra crazy this time of year."

"Then it's a good thing I called this emergency yoga session," Kathy said with a knowing glint in her eye.

Zoe took off her shoes and wiggled her toes. "After we finish this *emergency yoga*, we're going to have a serious discussion about your Buddha addiction."

The girls giggled, but Zoe had a point. Several of the candles burning were actual wax Buddha heads.

"All right," Kathy said, ignoring Zoe's comment. We're here today to rebalance and center ourselves. Let's find mountain pose as we slow our overactive minds and ground ourselves in today's practice."

Em closed her eyes and followed Kathy's instructions. After her morning in Garrett, a bit of centering and reflection wasn't a bad idea.

"Soften and relax your face and join me in Eagle Pose, Garudasana."

Em copied Kathy's pretzel looking pose as she wrapped her left leg around her right leg and then wrapped her left arm under her right arm.

"In Eagle Pose, we're drawing our energy into the midline of the body. We must draw inward before we can release all the things that distract us. All the things that lead us from our true purpose."

Em closed her eyes and settled into the pose. The hum of the town center bustling outside floated through the air like a gentle lullaby. She inhaled and exhaled, listening to a child's laughter out on the sidewalk. She opened her eyes and glanced toward the bank of windows. She blinked and took another look, not sure if her eyes were playing tricks on her.

A woman was peering inside the studio. Blond hair. Snub-nosed. She held a toddler in her arms while an older child with the same gently tilted nose stood beside her and pulled on her hand. Em met the woman's gaze, and, for a split second, she saw the teenage version of this person in tiny cut-off jean shorts holding out a red plastic cup.

Em blinked again, and the woman turned away and hurried across the street.

Twelve years had passed, but she had never forgotten the face of Tiffany Shelton.

26

"Mrs. Stein, I'm sorry. I've got to go."

Em lost her balance and fell out of the yoga pose. She headed for the door. Barefoot, she searched the street for Tiffany Shelton. The woman wasn't moving fast with two little ones in tow. They had crossed the street and were heading toward The Scoop Ice Cream Parlor.

"Tiffany!" Em called out. She gestured for a car to stop and ran across the street.

Tiffany stilled and straightened her spine before she turned to face her.

The color had drained from the woman's face. "Yes, can I help you?"

"Tiffany?" Em said. "Tiffany Shelton?"

"It's Tiffany Morrison now."

Em met Tiffany's gaze. "I know you recognize me."

The little boy pulled on the sleeve of Tiffany's coat. "Mommy, who's the lady with no shoes?"

"Just a lady Mommy knew when she was a little girl," Tiffany answered, holding Em's gaze.

"I'm not here to cause any problems, Tiffany."

Tiffany's face softened. She glanced at her older child who was entertained for the moment, peering inside the windows of the ice cream parlor. She shifted the toddler in her arms to her other hip. "I was sorry to hear what happened to you that night at Sadie's Hollow."

"Do you remember anything from that night?" Em asked.

The toddler fussed and pulled a strand of Tiffany's hair. "One minute, sweetheart," Tiffany said, jiggling the child. "It was a long time ago, Em."

"I know. I know. But you see, I'm trying to piece together what happened that night. I don't have any memory of being injured."

Tiffany's eyes widened. "I'd heard you'd had too much to drink and fell."

A lump formed in Em's throat. The whole town believed that story.

She swallowed past the emotion. "I don't know what happened that night. I only remember interacting with a few people that night, and you're one of them."

"I'm not proud of how I behaved that night, but I would never—"

"I'm not accusing you of anything," Em broke in. "But it would be a great help to me if we could talk. If you could tell me what you remember from that night."

Tiffany glanced at her child who was still amusing himself at the window. Then her gaze swept across the street. "Michael?"

Em turned and saw Michael jogging toward them.

"What are you doing outside without your shoes, Em?"

He joined them on the sidewalk, took off his coat, and wrapped it around her shoulders. He looked her over then glanced toward Tiffany. "Tiff?" he said like he couldn't believe his eyes.

Tiffany's cheeks bloomed crimson. "It's been a long time."

He nodded, and his gaze bounced from Tiffany to the child in her arms. "Are these your kids?"

The question dialed back Tiffany's blush. "Yes, Cal is four, and Lila's sixteen months."

He nodded and gave her a tight smile. "Are you two..." he broke off and gestured between Em and Tiffany.

"I was in the yoga studio when I saw Tiffany pass by. I thought she might be able to help us figure out what happened the night I was injured."

The little boy lost interest in the window and pulled on his mother's coat sleeve. "Mommy, you said we could get ice cream."

Tiffany patted the boy's blond curls. "Hold on, Cal."

"I can see this is a bad time," Em said, watching the toddler take another pull of Tiffany's hair. "Maybe we can grab a coffee this week?"

Tiffany met her gaze, and Em could see the exhaustion in the woman's eyes. "We're leaving tonight for Florida to visit my husband's family for a couple of weeks. I'm only in town because we stopped by my parents' place in Langley Park this morning to say goodbye before we left. I promised the kids we'd get ice cream after."

"What about when you get back from your trip?" Em asked. She knew Tiffany only had a few minutes before both her children went into meltdown mode.

"I don't think I'll be much help. I really remember very little about that night."

"Anything you remember could be helpful," Michael said, wrapping his arm around Em and rubbing her shoulder.

Tiffany smiled, but something melancholy colored her expression. "I always knew you two would end up together."

"Please, Tiffany," Em said. "Just a chat. Just a cup of coffee when you get back. It would mean a lot to me. To us."

Michael pulled her in a fraction closer and rubbed his hand down her arm. "Anything you can remember could be helpful, Tiff. Em's right. We could use your help."

Tiffany nodded and rummaged with her free hand through her purse. She handed Em a pen and notepad. "Write down your phone number. I'll call you when we get back in town."

MICHAEL TOOK HER HAND. "Let's go get your coat and shoes. You've got to be freezing."

Em watched Tiffany wrangle her children and enter the ice cream parlor.

"I thought you went home?" Em said.

"That was my plan, but I saw Nick coming out of the coffee shop, and we got to talking. He's decided to make Kansas City his home and wants to move to Langley Park."

"I thought he lived here already?"

"No, he's based out of Nashville, but he flies all over. Whenever he's got a layover in Kansas City, he stays with Sam or some aunt he's got nearby in Mission Springs."

Zoe came out of the yoga studio. She handed Em her coat and boots. "Was that who I think it was?"

"Yeah," Em answered, pulling on her socks and boots. "I couldn't believe my eyes. I had to try to talk to her. She's one of the handful of people I remember from the night at the hollow."

Zoe craned her neck to look into the ice cream parlor. "Last I heard, she was living in the suburbs. I think her husband's a firefighter. I've only seen her a handful of times since high school."

"I haven't seen her once in the last twelve years," Michael said.

Em released a tight breath, and a wave of relief sweep over her. She hadn't asked Michael about Tiffany. She knew it was silly to worry about some girl he'd hooked up with back in high school, but something deep in the darkest part of her still hated the fact that Tiffany and Michael had history.

"Do you want to go back in?" Em asked Zoe, tilting her head toward the yoga studio. "I think I'm done with yoga for today."

"Hell, no! I'll do yoga. Don't get me wrong. I understand all the benefits of it. But my mother and Jenna take it to a whole different level. They both have to put up with my brother a lot more than I do, so I totally see the appeal of zoning out like a rutabaga for two hours."

Em shook her head and wrapped her arms around Zoe. "I really missed you, Z."

"Right back at ya," Zoe answered with an uncharacteristic crack in her voice.

"We could go grab a cup of coffee at The Drip," Michael offered.

Zoe snapped her fingers. "Yes! Let's do that. I wanted to tell you, I spoke with the reporter who did the story on the ten-year anniversary of Tina Fowler's death a couple of years ago."

They walked the few paces next door to The Drip. Michael went up to order while Zoe and Em grabbed a table.

"Did he or she remember anything?" Em asked.

"It's a she, and yes, she remembered there were a couple of things that were weird about the Fowler hit and run."

Michael waved to them from the counter. "I know Em's drink. What can I get you, Zoe?"

"Dirty Chai. Three, no make it four shots of espresso," Zoe called back.

"Plan on sleeping anytime this week?" Em teased.

"I'll sleep when I'm dead. Now, listen. There were a few things that my reporter friend found interesting." Zoe leaned forward. "There were two sets of tire tracks at the site of the hit and run, and the police weren't sure which set hit Tina."

"Okay, that does seem a little strange. Could they determine the kind of car that hit her?"

"No dice. They can only determine the kinds of cars that go with certain tires. In this case, they were able to pinpoint it to several midsized sedans and a light utility truck."

Em frowned. "Sounds like ninety percent of the vehicles driving around Kansas."

"Yes, but there was another thing she remembered about the case," Zoe said, now perching on the edge of her seat.

Michael joined them and passed out their drinks. "What did I miss?"

"I was just getting to the interesting part." Zoe took a quick sip of her chai. "They found some jewelry near Tina's body. But the family wasn't sure if it belonged to her."

"Did your friend know what kind of jewelry?"

"She couldn't remember. The police wrote it off as some random roadside debris after the family said it wasn't hers."

Em touched her neck. "My pearl necklace broke that night. I'm not sure how many pearls are missing, but if the police had found pearls..."

"That's what I was thinking," Zoe said. "When we found you, the necklace was broken. We grabbed it because we knew how important it was to you."

"I could ask Clay Stevens to look into it?" Michael offered.

"Clay's the police detective?" Em asked.

He nodded. "Yes, he may know someone in the Garrett PD who wouldn't mind taking a look at the case file."

"Are you guys still checking out the list of bridges I found? Anything look or feel familiar?" Zoe asked.

Em lifted her flat white to take a sip, but the smell was off. She set the drink down. "We've been to several, but none of them felt like the bridge I went over."

Zoe nodded. "I've done a few searches for *tall men* and tried to localize the results to the Garrett area. All I've gotten so far are listings for clothing stores."

"You're sure it's the words "tall men" and not an actual bunch of tall guys?" Michael asked.

"I can see the words like they've been cemented into my brain."

"Maybe you drove by a clothing store on your way to the hollow?" Michael offered.

"I checked that, too," Zoe answered. "Em and I didn't drive by any Big and Tall Clothing stores on our way to the hollow that night."

"Did your reporter remember anything else?" Michael asked.

Zoe nodded. "Yeah, something kind of weird. There's a memorial near where Tina was killed, and nobody in the town seems to know who maintains it."

"We also found Tina's memorial Thanksgiving night," Em chimed in. "And when we went back today, someone had switched out the old flowers and left a fresh bouquet."

Zoe wrinkled her nose. "What were you doing there on Thanksgiving? I figured you two were living it up with the over eighty crowd on the Senior Living Campus."

"We started off at the campus," Em said, cheeks heating, "and then we—"

Michael wrapped his arm around her shoulders. "We needed to go to the hollow to make peace with some demons from the past."

Zoe's gaze danced between them, a wry glint in her eye. But then her gaze softened. "I'm all for putting old demons to rest." She paused and drummed her fingers on the table. "So, what's next? I forgot to ask. Did teen dream, Tiffany Shelton, remember anything? I assumed that's why you booked it out of the studio."

Em shook her head. "She said she didn't remember much. She didn't have any time to talk. She's leaving today to go to Florida with her husband and kids. But she agreed to meet with me after her family gets back in a couple of weeks. Maybe if I get her on her own, she'll open up more."

"That's assuming the two brain cells God gave her still work," Zoe said.

"I know you were never fond of her, Z, but she seemed genuinely regretful about that night."

"Possibly," Zoe replied. "But keep your guard up with her, Em."

27

"You're going to be late," Em called up the stairs.

"I'm never late," Michael answered, coming down the steps two at a time.

Em bit her lip, drinking him in as Cody bounced between them. Michael MacCarron in a three-piece suit could set off a five-alarm fire.

"I think I know why so many of your clients are old ladies," she said and straightened his tie.

He ran his hand down her back, letting it settle on her ass. "My enormous intellect?"

"I'm pretty sure it's something enormous. Maybe not your intellect?"

He dropped a kiss on her nose. "Enormous, huh?"

"You don't hear me complaining."

"Think you're up for an *enormous* lunch at Park Tavern? I could swing by and get you after my meeting."

She let out a breath. "I'd love to, but Ben's guys should be finishing up today. I want to be here if they have any questions."

Over the past three weeks, her Foursquare had gone from a work zone with a steady stream of tradesmen to looking like one of those HGTV dream homes.

She had moved what she needed into Michael's Foursquare. It made sense to stay there. She was out of the workers' way, Cody had his doggy doors and could come and go as he pleased, and Michael had a king-sized bed. While they had spent plenty of time over the last few weeks breathless and tangled in her tiny twin, Michael's king was more conducive to lazy Sunday mornings in bed.

"And my stomach's been bothering me a little bit this morning. I may skip lunch altogether."

He slid his hand from her ass to her stomach. "You do feel a little bloated."

Her eyes went wide.

Michael broke out into laughter. "Em, I'm kidding. It's probably the transition from Australia to America. I'm sure you're just getting used to all the bugs and viruses in the states. You could always ask Dr. Stein. Their party's tonight, right?

"Oh, yes, Zoe and Mrs. Stein have already texted twice this morning confirming that we'll be there."

"Wouldn't miss it for the world. Did you decide if you're going to play?"

Kathy had asked her to bring her violin. She'd been playing regularly at the Senior Living Campus and with Michael, composing tracks on the electric violin in the evening, but she still hadn't attempted the Paganini piece.

Her fingers twitched. "It couldn't hurt to bring Polly along."

Michael lifted her chin and pressed a kiss to her lips. "It couldn't hurt at all."

His phone chimed.

"Duty calls."

"Tell Mrs. Bigglesworth-Bucksdale the third that she can look, but she can't touch."

Michael's lips quirked into a crooked smile. "I have another meeting after lunch. I may need to just meet you over at the Steins if it runs long." He ruffled Cody's ears. "Take care of our Em today, boy."

She walked him to the door and smoothed out a wrinkle on his shirt.

He palmed her ass again and pulled her in close. "I'll let Mrs. Bigglesworth-Bucksdale the third know you send your regards."

She laughed and shook her head.

"I love you, Mary Michelle," he said, his sage green gaze softening as he pressed one last kiss to her forehead.

IT WAS BARELY HALF past ten when the last craftsman left the Foursquare. After the last few weeks of constant activity, the house was finally quiet. Em walked from room to room, admiring the espresso-stained baseboards, the freshly painted walls, and the new appliances. Several of the windows had been replaced, and upgrades were made to the electrical and plumbing systems.

The house was ready to sell.

She ran her fingertips along the top of the wainscoting. This house would always be dear to her heart, but she no longer harbored reservations regarding its sale. Home had never been a physical place. Home was Michael's smile. Home was Zoe's bubbling laughter. Home was spending hours signing with her grandmother. Home was the music flowing through her soul that anger could never stamp out.

Her phone buzzed with an incoming text. She smiled, thinking it must be Michael. But the text was from an unknown number.

I'm back from Florida. I can meet you at the Langley Park Botanic Gardens in fifteen minutes.

WITHIN A MATTER OF SECONDS, Em was out the door and headed toward the gardens. A brisk December chill had swept in overnight, and she looped a scarf around her neck as she made her way up Foxglove Lane. After their awkward exchange on the sidewalk, she had almost lost hope that Tiffany would reach out to her at all. Em doubled her pace. She didn't want to give the woman any time to second-guess their meeting.

Tiffany was standing at the entrance to the gardens with two coffee cups from The Drip in hand. "I wasn't sure what you drank." She passed Em a cup. "I figured herbal tea was a safe bet."

Em accepted the drink with a grateful smile. "That was kind of you," she said, taking a sip. She'd never been a fan of herbal tea. But it hit the spot today.

Tiffany shifted her stance. "I'm sorry it took so long for me to contact you. We got back from Florida, and both kids came down with a cold. Today was the first day I've left the house since we got back."

"Thank you for agreeing to meet with me. I know this whole situation is pretty strange."

Tiffany nodded. "Can we walk? I've been cooped up inside for days."

They walked in silence, following a stone path past grand juniper hedges and thick clumps of dormant prairie grasses glowing golden yellow in the winter sun.

"Are your kids with your parents?" Em asked, breaking the silence.

"Yes, we don't get to Langley Park much these days. With the kids being so small, my parents usually come to us." Tiffany took a sip of her tea then stopped walking. "I need to tell you something, Em."

Em gestured for them to sit on a bench overlooking Lake Boley.

"I lied to you the other day," Tiffany said.

"What do you mean?"

Tiffany fiddled with the lid of her paper cup. "I do remember that night at Sadie's Hollow. The night you were injured."

Em's pulse kicked up a notch. "What do you remember?"

"How jealous I was. How much I hated seeing Michael kiss you. How I went out of my way to make sure he was too drunk to come find you after he played his set."

Em's heart sank, but she tried to keep her expression neutral. "It was a long time ago. We were just kids."

Tiffany shook her head. "You know, he was always talking about you. Always telling everyone about all the amazing places you were visiting and about all of your performances with big orchestras and famous conductors."

Tiffany paused, but Em forced herself to stay quiet. She needed to give Tiffany space to talk.

"When I heard you were at the hollow that night, I wanted to scream, because I knew."

"Knew what?" Em asked.

Tiffany met her gaze. "I knew he would pick you."

Em took a shaky breath as something sharp and cold pricked at her heart. "Do you still have feelings for Michael?"

Tiffany shook her head. "No, I don't think I ever had any real feelings for him. He was more of a prize. I know that sounds awful. But it's the truth. It makes me sick when I think of the person I was back then."

"It looks like you're doing well now. You've got two beautiful children."

Tiffany smiled. "I grew up a lot after that night. I met my husband a few years later in college. That's when I figured out what real love looked like." She ran a finger over her wedding band. "I wanted to reach out to you, to apologize for my behavior. But, I'd heard you'd moved to Australia and then weeks turned into months and months into years."

"I'm not angry with you, Tiffany. I just want to figure out what happened that night."

Tiffany stared at the lake. "I've been going over that night in my head since you stopped me on the street. All I can remember is someone handing me a drink, and then I gave it to you."

"Do you remember who gave you the drink? Was it Gabe Sinclair? He handed me a drink when I arrived with Zoe."

"No, I would have remembered if it was Gabe—and Gabe was busy setting up the deejay equipment. No, somebody else handed me that drink."

Em nodded. "The last concrete thing I can remember from that night was taking that drink from you. After that, it's like everything became this crazy, distorted dream."

Tiffany gasped. "It sounds like you were drugged. I had this friend in college, and the same thing happened to her when she tried Special K."

"Special K?" Em echoed.

"Yeah, the real name is Ketamine. It can really mess you up. My friend was out of it for hours."

"Did kids do that at Sadie's Hollow?"

"Not usually, but that night was supposed to be the big blow out before everybody went off to college. I wouldn't be surprised if some-body got their hands on some Special K for the occasion." Tiffany paused, and her hand flew to her chest. "Jesus Christ."

"What is it?" Em asked.

"Nobody told me to give you that drink, Em. I just did because I wanted to get Michael away from you. But, if that punch was spiked with something, I don't think it was meant for you. It must have been meant for me."

"YOU THINK someone was trying to drug Tiffany?" Michael asked, pulling the Audi into traffic.

Em settled herself in the front seat. Michael's meeting had run late, but he had insisted on stopping by the house to pick her up.

She released a breath. "As far as we can tell, the drink had to have been spiked with some kind of drug. Can you think of any kids from high school that were into that kind of thing?"

"I can think of a few people from high school that could have been into that scene. Unfortunately, that shit wasn't hard to get. But I haven't seen any of them in years. I don't even know if they're still in the area."

Em picked at the edge of her sleeve. "Did anyone have it in for Tiffany back then? I know Zoe didn't like her, but it's a far cry from disliking someone to drugging them."

Michael shook his head but kept his gaze on the road. "No, I can't think of anyone. Tiffany was pretty popular, and she mostly stuck with her crowd. High school girls can get bitchy, but I never heard of anyone hating her enough to hurt her like that. What's this Special K, anyway?"

"The actual name is Ketamine," Em replied. "Tiffany mentioned a friend of hers tried it in college. She said the girl pretty much blacked out and didn't remember anything. I did a little research on it today. It's considered a date rape drug, like Rohypnol. It can make you feel like you're trapped in some dream-like state. It can distort sound and vision. People say they lose whole chunks of time they can't account for when they're on it."

"Christ! Zoe and I thought maybe somebody had given you acid or shrooms. That stuff was always around. I never touched it, but plenty of kids did. I can't remember anybody doing hardcore drugs like Ketamine."

Em stared out at the road. "I'm worried that my memories from that night may not be real. If I ingested this drug, anything could have happened to me. I wouldn't have been able to tell what was real and what wasn't. Has Clay Stevens heard back about the jewelry found at the scene of Tina Fowler's hit and run?"

"Not yet. I checked with him a few days ago. He said he would put in a call, but he hadn't heard anything. I know the Garrett PD is stretched pretty thin when it comes to dollars for law enforcement. Whoever he contacted might be swamped with cases. We can ask him again tonight. There's a good chance he'll be at the party."

"No, I don't want to spoil the mood. I know the Steins put a lot into their holiday gathering."

Michael took her hand. "Are you sure you're up for a party tonight? I know your stomach was bothering you earlier and now all this with Tiffany is pretty stressful."

She squeezed his hand. "I'm fine."

"I'm glad you decided to bring Polly," he said.

She glanced over her shoulder to where she had secured her Paul Bailly violin in the backseat. "I wouldn't want to disappoint Mrs. Stein."

"Do you have any pieces in mind you'd like to play?"

"Jingle Bells. Deck the Halls. That cute dreidel song. It's not that difficult of a playlist this time of year."

"You know what I mean," he said.

She had found her old paperback book containing Paganini's 24 Caprices for Violin, but she hadn't attempted to play any of them, especially not *Nel cor più non mi sento*. She hadn't even opened the cover. But she didn't need to. The music was seared into her soul. She'd tried like hell over the last twelve years, but she could never separate herself from the music.

Her fingers twitched. "We'll see. I'm sure I'll be able to come up with something."

Michael made the last turn onto the Stein's street, and they were met with a sea of cars lining the road. The Stein's Langley Park red brick colonial style home was decked with wreaths and twinkling lights just like Em remembered from years past. When she was in grade school, she and Zoe used to make hideouts and play secret agents under the ornate tablecloth that covered the buffet table.

Michael found a parking spot a few houses down, and they walked hand in hand to the Stein's.

"Do you want me to carry Polly?" he asked.

"No thanks, I've got her." Em tightened her grip. The violin's solid weight was as comforting as a child's cherished teddy bear.

They hadn't even knocked on the door before it swung open and Kathy Stein met them with an easy smile.

"Michael! Em! I'm so glad you made it."

Kathy ushered them inside and took their coats. She glanced down at the violin case. "May I?" she asked, gesturing to the case.

Em handed it over.

Kathy opened the latches, and, with a mother's gentle touch, lifted the lid. "I remember when you got this. Your parents were so excited when they found this violin."

Em nodded, knowing if she said anything her voice would crack with emotion.

Kathy closed the case. "How is your mother? I bet she's eager to get you back to Australia."

"My mother's doing well. I spoke with her earlier today, but I'm not planning on going back to Australia anytime soon."

Kathy's eyes widened. "You're staying?"

Em shared a glance with Michael. They hadn't told anyone about her decision to stay in Langley Park yet, not even her father.

"You're not selling the house?" Kathy asked.

"No, I'm still selling the house, but..."

"But, Em is going to be staying with me," Michael added.

Kathy's eyes sparkled. "For how long?"

Michael wrapped his arm around her shoulder. "I was hoping forever," he said.

Em met his gaze. "I like the sound of that."

"Oh, you two," Kathy said, extending her arms and pulling them both into an embrace. "I'm delighted. Just delighted. Does anyone else know? Zoe and Ben haven't mentioned anything to me."

"You're the first person we've told," Em said.

Kathy released them but held on to their hands. She closed her eyes, and the three of them stood in a circle, hands clasped.

"Do you feel that?" Kathy asked.

Michael shot Em an amused glance.

Kathy opened her eyes. "It's your energy. You balance each other out perfectly."

"I want to play Ring Around the Rosie," came a little girl's voice.

Kate Fisher appeared wearing a Harry Potter holiday sweater and ducked under their clasped hands to stand in the middle of their circle.

They released their hands and laughed.

"I like your Harry Potter sweater," Em said, signing as she spoke to the little girl.

Kate's face lit up, and she made the Harry Potter sign back.

Jenna Fisher joined the group with her husband, Ben, at her side. Ben was wearing a holiday sweater with Darth Vader in a Santa cap.

"We're a house divided," Jenna said with a grin.

"I heard the guys finished up work on your Foursquare today. I'd love to come by and check the final product," Ben said.

"Anytime! And thank you so much for all of your help. The house looks amazing," Em replied.

"I may even have a potential buyer for you," Ben added. "Mrs. G's goddaughter is looking to move to Langley Park."

"And don't forget about me. I'll be looking to buy in this area," Nick Kincade said as he and Zoe joined the gathering in the foyer.

Em looked from Ben to Nick. Nick was wearing the same *Star Wars* sweater as Ben.

"See," Michael said with a wry grin. "I told you they took this *Star Wars* thing seriously."

"This happened purely by chance," Nick said, shaking Michael's hand.

"And by chance," Zoe said, "he means totally on purpose."

Kate put her hands on her hips and pulled on Kathy's sleeve. "If we're going to stay in the foyer for the whole party, can I go get the candy bowl?"

Kathy clapped her hands. "Kate's right! Come on, everybody. Let's join the other guests."

Michael pressed his hand to the small of her back. "Are you doing okay?"

Em smiled. "I'm good."

They entered a large kitchen area that opened up into a spacious living room. Kathy's husband, Dr. Neil Stein, waved from across the room. He was speaking with an older woman who looked vaguely familiar.

"Em! Michael!" Neil said, gathering her into a warm embrace. "I'm so glad you made it."

"This is Eve Medina," Neil said. "I'm not sure if you remember her."

"Dr. Eve Medina," Michael added. "the soon-to-be medical internet sensation."

The woman shook her head. "It's so good to see you, Em. We met many years ago. I performed your tendon repair surgery."

Em searched her memory. Her time at the hospital was almost as much of a blur as the night she was injured. She took another look at Dr. Medina. Some gray was woven into the woman's jet-black hair now, but she did remember the woman's reassuring brown eyes.

"Dr. Medina," Em said, taking the woman's hand. "It's so good to see you. I wasn't at my best the last time we met."

"I don't remember it like that," the doctor said. "I remember you being a very brave young woman. May I?" She gestured to Em's injured hand.

She held up her hand for Dr. Medina's inspection.

"I do remember it was a clean cut." She flexed and bent Em's ring finger. "Did you keep up with physical therapy? It appears your tendon has healed beautifully."

"Not really," Em answered. "I left for Australia shortly after I was injured. I did some therapy, but nothing regularly."

"Huh," Dr. Medina said, continuing to manipulate her finger. "May I ask what kind of work you do? I remember hearing you were a musician."

"After I was injured I stopped playing music and went to work at a school for hearing-impaired children."

The doctor narrowed her gaze. "Did you use sign language?"

"Yes, every day."

Dr. Medina shared a look with Neil. "Are you thinking what I'm thinking?"

Neil smiled. "Your time working at the school and signing every day is probably what strengthened your finger and allowed you to regain full use. Sound about right, Eve?"

Dr. Medina nodded. "I would agree with that assessment, Dr. Stein."

Em swallowed back a lump in her throat. "That's amazing! All that time, I thought I'd lost my ability to play."

"And the whole time you were helping your tendon heal," Michael added.

"May I steal him away from you for a moment," Dr. Medina said, gesturing to Michael.

"Eve's looking into posting some of her surgeries on YouTube," Michael said. "I'm reviewing some of the language in the disclaimer."

"Michael is doing me quite a favor. Give me a ruptured extensor tendon, and I know exactly what to do. But when it comes to legal jargon, it's all Greek to me."

"I'll just be a second," Michael said, then followed Dr. Medina into the kitchen.

Neil gave her a knowing smiling. "Things have a way of working themselves out, don't they?"

Em swallowed back another lump. "They do."

Neil gestured to the violin case. "I was hoping you'd play for us this evening. Do you have anything in mind?"

"I do," she answered.

He patted her shoulder. "Everyone! Everyone, can I have your attention?" he called out as conversations quieted. "We've got quite a treat for you tonight. Our own Em MacCaslin has brought her violin and will be playing for us tonight."

Em scanned the room for Michael, but her gaze found Tom and Mindy Lancaster first. They had just arrived and were still in their coats.

Tom gave her a reassuring nod while Mindy remained frozen in place.

She blinked, and when she opened her eyes, Michael was moving toward her through the crowd of people who had gathered around her.

She opened the case and retrieved her violin and bow. "I thought I would start with a piece I haven't played in a very long time," she said, willing her voice not to crack. "This is a piece by Niccolò Paganini. It's titled *Nel cor più non mi sento*."

28

E m closed her eyes. Someone once asked her what went through her head before she played a piece of music. She could never answer the question because what happened didn't just happen in her mind. Before she struck the first note, her whole body ceased being a collection of blood and bone and organs. When she held a violin, she disappeared into a place where only sound and vibration dwelled.

She opened her eyes and met Michael's gaze before she vanished to that faraway place. Then, like an artist drawing the first brush-stroke of paint across the canvas, she played the piece. Her fingers remembered each note and each pluck of the strings. Paganini's music poured out of her like the rush of a flash flood over the sunbaked Serengeti. The bow wasn't just bits of wood, ivory, and horse hair. It was the living extension of her right arm. The rules of time seemed to bend. She could have been playing for five seconds or five hours when, with one final stroke, the piece came to an end.

She exhaled. She wasn't even sure if she had breathed while she'd played. Opening her eyes, she gazed down the length of the violin. The scar on her ring finger peeked out at her like a star athlete begging to be back in the game. Up until now, this scar had been the unwavering proof of her failure. Now, it was the unmistakable mark of her triumph.

She held the violin at her side and found Michael in the crowd. The entire room had gone still as if they weren't sure if what had happened was even real. He smiled and nodded to her, his sage green eyes glassy with emotion. He closed the distance between them and kissed her in front of the entire party.

She was home.

Michael pulled back a fraction. "You are amazing," he whispered against her lips before pressing another kiss to the corner of her mouth.

The room erupted in cheers. Em scanned the crowd. Zoe and Kathy were holding onto each other, tears streaming down their cheeks. Tom Lancaster met her gaze and patted his heart just as he did the last time she had played this piece over twelve years ago when she had performed at the symphony benefit before her ill-fated trip to Sadie's Hollow.

She stared down at her violin. "I did it. I really did it."

"Everything you went through has brought you here," Michael answered.

Tom joined them, and his teary-eyed grin spoke volumes. "I've never heard Paganini's piece played with more depth or with more emotion. The last time you played this piece—don't get me wrong—it was technically flawless. But now, now your music has an emotional component second to none."

The heat of a blush crept up her neck. "It felt different. I felt..."

"Grateful?" Tom offered.

She nodded. That was it. Before her injury, her gift was something she'd always had. From the moment she woke, to the seconds before she drifted off to sleep, her gift was with her like an inseparable twin. But after the accident, for the first time in her life, she was completely alone, stripped of her constant musical companion.

"Yes, I am grateful," she said. "I never thought I'd get it back. I thought I'd lost it forever."

"Your gift is still there. In fact, I don't think you've ever sounded better," Tom said.

"He's right," Michael added. "Listening to you play—it was like being transported to another world."

Tom nodded. "I think we should get you back on stage. I can talk to some people at the symphony."

"I agree," Michael said. He turned to Tom. "Em and I have been working on some music. It's a blend of classical pieces mixed with electronic and techno elements. It's cutting edge stuff. There's a huge following for that online. Many internet musicians have snagged lucrative recording contracts starting this way."

Tom nodded. "I've started listening to this kind of crossover genre. It's fascinating stuff, and really engaging the younger generation to explore classical roots."

Em's gaze bounced between Michael and Tom like she was watching a tennis match. The flurry of their words made her head spin.

"Hold on," she said, setting her violin carefully on an end table. She looped her arm through Michael's and leaned into him.

"Are you okay, Em?" he asked.

She was lightheaded. "It's all a little overwhelming," she answered, concentrating on her breath. "I'm not ready to play with the symphony right now. And I'm definitely not ready to be some internet sensation."

"Of course, Em," Tom said with the same gentle smile he'd given her as a child. "But you should know, it will all be there when you're ready. Just say the word. I'm not sure when you're heading back to Australia, but—"

Kathy Stein cut in and tapped a spoon to a glass of champagne. "I think this is as good a time as any to make a toast."

The room quieted as Neil, Ben, and Zoe passed out glasses of champagne.

Kathy smiled at her guests. "We have many things to be thankful for, don't we, friends?"

The room buzzed with murmurs of agreement as Neil put an arm around his wife.

"We're thankful for all your love and friendship. We're thankful for the many gifts life gives us each day."

Em looked up, and Kathy met her gaze. Kathy's eyes held a question. Em knew what she was asking and nodded.

"We're thankful to have Em home. I'm happy to tell you, she has decided to stay in Langley Park."

The room shifted its focus from Kathy and onto her. Michael wrapped his arm around her shoulders and pressed a kiss to her temple.

Kathy blinked back tears. "Sweetheart, it's so good to have you home. Let's all raise our glasses, and, with profound gratitude in our hearts, let's toast to Langley Park. It's not just where we live. It's where we love."

The tinkling of glass filled the air, and Michael tapped his glass against hers. "I guess it's official. You're here to stay."

She gazed around the room. Sam had arrived and was holding Kate in his arms. The pair gave her bright smiles and two thumbs up. Zoe was standing next to Ben and Jenna.

Her friend wiped away a tear and mouthed, "Love you."

Em mouthed back, "Love you, too."

She set her champagne down and rested her hands on Michael's chest. "It's good to be home," she said, pushing up on her toes. He met her in the middle and pressed another kiss to her lips.

"I HAVE a few last minute things I need to do before we head over to the Senior Living Campus," Michael said, zipping his coat. "And one of those things may or may not involve a certain Christmas present for you."

Em curled up on the sofa in Michael's living room. Her stomach was acting up again, but she didn't want to worry him.

"Lucky for me, I finished my shopping two days ago. You're cutting it close, aren't you? It is Christmas Eve."

They had gotten a tree from a vendor in Langley Park's town square a few days ago, fished out all their favorite childhood ornaments from dusty boxes, and hung their stockings over the fireplace in Michael's Foursquare. She'd purchased Michael's gift—a fancy keyboard for them to use in the carriage house recording studio—a few days after the Stein's holiday party. But she had no idea what he had in store for her.

"You can't put a time limit on perfection," he said. He looked her over. "Is it your stomach, again?"

"It's nothing," she said, patting Cody who was snoozing away on the couch next to her.

He gave her a dubious look. "I'll work as fast as I can. If I can get a few things squared away today, I won't have to do a lick of work for the next week."

She walked him to the door. "I'm sorry, did you just say lick?"

He bent down and pressed a kiss to her lips. "When I get back, we aren't leaving my bed for the next week."

She cocked her head to the side. "What about food?"

"Completely overrated. But with your stomach, we better make a couple of platefuls of grilled cheese. We can leave them next to the bed."

She shook her head. "I'll see you in a couple of hours."

"I may be a little longer than that. I'll work as fast as I can." He dropped a kiss to her forehead. "You should check out that old box I found in your carriage house when I was looking for the Christmas ornaments. I think it had some of your old music books and possibly a diary or two."

Em's eyes widened. "I certainly hope you didn't read anything."

"I think they're just your old practice logs."

She swatted his chest. "You did read them!"

"No, you know I wouldn't do that, Em," he said, squeezing her hand. "Take a look. I left the box in the kitchen."

Michael left for the office, and she padded into the kitchen. The old box was brittle and sun-bleached on one corner from where it must have sat exposed to the light over the last decade, maybe longer. She opened the box and waved away a puff of dust.

"Look at these," she said as Cody joined her in the kitchen. She had loved using datebooks to log not only her practice time but just about every aspect of her day. From the time she was eight and until her accident, she studiously recorded all her daily activities.

"I was a pretty thorough kid, Cody."

The dog tilted his head from side to side as if he understood.

"I recorded everything: when I woke up, when I practiced, even my—" She stopped her narration and ran her finger along a series of red dots, each appearing over five consecutive days.

"Oh my gosh," she whispered. Her periods had been irregular since she was a teenager. The red dots were her not so subtle way of tracking her cycle. She'd started taking birth control pills to combat this when she was eighteen, shortly after she moved to Australia. Then a realization nearly knocked the breath out of her.

She ran into the bathroom and rummaged through her cosmetics pouch where she had kept her pills. She'd stopped wearing heavy makeup and had barely touched the bag over the last few weeks.

Back in Australia, she had a set routine. First, she would take her birth control pill. Next, she'd apply her mask of makeup. But now that she was in Langley Park, that routine had been thrown off. How long had it been since she had even unzipped the pouch? She examined the pack. Nearly full, and it should have been almost empty.

Despite being on the pill, she had always insisted on using condoms with her sexual partners.

But she hadn't with Michael.

Em looked at herself in the mirror. Turning to the side, she stared at her abdomen. She didn't look any different. At least, she didn't think she did. She drummed her fingers on the sink and tried to think. Her last period started the day after Halloween and ended a few days later. She hadn't had one since then.

She closed her eyes and tried to organize her thoughts. She'd had bouts of nausea. She preferred herbal tea to her espresso laden flat whites, and she couldn't remember the last time she had wanted a sip of alcohol. She opened her eyes and surveyed herself in the mirror.

"Wow," she breathed, pressing her hands to her abdomen.

THE TIMER BEEPED. Em looked on as another bold pink plus sign bloomed under the strip of clear plastic. Ten home pregnancy tests had all come to the same conclusion: Mary Michelle MacCaslin was pregnant.

"Cody, you're going to be a big brother."

The dog tilted his head, and Em laughed, then cried, then laughed some more.

"A baby," she said, unable to stop smiling. She had never even considered motherhood. But the thought of having a baby with Michael only made her heart burst with joy.

"Should we call Michael?" she asked the dog. Cody tilted his head. "Oh, you're no help," she said, scratching between his ears.

"No! We'll surprise him."

Em collected all ten pregnancy tests and hid them throughout the house as Cody watched her with a perplexed expression.

She held up the last one. "We can't forget the carriage house."

She pulled on her boots and walked the short distance across the backyard. She flipped on the carriage house light, and a warmth bloomed in her chest. Sheets of paper scribbled with musical notations were scattered across the desk next to their digital audio workstation equipment.

She wanted to hide this last pregnancy test under the sheet music for their Chopin Nocturne 20 remix, but an orange piece of paper stuck to the side of the workstation caught her eye.

Upload all files of EM project

She plucked the note from the desk. Crushing anger replaced the rush of joyful euphoria. He had promised he wouldn't do anything with their music until she was ready. She grabbed a pencil and wrote a message on the bottom of Michael's note:

So much for being BETTER TOGETHER!

Angry tears blurred her vision. Rubbing her eyes, she left the note and the pregnancy test on the desk and ran out of the carriage house. Her gaze bounced between the two American Foursquares. All their shared history closed in around her. Suffocating her. Smothering her with his deception. He had gone behind her back. He'd lied. She shook her head. It couldn't be true. Michael wouldn't do that. *Would he?*

She had to get out of there. But where would she go? She took her phone out of her back pocket. It was only a little after three in the afternoon, but it was Christmas Eve. She glanced over at her carriage house. The cherry red Mercedes coupe peeked out through the set of square windows.

She would go for a drive. Clear her head. She opened the garage, fished her keys out of her pocket, and fired up the engine. Gravel crunched and spewed out in an angry screech of sound as she tore down the driveway and onto Foxglove Lane.

Dark clouds rolled in as the temperature dropped. She cranked up the heater and aimlessly drove in circles around the Langley Park town center, careful not to drive past Michael's office.

What was he thinking? Did he really believe she would be pleased with this? Was this betrayal supposed to be her Christmas gift?

She blinked back the hot tears threatening to spill down her cheeks. She didn't have the luxury to wallow in anger. Not this time. She was pregnant. There was another life to consider. Em rested a hand on her stomach, and the tears she had kept at bay came trickling out in angry streaks.

She turned onto Mulberry Drive, and an icy drizzle blurred her windshield. She switched on the wiper blades just as her phone chimed, alerting her to a new text message. She pulled over near the coffee shop and looked at the screen. It was a text from Michael.

I found your note. It's not what you think. EM is Eve Medina. Dr. Medina. The files I uploaded were her surgeries. Come home, Em. We need to talk. I need to see you. I found all the tests. I love you, Em. I would never go behind your back. We are always better together.

She stared at the text as tears of relief replaced the tears of anger. She wiped her face with her coat sleeve then texted her reply:

Just driving around. I'll come right home.

She set the phone on the coupe's console, turned the steering wheel, and hit the gas. Immediately, she slammed on the brakes. A man had stepped out to cross the street. She threw the car into park and got out.

"I'm so sorry," she said, shielding her eyes from the wind and icy rain that had kicked up in intensity. "I didn't see you!"

The man lowered his hood.

"Kyle?"

Kyle Benson met her gaze. "Yeah, it's me."

"I'm so sorry. Are you all right?"

"I'm okay." He glanced up at the sky. "Would you mind giving me a ride home. It's coming down pretty good now."

She gestured to the coupe. "Of course, of course."

They got in the car, and Kyle took out his phone.

"Do you have any plans for Christmas?" she asked, guiding the old Mercedes into traffic.

Kyle was typing something on his phone. Em glanced over. She couldn't tell if it was a text or email. She waited for him to answer, but he didn't respond.

"Kyle," she tried again. "Is everything okay?"

He looked thinner, hollowed out.

"Are you sick?"

Kyle's head whipped up. "No."

Em turned down his street and pulled up in front of his house. "We're here," she said, eyeing her phone. Michael would be wondering why she hadn't made it back yet.

"Do you have a minute to come up, Em?"

Kyle looked like a ghost. His usual healthy glow was replaced with a pallid, dishwater gray tinge. And from the looks of it, he hadn't shaved in a few days either.

"I really don't have much time. I better go. Michael is expecting me."

"It'll only take a second. I've got some photos I'd like to show you. I've been spending a lot of time near Sadie's Hollow lately. I thought you'd like to see them."

Her eyes widened with the mention of the hollow.

"Remember? I've been doing some work for the Kansas historical society."

He smiled, but something in his voice made the hairs on the back of her neck prickle.

"I better go, Kyle. I'd love to do this some other time."

"Five minutes, Em. I'm sure Michael can fend for himself."

She glanced at her phone then back over to Kyle. The rain pinged off the hood of the coupe with a growing urgency.

"All right, but only for a few minutes. I really should be getting back home."

They covered their heads and jogged down the driveway to Kyle's carriage house. He unlocked the door and ushered her inside.

"The pictures are in my room. Give me a second." Kyle disappeared into his room and pulled the door partway closed behind him.

She paced the length of the studio apartment a few times. The photograph she had found last time she was here was laying on the counter. But now, it was held together with tape like someone had ripped it up and then tried to piece it back together.

She fingered the edge of the photograph. There was a building in the background she hadn't noticed the first time she had looked at it. She'd been so amazed to learn Anita Benson was married to Mindy Lancaster's brother. She had completely missed it. She stared at the building. There was something familiar about it.

A noise pulled her attention from the photo, and she glanced out the window. A car had pulled up behind the Mercedes and sat idling on the street.

"Are you expecting someone?"

Kyle didn't answer.

She walked over and peeked through the crack in the door. He was typing something furiously on his phone.

This felt wrong. Em reached for her phone but cursed under her breath. It was back in the car.

Kyle looked up and caught her watching him. He didn't say anything. He didn't even move a muscle.

"I really have to go, Kyle. Merry Christmas."

She left the apartment and rushed down the stairs. She opened the door and stopped short, dropping her keys. The woman standing in front of her with mousy brown hair produced a saccharine smile.

"You better pick those up," Mindy Lancaster said, revealing a small, shiny revolver tucked inside her purse. "We're going for a drive."

29

"Em, I know I've already left a shitload of messages, but I really need you to call or text me back as soon as you get this."

Michael pressed the end call button on his phone and looked out at the steady stream of freezing rain as he navigated the ice-slicked road. After half an hour of driving around Langley Park looking for Em's red Mercedes coupe, he was no closer to finding her than when he started. He pulled over in front of Park Tavern. Maybe Em stopped in to say hello to Sam.

But where the hell was her car?

He entered the tavern and nodded to Sam. "Have you seen Em?"

Sam met him at the corner of the bar. "No, cuz, was she supposed to come by? You know I'm closing down in thirty minutes."

"I can't reach her. She's not answering any texts, and all her calls are going to voicemail."

"Did something happen?" Sam asked.

Michael ran his hands through his hair. "We had a miscommunication, but I texted with her. Everything seemed okay."

"She probably stopped by the Steins," Sam said, crossing his arms. "I wouldn't be too worried."

"You think I didn't already go by there?" he bit back.

Sam put his hands up. "What the fuck? What's going on? Do you think Em's in trouble or hurt?

Michael shook his head. He wanted to scream. He just found out the woman he loved more than life itself was pregnant with his child, and somehow, between her texting him she was on her way home, she had fucking disappeared.

He released a shaky breath. "I just need to find her."

Sam put a hand on his shoulder. "Let me tell Benson we're closing up now, and I'll help you look."

Michael's gaze flicked to the man downing shots of tequila. "When did Kyle get here?"

"I don't know. Half an hour, forty-five minutes ago. The dude has been pounding Cuervo since he got here. It's like he's on some kind of mission."

Kyle glanced over from the end of the bar then tossed back another shot. The guy looked like shit.

"Kyle," Michael called out. "Have you seen Em?"

Kyle leaned forward. He was shaking his head and murmuring.

Michael walked to the end of the bar. "Kyle?"

"I never wanted anything to happen to either of them," he said, rolling something small and white between his fingers.

Michael stared at the tiny object, and the breath caught in his throat. He reached into the breast pocket of his coat and took out a slim rectangular jewelry box. His Christmas present to Em. He'd had a jeweler repair her grandmother's pearl necklace.

Sam joined them and crossed his arms. "What the fuck do you have in your hand, Kyle?"

Kyle set the tiny sphere on the table. One delicate pearl sat buttery-white against the dark Cherrywood bar.

Michael picked up the pearl and compared it to Em's necklace in the jewelry box.

A perfect match.

He grabbed Kyle by the collar and swung him around. "How did you get this, Kyle?"

Kyle didn't resist. He hung limply in Michael's grip. "It was never supposed to be Em."

"What the hell are you talking about, Benson?" Michael growled.

Kyle met his gaze with bloodshot eyes. "It was supposed to be Tiffany. Em should never have gotten that drink."

"You spiked Tiffany's drink that night? Why?"

A muscle ticked in Kyle's jaw. "Because of you. Because you always got everything. The hottest girl in our class. Everybody clamoring around you, telling you what a great deejay you were. I wanted Tiffany out of commission that night. I wanted to see you fucking alone. I wanted you to get a taste of not being top dog for once." His face fell, and he stared at the ground. "I didn't know Em was going to be at Sadie's Hollow that night. I never meant for her to get hurt."

"Where is Em? I know you know, Kyle. You wouldn't be sitting here fondling this pearl and drinking yourself into fucking oblivion otherwise."

"She's with my aunt."

"Mindy Lancaster?" Michael asked. "Why the hell would she be with Mindy?"

Kyle gave a pitiful yelp as Michael tightened his grip.

"Why Mindy?" Michael asked again.

"You know how much I hate you?" Kyle asked, his wobbly eyes working to stay focused.

Michael grimaced.

"Mindy hates Em a thousand times more."

Michael pulled Kyle in so they were nose to nose. "Where is Em?"

Kyle sniffed. "You guys were getting too close. You were spending all that time at the hollow. Then you found Tina's memorial."

"Is that where Mindy took Em? To the hollow?"

Kyle shook his head. "No, the cement plant."

"What fucking cement plant?" Sam demanded.

Kyle lifted his gaze. "The abandoned plant in LaRoe."

"The old Hale cement plant?" Sam asked.

Michael turned to Sam. "What did you say?"

"The old Hale cement plant. It went bust years ago and left a lot of people in Garrett, LaRoe and Lyleville shit out of luck. From what I remember, the Hales running the place were pretty shady and ran it into the ground."

Michael narrowed his eyes. "Eunice Teller called your mother, the young Mrs. Hale. I thought she was confused. But she wasn't, was she?"

Kyle didn't answer, but the pathetic look in his eyes revealed Michael was right.

Michael released Kyle's shirt collar and grabbed him by the arm. "I'm taking this sorry sack of shit with me to this Hale cement plant," he said, meeting Sam's gaze.

"Do you want me to come with you?" Sam asked.

"No, call Clay Stevens. See if he's heard from the detective from Garrett. Let Clay know what's going on. I've got to help Em. And Kyle's going to show me the way."

EM TIGHTENED her grip on the steering wheel. The coupe's bald tires skidded and slipped on the icy country road as she drove past Tina Fowler's roadside memorial. Mindy sat in the passenger seat, seemingly unaware of the treacherous conditions, humming a tune under her breath. The gun rested in her lap, and the bright pink of her cast looked cartoonish in contrast to the shiny metal.

The windshield wipers pushed sleet and icy rain from side to side, and Em squinted her eyes. "I should pull over. It's getting pretty bad."

"Keep driving," Mindy directed. "We're not far now."

Em glanced at the gun. "Why are you doing this, Mindy?"

Mindy tapped the hard plaster of her cast against the revolver's barrel and stared out the window. "The men in my family ruin everything. My father, my brother. I thought my nephew might be different."

Em released a shaky breath. "I don't understand. How does any of this have anything to do with me?"

"You! It's always about you, Em."

Em kept her eyes trained on the road.

Mindy's taps on the gun increased in tempo. "You know, when I met Tom, I was his entire world. He was my fresh start away from this godforsaken place. Then he got the offer to play with the Kansas City Symphony. I didn't want to come back here. But I did it for him." The tapping stopped. "We were barely making enough money to make ends meet. I suggested we start teaching to try and make a little extra money on the side. Once he met you, he couldn't stop talking about you. *Langley Park's little Wunderkind.* Isn't that what they called you?"

"I was a child. Tom was my teacher. It was never more than that."

"He just couldn't shut up about you. 'Em's playing with this prestigious orchestra. Em's traveling the world learning from the best of the best.' It was nauseating."

"So you had Kyle drug me and cut my finger so I couldn't play?"

Mindy released a dry laugh. "You think Kyle could plan something like that? Kyle didn't even know you were going to be at the hollow that night. You weren't supposed to get that stupid, spiked drink. He was saving it for some other girl. No, Kyle, like his father and grandfather, only knew how to screw things up. Kyle was so scared when he saw you drink the spiked punch. He didn't know what to do. He panicked and brought you to our family's old cement plant. But you kept getting worse, and after a couple of hours, he started to freak out. He was on his way back to the hollow to fess up when that little bitch on a bike got in his way."

Em dug her nails into the steering wheel, and hot bile rose in her throat. "How do you know all this?" But just as the question escaped her mouth, the car heaved and bounced.

"Watch it," Mindy yelled, bracing herself. "We're crossing over the railroad junction."

"Railroad junction?" Em whispered.

Her body tensed. She knew this sensation. The motion had ground itself into every cell of every muscle in her body. All this time, she'd thought she'd gone across a bumpy wooden bridge, but the rise and fall of the old sets of railroad tracks couldn't be mistaken. This was the jostling sensation her body could never forget.

The buzzing was back. But this time, the sound was amplified and ripped through her mind like a chainsaw. She jammed her foot against the gas pedal. Instead of slowing down, the coupe's wheels skidded over the tracks in violent disjointed jolts, and the car flew forward onto the icy road.

Mindy was saying something, screaming something, but Em's gaze was locked on a large structure in front of them. The car's headlights illuminated faded, white letters printed on the side of a building. Years ago, it must have said HALE CEMENT, but the lettering of the *H* and *E* had faded, making the *H* look more like a lowercase *t* and the *E* into an uppercase *L*.

tALL

The *C* and *E* in "cement" had faded along with the final *T* revealing only the letters *M, E, N.*

tALL MEN.

The two words that had haunted her for over a decade stared down at her like the forgotten cover of an old book.

Em closed her eyes. Flashes from the night of her injury reeled through her mind. Zoe's laughing eyes and Michael's lips against hers morphed into a barrage of images of Kyle's worried face, urging her not to fall asleep as headlights illuminated the side of a stark gray building, and the words *tall men* etched themselves deep inside her mind.

She opened her eyes as the car careened off the road and skidded into a ditch. She turned to Mindy. The gun wasn't on her lap anymore. Mindy's gaze bounced from her lap to the backseat. She twisted around and tried to reach the gun that had settled directly behind her. She was fighting with her seatbelt, bouncing wildly to try and get free.

The seatbelts in the coupe could be temperamental. With trembling hands, Em reached down, pressed the release button on her belt, and gave it a quick jiggle. The belt released and she scrambled out of the car. It wasn't dark out yet, but the heavy cloud cover and freezing drizzle cast a dark shadow on the cement plant. Overgrown weeds and long-neglected bushes and trees encased the structure like a snake constricting around its prey.

Em ran toward the plant, and her boots grew heavy with caked mud and earth. She didn't want to go inside, but it was the only place that could provide somewhere to hide. It was an enormous facility. Several tall silo structures stood side by side. She spotted a three-story rectangular structure littered with broken windows. Fighting the overgrown talons of bare branches, she found an opening and ran inside.

Even in the dim light, she could see the ground was covered with debris. Years upon years of dead leaves and branches mingled with rusted metal, broken glass, and water stained cardboard boxes. She pressed her body against the wall, trying to steer clear of the ominous pieces of jagged wood jutting up from the floor. She inhaled and stifled a cough. The gray powder that had coated her clothes the morning she was found injured on The Steps to Hell was caked to her hands and clung to her skin where her body had pressed up against the wall.

"There's nowhere to go, Em," Mindy called out. Her voice echoed against the concrete walls. "I followed your footprints. I know you can hear me."

Em crouched down behind a half wall. The acoustics of the abandoned space wheezed and creaked as Mindy kicked debris out of the way.

"I know this place like the back of my hand. My great-grandfather built and ran this plant. Once upon a time, the Hale family employed all of LaRoe. Even people from Garrett and Lyleville worked here. The Hales were respected. Revered."

Em peeked over the side of the wall. Mindy dragged a rusty chair to the middle of the room, and the sound of metal scraping wood screeched like a wounded animal. Mindy sat down and inspected the revolver.

"I'm sure you can tell from the state of this place, the story of the Hale family isn't a happy one. You see, my father and my brother weren't cut from the same cloth as my grandpa. My father almost ran this plant into the ground. He was greedy. He wanted to suck every penny he could out of this plant. He started dumping polluted wastewater right out there into the creek to cut costs. After he died and my brother Bobby took over, I prayed Bobby would turn things around. He had Anita, and Kyle was just a baby. But he was no better than my father. Except, not only was he still dumping waste into the creek, but he was also funneling money from the plant to feed his little gambling habit. He shot himself in this very building. He locked himself in his office and just as the authorities were about to bust down his office door to take him in, he pulled the trigger."

Em pressed her face against the side of the wall and held her hands over her mouth. The fine dust particles tickled her nose. With each breath, her throat convulsed as her body begged to cough.

Mindy fired the gun.

Em screamed, and her cries mingled with the sounds of shattering glass.

Had Mindy shot herself?

Em closed her eyes and pressed herself harder into the wall, begging the lifeless structure to swallow her whole.

The sound of dried leaves crunching underfoot filled the concrete chamber. Em looked up to see Mindy peering over the crumbling half wall.

Mindy let out a bark of laughter. "What? Did you think I shot myself? I'm not weak like my brother." She pointed the gun at Em's head. "Get up."

Em rose to her feet and put her hands out defensively. "You don't have to hurt me. We can end this right now. Please, let me go home."

"Oh, I'd love for you to go home...to Australia. But that's not the plan, is it?" Mindy asked, waving the gun. "When Kyle told me you and Michael MacCarron were poking around the hollow, I knew it was only a matter of time until you remembered what happened that night." Mindy gritted her teeth. "And I am not losing Tom. And I am not going to live in a world where every waking moment all he wants to talk about is *you*."

"Why would you lose Tom? Mindy, you're not making any sense?"

Mindy raised the gun, and that saccharine smile slid across her lips. "Who do think gave you that scar?"

Em glanced at her left hand and the zigzag seam of raised skin running the length of her ring finger. "It was you? Why? How?"

"Kyle turned to me for help after he hit that Fowler girl. He couldn't tell his mother. You know what she's like. No, he called me. I met him at the hollow. I told him to drive home and tell his mother he'd hit a deer or a coyote."

Em rubbed her eyes. The image of a tree with a makeshift ladder next to a mangled bicycle bathed in the first rays of dawn flashed through her mind.

Mindy took a step closer. She knocked Em's hands from her face. "I was the one who dragged you over to The Steps to Hell. I'm the one who took that shard of glass and butchered your finger."

Before Em could respond, beams of light shot past her through the broken glass, turning Mindy's mousy-brown hair halo white. Mindy shielded her eyes and turned away.

Em ran for the exit. "I'm in here! I'm in here," she screamed, dodging a pile of twisted metal as a bullet ricocheted off the cement wall.

She dropped to the ground and covered her head.

"Em? Em, where are you?"

It was Michael, but she couldn't answer. Mindy had grabbed a handful of her hair and dragged her back to the center of the room. The revolver dangled from her hand sheathed in the hot pink cast.

Mindy tightened her grip. "Looks like I'm going to get to kill two birds with one stone tonight."

30

Michael ran inside the crumbling room. "Em!" he called out. He froze when Mindy pointed the gun at him.

"You can stop right there, Michael," Mindy said, giving a sharp pull to Em's hair.

He raised his hands. "Mindy, it doesn't have to be like this."

Kyle entered the room.

Mindy's eyes went wide. "What are you doing here, Kyle?"

"We can't do this, Aunt Mindy. It's got to end," he said and walked slowly toward her.

"Stop!" Mindy yelled, her gaze dancing wildly. She released Em's hair. "Michael and Em, I want you both right where I can see you." She gestured toward a bank of broken windows.

Em got to her feet, gave Mindy a tentative glance, and met him at the wall.

He cupped her face. It was smudged with dust and gray powdery streaks. "I saw the car. Are you hurt?"

"Shut up!" Mindy screamed, pacing back and forth.

Em gave him a quick nod. "I'm okay."

"Kyle," Mindy groaned. "I told you I'd take care of this."

"No, you told me you needed to talk to Em alone. When I texted you, you didn't say anything about taking her at gunpoint."

Mindy shook her head. "You're the one who told me they'd been poking around the hollow for weeks. I saw them at the diner in Garrett asking all about Tina. They'd found the memorial on the side of the road. I told you to stop maintaining that little shrine to your guilt."

"I've told Michael everything," Kyle said, bloodshot eyes meeting his aunt's gaze. "He knows I took Em here after she drank the spiked punch. He knows I killed Tina Fowler. He knows you cut Em's hand."

Mindy looked at the ceiling and let out a primal cry. "She doesn't get to have everything! Have you heard her play? Tom can't stop talking about her. He thinks she's even better than she was before. And him." She pointed to Michael. "Wasn't he the reason you wanted to spike that girl's drink to begin with? Isn't he the reason this whole charade started? Both of them have stood between us and our happiness, Kyle."

Kyle kicked a mound of crumbling cement. "We can't do this. It has to end. This has haunted me my entire life."

Mindy took Kyle's hand. "This can all be okay. You have a chance to run for state office. You have a chance to bring some honor back to our family. All your mother ever wanted was for you to make something of yourself—to not end up like your father." She turned to Em. "You should have never come back to Langley Park. You should have stayed holed up half a world away."

The whine of a siren carried in through the room on an icy breeze.

Mindy turned toward the bank of broken windows. "What is that?"

"I called the police when Kyle and I found Em's car," Michael said. "It's over, Mindy. Put the gun down."

Mindy turned to Kyle. "You let him call the police? It's not just your ass that's on the line. Did you think about me? About Tom? About your mother?"

Kyle dragged his hands over his face. "I didn't want any of this to happen. Hitting Tina was an accident. I was exhausted. I was worried Em was going to overdose. I wasn't paying attention. But it happened, Aunt Mindy. I killed Tina Fowler. I should have gone right to the police."

Mindy barked out a laugh. "My brother failed you and your mother. I'm not going to fail you now." She lifted the gun and pointed it at Em. "You don't get to have everything, Mary Michelle MacCaslin. You don't deserve it. You never worked for it."

The police cars advanced up the drive. Sirens blared and lights flashed in a tangle of red and blue.

Mindy aimed the gun and fired. Michael threw his body in front of Em as a hot burn seared his shoulder.

"No!" Kyle yelled, wrestling the gun from Mindy's hand.

"Did you get hit?" Michael asked.

Tears streamed down Em's cheeks. "No, you did. You're bleeding."

Another shot echoed through the room. They looked up to see Kyle, holding his stomach, blood soaking through his shirt. A shocked Mindy stood slack-jawed, the revolver clutched tightly in her hands.

Car doors opened and closed in a cacophony of sharp pops. A voice cut through the air. "Garrett Police. Drop your weapon."

Mindy dropped the gun as Kyle fell to the ground, clutching his stomach.

Michael rose to his feet and kicked the gun to the corner of the room. "We need a medic. A man's been shot."

"Two men," Em called out. She took off her coat, balled it up and pressed it to his shoulder.

"Em," Kyle said, in a hoarse whisper.

They turned to where Kyle lay in a pool of blood. He raised a blood-soaked hand toward Em. "I'm sorry. I never meant for you to get hurt."

She clasped his slippery hand. "I know, Kyle. I know," she said. "Hold on, Kyle. An ambulance is on the way."

"Let the Fowlers know I'm sorry. Let them know it was an accident. She didn't suffer. She was gone by the time I was able to check her pulse."

"Kyle!" Mindy cried out.

His features relaxed and the corner of his mouth lifted into one last smile. "It's over, Aunt Mindy. It's finally over."

MICHAEL EXHALED and listened to the array of beeps and low chatter that floated in from the hospital corridor. An ambulance had brought both himself and Em to the Garrett Community Hospital, and she wouldn't leave his side. She lay asleep in the tiny hospital bed curled around him.

A nurse gave a quick tap on the door then entered and checked the monitors. "Everything looks good, Michael." She lifted the dressing covering his right shoulder. The bullet had only grazed him, and there was no muscle damage. "The wound isn't showing any signs of infection. As long as you apply the topical ointment and change the bandage, you should be as good as new in no time. We're still going to keep you both overnight just as a precaution."

"Can you tell me if Kyle Benson made it?" A lump formed in his throat. The image of Kyle's bloody hand clasping Em's was tattooed on the back of his eyelids.

The nurse shook her head. "No, he was deceased when he arrived at the hospital. I'm very sorry."

Michael exhaled and tightened his grip on Em.

The nurse gave him a sympathetic smile. "There are a few people out in the waiting room who would love to see you. Would you like me to send them back?"

He nodded. The nurse went to the door and waved. Within seconds, Sam, Nick, and Zoe filed into the room.

"Hey cuz! How's the shoulder?" Sam asked, laying a protective hand on his leg.

"It's going to be fine. It was just a graze," Michael answered.

"And Em? Is she going to be okay?" Zoe asked.

Michael brushed the waves of auburn hair from her sleeping face. "She's a tough little thing. She'll be okay."

"We heard about Kyle Benson," Nick said.

Michael nodded. "The nurse just told me. I wonder if anyone's contacted his mother?"

Nick crossed his arms. "They must have. We saw her come into the hospital with a deputy."

A heavy silence swallowed the room. Anita Benson, once Anita Hale, had tried to break free of the Hale name, only to have her son and sister-in-law fall victim to the Hale curse.

"How did Mindy Lancaster play into all this?" Nick asked.

"She was Kyle's aunt." Michael glanced at Em and lowered his voice. "The night of her injury, Em accidentally drank a spiked drink Kyle had meant for another girl. He freaked out and took her to the Hale Cement Plant so nobody would find out she was drugged. He panicked when she got worse and decided to take her back to the hollow. He hit a local girl named Tina Fowler on the way back. She died right there on the side of the road."

Zoe gasped. "The Fowlers never knew what happened."

"Now they'll know," Michael said with a weak smile. He took a breath and exhaled. "Instead of calling the police, Kyle called Mindy. She met him at the hollow. She told him she would get Em back to her tent and sent him home."

Zoe raised a hand to her chest. "Mindy purposely injured Em's hand?"

"She dragged Em over to The Steps to Hell, found a broken bottle, and..." He couldn't go on.

"But, why?" Sam asked.

Michael shook his head. "Jealousy. Deep-seated resentment. Mindy's husband, Tom, was Em's first violin teacher. He was the driving force behind Em becoming a world-class musician. Mindy hated feeling second best. She was terribly jealous of Tom's connection to Em."

"It's hard to believe she could do something so cruel," Zoe said, taking a seat on the corner of the hospital bed. "You think you know someone; then you find out it's all a lie."

Sam took a step back and stared out the window.

A slight man in a white coat walked into the room reading a chart. He pushed a pair of glasses up the bridge of his nose. "I wanted to let you know that the blood work for Ms. MacCaslin came back. Everything looks perfect for both her and the baby."

"Baby!" Zoe, Sam, and Nick all said in unison.

The doctor startled and looked around, seemingly oblivious to the three adults standing inches away from him.

Michael chuckled. "We've got some news."

Em turned her head from side to side and opened her eyes. She scanned the room then met his gaze.

He pressed a kiss to the top of her head. "The gang's all here."

"Ah, good, Ms. MacCaslin. You're awake," the doctor said.

"I was just telling Mr. MacCarron your blood work is completely normal. The chart says you're about six weeks along. Would you like to hear your baby's heartbeat?"

Em looked past the doctor and gave a small wave to Zoe, Sam, and Nick. "Hi, guys. I'm pregnant."

"Yeah, we got that," Zoe said.

"How long have you known?" Sam asked, his wide-eyed gaze locked on Em's stomach.

"What time is it?" Em asked.

"About half past ten," Nick answered.

Michael looked down at Em. "About eight hours."

"Sounds about right," she answered. Her blue eyes sparkled as she gave him a shy smile.

"Holy mother of pearl!" Zoe exclaimed.

A nurse entered the room with a portable ultrasound.

"Is everyone staying for this?" the doctor asked.

"Hell to the yes, we're staying," Zoe said. She sat down on the edge of the bed and patted Em's leg.

The doctor gestured for Em to raise her shirt. He squirted a jellylike substance on her abdomen and pressed the ultrasound wand to her belly. A grainy black and white picture appeared on the monitor.

"Ah," the doctor said. "There you are."

Michael stared at the fuzzy screen. "That's our baby?"

"Yes, it is. I see the heart and the yolk sac. That's what's going to give your baby nourishment until the placenta forms." He pressed a button, and a rapid whooshing beat filled the room.

Em squeezed Michael's hand.

"That's the baby's heartbeat?" Em's voice was thick with emotion.

"It is. Ninety-eight beats per minute. Perfectly normal."

"It's going to be a whole new world for us," Em said, her voice tinged with wonder.

Michael looked around the room. All eyes were glued to the monitor and the tiny, peanut-sized life pulsing in fuzzy waves of black and white.

Em tilted her head and met his gaze. In her deep blue eyes, he saw the laughing girl with auburn braids. She was beckoning him to run through the pouring rain and stand by her side.

"I can promise you this, Mary Michelle," he said, his voice barely a whisper. "No matter what happens, we're always better together. But now, it's going to be the three of us."

EPILOGUE

Em's pearl necklace bobbed between her naked breasts. "We're never going to get this crib put together."

She pressed her hands against Michael's chest, her pelvis grinding into him in smooth, steady thrusts. He gripped her hips and guided her body as she rode his cock. The late morning sun sent streams of golden light through the room. It highlighted her auburn hair and cast a soft glow on the gentle rounding of her stomach.

Em was almost twenty weeks along, and Michael loved everything about her pregnant body. The added weight of her breasts. The curve of her hips. To him, there was nothing sexier than Em, pregnant with his child. And he certainly did not mind her ramped-up pregnancy sex drive.

"You're the one who came into the nursery wearing nothing but a necklace," he breathed.

Her lips drew into a wicked grin. "I don't see you complaining."

He answered her taunt by rolling his hips. She gasped and arched her back as he dug his fingertips into the flesh of her sweet ass. She was stunning. Head thrown back in ecstasy. Body writhing. Biting her bottom lip and purring with lusty moans.

She gazed down at him with sated eyes. His body tightened, and the base of his cock tensed and prepared for release. He met her gaze, let out a primal growl, and lost himself in the depth of her blue eyes and in her tight, wet heat gripping him like a vice.

He took a breath and ran his fingertips along the length of her belly. He slid them down to squeeze her thighs, pressed flush against his.

Em scanned the room. A half-painted room. A half-constructed crib. And the floor, awash with tiny pillows and creamy white bedding.

"I know what you're thinking," he said, sitting up, but not breaking their connection.

A worried look crossed her sex-flushed face. "We don't have much time."

Em's mother was coming in from Australia to attend the twenty-week ultrasound where they were hoping they would find out the sex of the baby.

"It's a busy life being an internet sensation," he teased.

She gazed at the ceiling. "We need to change something with the Shostakovich remix. I just can't put my finger on it yet."

He smiled. In a matter of weeks, they had amassed thousands of followers online. There was quite an appetite for classical pieces remixed with modern electronic elements, and the world had fallen in love with the entrancing redheaded violinist at the center of each remix.

Em reclined on her side. "Are the guys coming over?"

"They should be here any second. I wanted to show them the finished carriage house, then bribe them with beer to help me put together the rest of the nursery."

She kissed his neck. "Good plan."

They had decided to pop the top of the carriage house and build a studio apartment on the second floor for when Em's mother came to visit.

Em ran her hand over his chest and let her fingertips travel south toward his cock. "You smell so good."

He smiled. He fucking loved her sex-fueled pregnancy hormones.

A knock on the front door stopped her hand's descent.

"The guys are here," Em said with a sigh. "I should probably put on more than just pearls."

"I'm sure I could find a potato sack that could work." He'd become more protective of her over the last few weeks. He blamed it on whatever was the male equivalent of pregnancy hormones. If another man even glanced Em's way, he found himself ready to pounce on the unsuspecting guy.

Em threw him a dubious glance and padded into their bedroom. Along with finishing out the carriage house, they'd had the staircase professionally rebuilt and remodeled the master bedroom.

The Foursquare would always be his childhood home. But with Em making it her home now, the energy in the house had shifted. The Foursquare wasn't the place he was forced to live. It was the place he chose to live, and he couldn't think of a better place to start his family.

Michael made sure the door to the bedroom was closed, grabbed a hat, and made his way to answer the door.

"What the hell's going on in there?" Sam asked.

Nick mouthed, "Holy shit, dude."

Michael joined the guys on the porch. "Don't let anyone tell you pregnancy is the pits, boys," Michael said, pulling the ball cap over his tangle of ruffled hair. "I may be making two a.m. trips to Pete's Organic Grocer for ice cream, bananas, bacon—"

Nick and Sam grimaced in unison.

"But, it certainly has its perks," Michael finished, grinning like an idiot and not giving one single fuck.

"You and Em are the last hope for the ginger race. Science says we're a dying breed. So, by all means, go make all the redheaded babies you two possibly can!" Sam added with a playful shove.

Michael shook his head and laughed.

Nick gestured to Em's Foursquare. "Have the new owners moved in yet? You know, into the Foursquare you didn't sell to me."

They hadn't even needed to put the house on the market. Mrs. G, the beloved retired Langley Park Elementary school teacher and current office manager for Ben Fisher's architecture firm, had bought the home.

From a legal standpoint, it was a creative purchase. Mrs. G had paid for the Foursquare with funds from a trust set up for her goddaughter to which she was the executor. Mrs. G explained that her goddaughter was engaged in a "messy" breakup and needed to act with discretion. Had it been anyone other than Mrs. G, Michael would have been wary of the circumstances. But he'd known Mrs. G his entire life. If her goddaughter needed a home, he was happy to oblige.

"Dude," Sam said with mock surprise. "You don't like crashing at my place?"

"You know I appreciate your hospitality, buddy," Nick said with a grin. "But now that I'm going to be in Langley Park permanently, I need to find a place that doesn't include waking up to you singing, 'Oh, What a Beautiful Mornin'.'"

"You have something against Rodgers and Hammerstein's *Oklahoma*, Kincade?"

"You got the job?" Em asked, joining them on the porch.

"You're looking at Kansas City Downtown Airport's newest Director of Aviation," Nick said with a grin. "I start next week."

"Hearts are breaking at every port. Airports, that is. Captain Nick is putting down roots," Sam said, clapping his friend on the back.

"Are you going to miss flying?" Em asked.

"I'll still get to fly. I'll run the airport, but I'll also do some flight instruction. I may even pick up some corporate flights if the opportunity presents itself. Right now, I need to figure out a more permanent living situation."

"Seriously, dude," Sam said, "you're always welcome at my place. You know that."

"Wait a second," Em said and shared a look with Michael. "Nick, you should move into our carriage house apartment until you find a place in Langley Park."

"Absolutely," Michael said, wrapping an arm around Em's shoulders. "Em and I grew up listening to Sam belt out show tunes. It's a miracle you've survived this long."

Sam shook his head.

"What about your mom? Isn't she arriving soon?" Nick asked. "Won't she need the carriage house?"

"She can stay in our guest room in the Foursquare," Em answered.

"If you're sure you don't mind, I'd appreciate it. I'm ready to jump when something goes on the market in the area—so I shouldn't be in your hair for too long. I do have an aunt nearby in Mission Springs. She's offered to let me stay with her, but that would involve weekly Euchre tournaments with her Junior League ladies. I politely declined."

"Understandable," Michael said.

"Really, Nick, it would be no trouble at all. You can stay as long as you need to," Em added.

"Thanks, guys," Nick said. "You know I love you, Sam. But with my new job and the crazy hours, it may be good to have a place to myself."

Sam clapped Nick on the back. "Whatever works, bud. I'm just glad you're making Langley Park your home."

Michael gestured toward the door. "Let's head inside. We can hammer out the details while we try to figure out how the hell to put this nursery together. Who writes these directions?"

But just as the group was about to go inside the house, a sedan turned onto Foxglove Lane and caught their attention. The car drove past them, but within a matter of minutes, it was back and pulled up in front of Em's old Foursquare. There was a woman inside the car. She was wearing sunglasses and a hat. A long cascade of chestnut brown hair fell past her shoulders.

"Do you think that's Mrs. G's goddaughter?" Em asked.

"I'm not sure," Michael answered. "I've never met her. Mrs. G said she'd spent a summer in Langley Park when she was sixteen. She worked at the Langley Park Community Center's summer camp. Did you ever meet her, Sam? Mrs. G said you guys are the same age."

Sam shook his head. "No, I don't think so."

Nick stared at the woman. "I worked at the Langley Park Community Center's summer camp when I was sixteen."

"You did?" Sam asked. "How the hell did I not know that?"

"My mom sent me to stay with my aunt in Mission Springs. I pretty much kept to myself," Nick answered, gaze locked on the mysterious woman.

The woman got out of the car and stared up at the Foursquare. She must not have noticed them on the porch and kept her gaze locked on the house. She was wearing a baggy sweatshirt and worn jeans. Nothing about her said *look at me*, but Nick couldn't take his eyes off her.

"Hello!" Em called out, stepping off the porch and crossing the yard as the men followed behind.

The woman let out a startled gasp, and her hands went up protectively.

"I'm so sorry! We didn't mean to frighten you. I'm Em MacCaslin. This is Michael MacCarron. We're your neighbors. And this is Sam Sinclair and Nick Kincade. They're our friends, and they live in Langley Park, too."

The woman's hands were shaking. She clasped them in front of her and produced a tight smile. "It's nice to meet you all. I'm Lindsey—"

"Lindsey Hanlon," Nick said.

"It's Lindsey Davies, now," she said, looking away. But she wasn't wearing a wedding ring.

"Do you two know each other?" Em asked.

Nick had gone pale. "We both worked at the Community Center's summer camp. That was the summer I was just telling you about."

A blush crept up Lindsey's neck. "I hardly remember that summer. It was such a long time ago."

Lindsey took a step back. "I don't mean to be rude, but I've had a long trip. I'd like to get settled inside."

"Of course," Em said. "Were you able to get the key from Mrs. G? She's your godmother, right?"

Lindsey nodded.

"Are your things being delivered today?" Michael asked. "If you need any help carrying boxes or moving furniture, just let us know. We're happy to help."

"There's no moving truck," Lindsey answered and took another step back.

A pregnant silence hung in the air.

"Well," Em said, taking Michael's hand. "You know where we'll be. You're welcome at our place anytime."

Lindsey gave a quick nod then turned and hurried inside the Foursquare.

"I don't think she remembers you, Nick," Sam said.

Nick stared up at the house. "No, I know she remembers me. She only wishes she didn't."

ACKNOWLEDGMENTS

It was an absolute joy writing this book.

To Chris and Kendra, who have been with me from the beginning, thank you. Thank you for listening to my crazy ideas. Thank you for providing spot-on edits and feedback. Thank you for always being in my corner.

To Dawn, who introduced me to the world of happily ever afters. My entire writing journey started with your kind gesture.

To Corinne and Tera, your careful eye and attention to detail made Michael and Em's story stronger.

To Brandi, for helping me with the *Star Wars* references and dialogue.

To my mentor, friend, and gifted author, Michelle Dare, I don't know where I would be without you. Thank you for encouraging me and guiding me through the beautiful world of romance.

To my father, Joe, who, in a million years, never imagined he would be reading romance novels written by his daughter.

To my husband, David. My true love. My best friend. My home.

And to you, the reader. It's the highest honor and the most humbling gift to have you read my book. Thank you for visiting Langley Park. I hope you come back soon.

ABOUT THE AUTHOR

 If there's one thing Krista Sandor knows for sure, it's that romance saved her. After she was diagnosed with Multiple Sclerosis in 2015, her world turned upside down. During those difficult first days, her dear friend sent her a romance novel. That kind gesture provided the escape she needed and ignited her love of the genre. Inspired by the strong heroines and happily ever afters, Krista decided to write her own romance series. Today, she is an MS Warrior and living life to the fullest. When she's not writing, you can find her running 5Ks and chasing after her growing boys in her adopted home of Denver, Colorado.

Never miss a release, contest, or author event! Visit Krista's website and sign up to receive her exclusive newsletter.

https://kristasandor.com

facebook.com/krista.sandor

twitter.com/Krista_Sandor_

instagram.com/kristasandor

ALSO BY KRISTA SANDOR

The Langley Park Series

The Road Home: Book 1

The Sound of Home: Book 2

Coming Soon

The Beginning of Home: Book 3

The Measure of Home: Book 4

Made in the USA
San Bernardino, CA
29 October 2018